To Save the Nation

A Novel

Robert E. Kass

Praise for *To Save the Nation*

"Forced disappearance is not only a serious human rights violation but also an international crime, punishable as a crime against humanity under the Rome Statute of the International Criminal Court. Unfortunately, this crime is notoriously under-prosecuted and many forced disappearances remain unpunished.

"Bob Kass' novel is a great legal page-turner but also a courageous book, bringing out horrendous crimes from a recent past, which were justified in the eyes of their perpetrators as something they had to do 'for the nation.' In drawing attention to crimes of this nature and the political intricacies behind them, he contributes to public awareness as part of a much needed international fight against impunity."

—*Christine Van den Wyngaert, former Judge at the International Criminal Court, the International Criminal Tribunal for the Former Yugoslavia and the International Court of Justice, currently Judge at the Kosovo Specialist Chambers*

"My father was one of the 'disappeared' in Argentina's Dirty War of the 70s. My mother fled the country with me and my sister and we eventually found asylum in Switzerland. Kass' book, *To Save the Nation,* is a reminder of what happened back then. Unfortunately, 'enforced disappearances' continue in nearly 100 countries today. This book in a contribution to the conversation about how far a country should go in violating human rights when its leaders feel the nation is under a threat from dissidents."

—*Antonio Hodgers, Swiss politician, Conseiller d'Etat of the Canton of Geneva, Switzerland. As a member of the Swiss Parliament, Mr. Hodgers voted for the adoption of the International Convention for the Protection of All Persons from Enforced Disappearance.*

"The respect of fundamental rights, individual liberties and the rule of law is the guarantee for every human being to be protected against arbitrary action of a State. Enforced disappearances are among the worst of the illegal actions a State allows itself to take against its own citizens, supposedly in order to protect the State in question, or any alleged greater value.

"Today, in our democratic countries, in the name of the fight against terrorism, States are making their populations accept restrictions on their liberties, invoking the need for greater security. Those breaches in our fundamental liberties are not to be taken lightly. We citizens deserve liberty as much as security, within a democratic state fully applying the rule of law. Any step that restrains our human rights is a dangerous step toward the risk of being submitted to the arbitrary power of the State, towards one of the most terrifying illegal actions: enforced disappearances.

"Bob Kass' book reminds us of those terrible crimes committed by the power of a State against its own population. Let us not forget the danger of any unregulated power within a State. Let us also be fully aware of those dangers in order to be able to recognize and challenge any breach that threatens the rule of law, our rights and our liberties."

—Olivia Venet, Belgian Attorney, specialized in criminal law, criminal procedure, international criminal law, international humanitarian law and human rights. President of the Belgian Human Rights League.

"In Kass' debut thriller, a lawyer takes a case that pulls him into the dark world of organized crime and the grim legacy of a past Argentinian conflict.*** A feast of political intrigue and an astute exploration of Argentina's nefarious past."

—Kirkus Reviews

TO SAVE THE NATION

A NOVEL

ROBERT E. KASS

CAROB TREE PRESS

DETROIT

Robert E. Kass/Carob Tree Press, LLC
333 W. Fort Street, 12th Floor
Detroit, MI 48226
www.robertekass.com
Cover design by Bespoke Book Covers
Audiobook production by ReelMusicianPro

To Save the Nation / Robert E. Kass — 1st ed.
Audiobook ISBN-13: 978-0-9856814-1-8
E-book ISBN-13: 978-0-9856814-3-2
Print ISBN-13: 978-0-9856814-2-5

This book may be purchased in quantity for
educational purposes and for reading groups.
For further information, see www.robertekass.com.

Look for the Discussion Guide in
the back of this book. To access the
Discussion Guide online, go to www.
robertekass.com.

"In every war, there are people who disappear."

Argentine General Leopoldo Galtieri,
1949 Graduate, U.S. Army School of the Americas

"As many people will die in Argentina as is
necessary to restore order."

Argentine Army Commander-in-Chief
Jorge Rafael Videla, October 1975
He became President five months after
overthrowing the civilian government.

"First we will kill all the subversives.
Then we will kill their collaborators.
Then their sympathizers.
Then those who remain indifferent.
And finally we will kill the timid."

General Iberio Saint Jean,
Military Governor of Buenos Aires,
May 1976.

"Those who cannot remember the past
are condemned to repeat it."

George Santayana

Dedicated to the memory of attorney
Jorge Rubenstein,
who died in 1977 while in the custody of
security forces in La Plata, Argentina,
the capital of Buenos Aires Province

CHAPTER 1

November 25, 1976

IT WAS A RELATIVELY QUIET NIGHT in the air traffic control tower at the Alvarez International Airport in Acapulco, Mexico. No more commercial flights were scheduled for that evening, and the small charter jet from New York was the only flight scheduled to arrive. Two controllers were on duty. A third had taken sick earlier in the evening. Because traffic was light, the supervisor didn't call in a replacement. Although the shift wouldn't end for three hours, at midnight the supervisor asked his second-in-command to bundle up their reports for the day and take them downstairs to the office.

The supervisor cleared the charter jet for landing, gave instructions in English, and watched the plane descend to 9,000 feet on his radar screen. Suddenly, the aircraft disappeared from the screen. He repeatedly called to the aircraft, to no avail.

The supervisor picked up the phone and called the airport office of the Mexican Federal Police to report a suspected crash of Executive Air Flight 83, in the Sierra Madre Mountains to the north and east of Acapulco, approximately thirty miles from the airport. His voice had a sense of urgency, but not panic.

The police procedure was extremely cumbersome. First, they couldn't authorize a search party without a written report from the control tower. One of the two staff members coordinating airport office operations that evening took it upon himself to walk over to the tower to pick up the report and brought it back to his office. He then made his own report and recommendations for a search and rescue operation, which had to be passed on to his regional command and required the approval of the central commander before allocating resources.

The apparent crash had occurred at approximately nine fifteen that evening, and it was almost one in the morning when all the required approvals were finally obtained.

In the meantime, local police officials on the ground received numerous reports of a possible air crash and massive explosion in the general vicinity where the aircraft was suspected to have gone down.

The Regional Commander of the Mexican Federal Police directed the search team to start the search only at daybreak and to be fully armed. The likely crash site was in a remote mountainous area, accessible only by four-wheel drive vehicles over narrow, winding mountain roads, and armed bandits were known to operate in the area. The United States National Transportation Safety Board was notified of the incident, since the flight was of U.S. origin, but the search and rescue mission would be undertaken solely by Mexican authorities. The NTSB and the manufacturer of the aircraft would decide later how to handle their own investigations, depending in part on what the Mexican investigation found.

CHAPTER 2

Buenos Aires, Argentina, October 1975

THE BLACK MERCEDES SCREECHED TO A STOP in an isolated area in the forest in the Parque Sarmiento, a large park on the north edge of Buenos Aires, and a man dressed in a rumpled tuxedo was dumped out onto the ground. Hands securely bound behind his back, legs tied together, mouth taped shut, and head covered by a black sack, he grunted frantically as his face hit the gravel at the road's edge. It was a rainy Friday, five days after he was taken at gunpoint on his way home from a lavish party at the United States Embassy.

Kidnaping was a common occurrence in Argentina. The Montonero guerrillas took their time and chose targets whose companies or families would be certain to pay large ransoms, a major source of financing for their operations. They attacked businesses and political figures, assassinated corporate executives and bombed their homes, killed police and raided military bases for weapons and explosives. All of this was intended to destabilize the right-wing military regime supported by the United States.

It was almost a game:

Snatch the target, maintain silence for several days to cause the family fear and concern, then make a huge ransom demand. They would prove the target was alive by letting him say a few words on the phone. If they chose right, it would take only two more days for the guerrillas to have their money in the bank. Ransoms for important businessmen generally ranged from $500,000 to $2 million; however, in one major score they'd kidnapped an Exxon executive and obtained over $14 million in ransom.

The guerillas never negotiated the amount and didn't deal in cash; cash would require delivery to a physical location, increasing the danger of getting caught. Also, the bills could be marked and traced.

Instead, payments were made by wire to an offshore bank, from which the money would be immediately transferred to another, then on to another. Bahamas, Bermuda, the Caymans, Switzerland, Liechtenstein, the Channel Islands. The offshore locations were different each time, or at least the first one was, because that was as far as the authorities could track the wire transfer.

Each location was chosen because of its strict bank secrecy laws and the lack of applicable treaties with Argentina. The system put a veritable brick wall between the guerillas and authorities. Usually the family wouldn't even contact the police for fear that the victim would be killed or the kidnappers would have accomplices in the police or military.

This time, the guerillas had scored a huge hit: The target was the brother of a big-time international banker, whose family members had been kidnapped many times before— seven times, to be exact—over a period of five years. For the guerrillas, kidnapping one of the members of this family was a challenge, because of the high level of security that generally surrounded them. At the same time, the likely ransom would be large enough to buy off security guards, who sometimes demanded hundreds of thousands of dollars.

Each time, the target was kept in a different location. Blindfolded, his mouth was taped shut, except for brief periods for meals, to limit his ability to establish a relationship with his captors. He was allowed to speak only to confirm that he was alive so the ransom would be paid. If the target attempted to say more he would be severely punished by beating, cutting, electroshock or other forms of torture.

This time, the head of the guerrilla group felt $3 million was the right price.

The target was taken on Sunday night, first contact was made with the family on Wednesday morning, and they were given until nine thirty Friday morning to wire the funds to a numbered account at the Caribbean Trust Bank of the Bahamas, Ltd. The transfer was made at nine. Just before noon local time, the member of the guerrilla group who handled finances received confirmation from their banker at the Zurich Private Bank that the funds had arrived, after transiting through accounts in several other countries.

"Good day, sir," said the voice from Zurich in a sing-song Swiss-German accent.

Though it was late afternoon in Zurich, the banker said nothing to give away the client's identity or even the time zone of his location. The caller's voice was familiar to the banker, but he still followed strict bank procedure, addressing each checklist item, including coded account number and passwords, as he did each time he provided information to a depositor by phone.

"You would like information on the transfer just received?"

"Yes, please. And the current principal balance in the account."

"Per your request, sir, we maintain this account with a principal balance, which represents the running total of all deposits to the account, reflected at current fair market value for the investments, less withdrawals. We have a separate account to which all interest and dividends are transferred. We hereby acknowledge receipt of a wire transfer today in the principal amount of U.S. dollars three million. This will bring the running total of all principal, less withdrawals, to U.S. dollars one hundred eighty million."

"Thank you very much," said the caller, who then put down the phone and dialed his associates to tell them they could deliver the target, which they did within the hour.

After pushing him out of the rear seat, they pulled the door shut, and the Mercedes sped away via Highway 9 to the north, direction Cordoba. About fifteen minutes later, another member of the guerilla group, using a pay phone in Mendoza, on the other side of Argentina, notified the family where they could find him.

CHAPTER 3

November 25, 1976

THE PRIVATE CHARTER JET was ready for the second leg of its flight from New York City to Acapulco, Mexico, with stops in Memphis and Dallas/Fort Worth for refueling.

The sole passenger, a burly, bearded, good-looking gentleman in his late thirties, had disembarked for the half-hour service stop in Memphis. He waited in the Flight Ways Aviation lounge, where two pilots were waiting either for their clients or planes to be readied, and a would-be pilot poured over maps and flight manuals as he waited for his flight instructor.

The flight lounge was small, with four small tables and a large window to the runway. The waitress, a long-time employee, remembered having seen the passenger on numerous occasions before. Extremely well-dressed, he wore a dark suit with black shirt and sharply contrasted tie, and highly polished shoes. He spoke some English, but with a heavy Spanish accent, and she imagined he was a drug lord but really had no idea of his business. He never discussed anything of substance.

He ordered a cup of black coffee, read his Spanish language newspaper for a while, then ordered a refill, keeping an eye on the clock on the wall. As the time for re-boarding approached, he left a five dollar tip on the table, huge by Memphis standards. After a brief visit to the men's room, he rushed out to the waiting plane, turning only slightly when the waitress wished him a good trip.

At the Dallas/Fort Worth airport, the passenger again waited in the airport lounge but remained silent. He bought a can of Coke from a vending machine and a local newspaper and stood at the window, watching the plane while it was being refueled. As the fuel truck pulled away from the aircraft, he walked back to the plane.

The co-pilot was waiting at the foot of the stairway as the man approached in the shadows of the lights beaming from the flight lounge building. The plane's jet engines whirred as they readied for takeoff. The co-pilot and passenger each nodded at the other as the passenger started up the stairway. The passenger then took a different seat than the one he previously occupied, putting aside the newspaper.

When the plane was ready to leave, the co-pilot came out of the cockpit and signaled that they were about to take off. The passenger fastened his seat belt. The pilot received clearance from the tower, taxied down the runway, and within a few minutes the aircraft was airborne for Acapulco.

This time, however, Executive Air Flight 83 wouldn't reach its destination.

CHAPTER 4

HE WAS BORED SILLY. Armed with a degree in journalism from Columbia University, Alex Ginsberg continued to hold out hopes for a choice assignment as a journalist. He had two jobs prior to this one: The first was a brief stint at Dell Publishing, working out crossword puzzles. That was followed by a year at *New Yorker* magazine, proofreading articles written by others. He then landed what he thought was the assignment of his dreams: A job as a reporter with United Press International, assigned to the UPI desk in Mexico, primarily covering financial news.

Until now, however, it had all been humdrum. Inflation. Free trade. The occasional multi-national merger. But how could he really show his investigative skills and literary talent writing about the everyday happenings of business and economics? Had he made a terrible choice to major in journalism? How could he hope to move up the professional ladder and maybe even someday be worthy of a Pulitzer Prize—by essentially relating facts?

By nature, Alex wasn't a complainer. But while the UPI job certainly paid the rent for his one-bedroom apartment in Mexico City, and would probably look good on his resume, if he could just get a juicy assignment, he thought, he could really show them his potential.

His boss, Hal McDonald, was the one who doled out the work, usually based on seniority or, in Hal's words, "experience." Alex had been lobbying Hal for weeks to give him a try on something more challenging, a story with real meat. Hal had no imagination and kept telling Alex his job at UPI was just to report the facts, not dig them up.

Frustrated, Alex decided to take a long weekend in Acapulco, soak up some sun, have a little fun, and reflect on how working in Mexico wasn't so bad at all. His long-time friend, Jim Ferguson, was on assignment in Acapulco to close a multi-million dollar condo financing deal. Jim was an attorney in the Dallas office of the international law firm of Prescott & Wilson, and one of the firm's rising stars. It had taken Jim weeks to get all the ducks in a row, but everything had finally come together to wrap up the financing, and Jim, too, was ready for a few days of R&R himself.

Jim was staying at the Fairmont Acapulco Princess, overlooking the Pacific Ocean and Revolcadero Beach with its famous white sands. He'd been upgraded to a two-bedroom deluxe suite, with plenty of room for Alex, which made the decision to spend a few days in Acapulco an easy one. Jim had been down there several times and knew all the best drinking holes and choicest beaches.

It was Thursday, Thanksgiving day, and Alex arrived on the first flight from Mexico City, landing at nine that morning. He and Jim spent the day in the sun, drinking Margaritas and ogling some of God's finest creations. The sun was hot, and they were physically exhausted from doing absolutely nothing.

After a brief siesta, they went out for a dinner and enjoyed a fantastic four-course meal at one of Jim's favorite French restaurants, Chez Joseph. Escargots from Burgundy in garlic and butter sauce for starters. They shared a tureen of Joseph's signature cream of tomato soup, with fried polenta croutons and fresh basil. For the main course, Alex had poached Chilean sea bass in a light cream sauce, with wild rice pilaf, and Jim had medium-rare New Zealand rack of lamb, with garlic mashed potatoes and sautéed green beans with almonds.

They accepted the sommelier's recommendation of a bottle of the best Côtes du Rhône, Châteauneuf du Pape, which was powerful, complex and certainly not bone-dry, to accompany the meal. And for dessert, they ordered crêpes flambées with Cointreau, mandarin oranges and vanilla ice cream, prepared table side.

Flawless service, exceptional presentation, with each plate arranged as only a master chef could do it, a true work of art. The finest quality ingredients and preparation.

Jim was still on the firm's expense account, as he had another day or so of work to complete the last details of the closing and put together sets of documentation for all the parties—the property owners, developers, various financing institutions and their legal counsel.

Jim considered his dinner with Alex a client development expense. Who knows? Maybe someday Alex would be able to steer a major corporation his way—or perhaps alert him to a breaking story so he could get his firm's marketing people on the case before other law firms even knew what was going on. A major new case might even convince the firm's Management Committee that Jim was partnership material.

Back in Jim's suite, they were ready to turn in for the night when Alex noticed the blinking red light on the phone. He'd left word for his boss where he would be, and he now had several frantic messages to call back as soon as possible.

Alex immediately called Hal McDonald.

CHAPTER 5

"ALEX, I'VE BEEN TRYING TO REACH YOU FOR HOURS. I hope you're not too drunk to focus, because I've got a hot one for you. This may be the chance you've been waiting for." Alex had never before heard Hal McDonald so energized. "Grab a pen and pad so I can fill you in."

Alex took a yellow legal pad from Jim's desk, gave Jim a thumbs up, and with the phone perched on his shoulder started to take detailed notes. Ten minutes and six legal-sized pages later, his head was spinning.

"Sure, Hal, I'll do exactly as you said, and I'll report back to you as soon as I'm back in town. And I really do appreciate your giving me this opportunity. I won't let you down." He hung up the phone, took a deep breath, and shook his head in amazement. "You won't believe this," he said. "Because I happen to be here in Acapulco, right now, when there's a breaking news story, I get the chance of a lifetime to break out of politics and finance. This is incredible! Let's go downstairs for a drink, and I'll fill you in."

"Fine with me," said Jim.

Alex tucked the yellow pad under his arm, and they headed for the elevator. Their suite was on the top floor, and once in the elevator, Alex pushed the button for the lobby level. The door closed, and Alex was about to start relating what Hal had told him, when an English-speaking couple entered the elevator on the floor below. He glanced at Jim, and they maintained strict silence between them for the rest of the ride down.

THERE WERE SEVERAL BARS on the main floor of the hotel, and Alex looked for a place free from the loud music of the mariachis, quiet enough to have a discreet conversation, yet not so quiet that they could be overheard at the next table. The Flamingo Bar fit the bill.

They took a booth in the far corner, away from the bar, a good distance from the TV, and with no one sitting at any of the tables nearby. They could hear each other, yet there was no one close enough to hear them. They each ordered a local beer.

"I'm going to break the first rule Hal laid out for me," said Alex. "'Don't tell anyone about this story.' How can I not tell you, when you were sitting there as he told me what happened? When I took my notes on your legal pad—which I'm going to keep, by the way. I wouldn't even have gotten the call if I hadn't been here this weekend, and I'm only here because you invited me down! Jim, I must tell you, but this has to stay between just us, OK? I'll consider this something like attorney-client privilege, and you can't peep a word to anyone, under any circumstances. Agreed?"

"No problem. I certainly have no connections in the news biz and wouldn't do anything to hurt you or your position. Mum's the word."

"So, tell me if you don't think this is the most incredible lead a reporter at my stage of the game could ever get: Earlier this evening, a private charter jet carrying a pilot, co-pilot, and passenger slammed into a mountainside in the Sierra Madres on its final approach into Acapulco. Hal's friends at the Mexican Federal Police immediately tipped him on the story, which they thought might be of interest because the flight originated in New York City and involved an American-made aircraft."

"So, how does a charter jet air crash with at most three dead become an international story worthy of an ace UPI reporter like you?" Jim said with a smile.

"The passenger, Jim. The passenger, that's how. Hal already had our New York office do some quick background research. The passenger was a major international banker, Ricardo Guttmann. Guttmann, an Argentinian, was in the process of buying up banks on three continents—New York, Brussels, Luxembourg, and Tel Aviv—and may have a dark side to him, but that's not clear.

"Our clipping files don't show too much, except that his banks in Argentina have been shut down for a day here and there for violating currency laws and members of his family have been kidnapped and huge ransoms paid to the left-wing Montonero guerillas, who oppose the current right-wing military regime in Argentina. There could be an angle here."

"So, Alex, do you think something about his business dealings could have caused someone to want to take him down?"

"I have no idea, but he certainly was high profile. Why would his plane just drop out of the sky, with no distress call and no reports of any difficulties in communications between the cockpit and Acapulco tower? The aircraft was a Gates Learjet 24B, first class equipment. It's the small business jet of choice for many top execs and corporate air charter companies. Seats up to six and has a range of anywhere between 1,250 and 2,000 miles, depending on how heavy it's loaded and how much fuel it's carrying."

"I didn't know you were into aircraft specs, Alex!"

"I'm not—but the guys in New York dug that up as well. Deliveries of the 24 began in '66, and the current version, the 24B, was certified in '68, which is eight years ago.

They've been flying the 24 and its predecessor, the 23, since '63. There are nearly 1,000 of all versions in service, and only a couple have gone down.

"I'm sure a lot of people will want to know why this plane crashed. If a bomb took it down, this will crank up the interest level. If it was equipment failure, that could have an adverse financial impact on the manufacturer if they can't figure it out quickly. Corporate America will be very interested in following this story."

"Slow down. Alex. Your imagination is working overtime. Ever hear of pilot error?"

"Sure, that's possible, but given who they were carrying, somebody may have wanted it to go down. I wouldn't assume pilot error without seeing the full report, finding out what the cockpit recorder said, and exactly what the tower told these guys. Charter jet pilots are well-trained and fly these babies for a living. Slamming into a mountain at 9,000 feet, shortly before arrival, would be the last thing experienced pilots would do."

"No kidding! For these guys, it was definitely the last thing they did!"

"Cut the comedy, Jim. You know what I mean. There was no weather involved here, that's for sure. We haven't seen a cloud all day. So far, there's not even a suggestion of another aircraft being involved, and the reports from the ground say nothing about an explosion prior to the crash, although nothing can be ruled out.

"The Mexican authorities are taking the lead on the investigation because the crash happened on Mexican soil, even though the plane was made in the U.S., the pilot and co-pilot were Americans and the passenger wasn't Mexican. The Americans have to stand by and wait for an invitation to get involved. At this point they don't know if there are survivors, but based on reports from peasants on the ground, there was a huge explosion and fire after impact, in a remote mountainous area."

"So, how are you going to report on the crash? You're not heading out into the mountains alone, are you?" Jim was legitimately concerned about his friend's safety.

"Certainly not. I don't get paid enough to do something so foolish. But Hal has contacts at the highest levels of the Mexican Federal Police. Not only did they make him aware of the accident shortly after it happened, they're also letting me accompany the investigating team. I think they're a big part of his budget for T&E. He made it perfectly clear that turf and image are really important to them. I'm to go along for the ride and do as I'm told but keep out of their way and not report anything that could be an embarrassment to them."

"So, when do you leave?"

"I have to be at the regional outpost of the Mexican Federal Police on the highway just outside the airport, at six in the morning," Alex said, looking down at his watch.

"That's just a few hours from now. I'm supposed to ask for Capitán Ramírez, the head of the investigating team. I don't know if I'll be able to sleep, but if I don't get at least a couple of hours, I'll be miserable. My guess is, tomorrow is going to be a very long day."

"Far be it from me to keep you up drinking," replied Jim.

They finished their beers, left some greenbacks on the table to cover the bill, and headed back upstairs.

CHAPTER 6

ALEX TOSSED AND TURNED FOR HOURS as his mind raced. What must it have been like to be in that plane when it crashed? How long would the trip to the crash site take? Would they run into trouble along the way? He'd heard of bandits ambushing groups passing through, even armed police convoys.

What dangers would he meet as they chopped their way through the heavy forest to arrive at the scene of smoldering wreckage, jet fuel, and burnt corpses? Would he puke his guts out because of the smells and the sight of burnt bodies?

Would the police really let him see what they found, or was he to be a journalistic puppet, reporting only what he was told he could report? Why was Hal McDonald so adamant that he had to keep out of their way and not report anything that could be an embarrassment to the authorities? Was this just a general admonition, or did Hal suspect something about the crash that could cause a stir?

What would be the implications of the death of the banker, Ricardo Guttmann? Was there someone in his organization who would take over at the helm? Did he personally guarantee any of his companies' debts? What would happen to pending bank deals around the world? Would there be ripple effects if the deals were aborted?

Why did the plane go down in the last minutes of what was otherwise a routine flight? If there was foul play, would the Mexicans dig it up, or would they gloss over it and quickly close their file? Why should they care anyway?

No Mexicans died, and no Mexican property was lost. But what if the plane was carrying drugs, or drug money? How would the Mexicans deal with that in his presence? Would the police scavenge the plane's cargo? How would they deal with him being there? His heart pounded.

Alex finally dozed off around four, to be awakened by his alarm at five fifteen. Groggy but still hyped, he was ready for what would certainly be the most challenging day of his professional life. He quickly splashed some cold water on his face and put on the only non-beach clothing he'd brought with him: A pair of khakis, sandals, and a T-shirt. He threw a camera, notepad, and small tape recorder into a backpack and jumped into the lone cab at the taxi stand in front of the hotel.

THIRTY MINUTES LATER, the cab arrived at the regional outpost of the Mexican Federal Police. Alex pulled a slip of paper out of his shirt pocket.

Ramírez, he thought to himself as he took a deep breath. I sure hope he speaks English.

There was no question he was at the right place. Outside the building a convoy of Jeeps lined up, the first and last of which were crowned with machine guns. About fifteen uniformed men were milling around the vehicles, drinking coffee. All were armed with rifles or machine guns.

Alex asked the first one he encountered where he could find Señor Ramírez.

"*Sí, el Capitán Ramírez, está par allá.*" "Over there," Alex understood, as the man pointed to the door of the building, a stucco-covered two-story structure which had seen better days, with iron bars over the windows and a large gate leading to the inner courtyard. The official seal of the Mexican Federal Police hung over the doorway.

At that very moment, two uniformed men came out, followed by two others in street clothes with what he later learned were kits containing crash investigators' tools of the trade: Cameras, notepads, measuring devices, and hundreds of plastic bags, vials, and labels to bring back any evidence they might collect. Alex stepped forward and introduced himself.

"Capitán Ramírez?" Alex held out his hand to the older of the two men, hoping he'd picked the right one and he'd been fully briefed about Alex joining their team.

"Buenos días, Señor Ginsberg, we are glad to have you with us," Ramírez said without hesitation but with a heavy Mexican accent. His voice was rough, that of a smoker. "I was notified last night by my superiors that you would be joining us, which is highly unusual, you must know that, but you are most welcome to observe. I hope you have a good stomach. I've seen many automobile crashes, but never an airplane crash, and I would expect that it will not be a pretty sight. You are sure you really want to go?"

"I've prepared myself for the worst. Yes, sir, I know this won't be a picnic, and I'm definitely up for it." What could he say? He couldn't back down now. McDonald would think he was a wimp and never give him anything challenging again.

"Well, then," Ramírez continued. "May I have the pleasure to introduce you to my second-in-command on this investigative mission, Señor Gonzalez. He will ride with you and make sure you stay out of trouble. He speaks English also."

"A pleasure to meet you, Señor Ginsberg," said Gonzalez.

"Please, you can call me Alex, if you don't mind. And may I ask who those fellows are, the ones who aren't in uniform?" Alex pointed to the two men in street clothes who had gotten into the rear seat of the third Jeep, where they'd loaded their kits and were studying maps while they waited.

"They are the official government crash investigators. Our job will be to get them —and you—to the site safely and retrieve any valuables and evidence we may find. Their job will be to investigate the crash and make a report. We will certainly lend a hand, if necessary, but the conclusions will be theirs."

"Will I be able to interview them?"

"I do not think so, Señor Alex. That is not our *sistema*— our protocol. They make a report, in writing, which may be public, but they do not make statements to the press. Also, they do not accept anyone other than their team or our people assisting in the investigation. That means that you are here strictly to observe, you understand, and if I say you must keep a certain *distancia*, then you must do that. And no photos. *Comprende*?"

"Sure, I get it. No problem. And if I have any questions, I'll just direct my questions to you, OK?"

"Ask anything you want, Señor Alex, there is no *problema* to ask. But understand that I may not always be able to give you an answer."

"Fine. When are we leaving?"

"We are waiting for one more group, the people from the funeral directors. They are coming with us to pick up the remains. The families have already been contacted, and they have given instructions."

A black hearse, more like a station wagon, turned the corner and pulled up alongside the convoy. Capitán Ramírez got into the passenger seat of the second Jeep, the crash investigators were in the third Jeep, Alex and Gonzalez climbed into the fourth Jeep, and the waiting Federal

Police officers filled in all the seats of the other Jeeps. As the convoy pulled away, the hearse fell in line, just before the last Jeep.

"How long a trip do we expect?" Alex asked.

"Based on the information we have at this moment, my guess is less than an hour until we leave the road, then who knows how long off the road until we reach the site. We will be in touch with local people who can direct us as we get closer. Depending on what we find, you may not be back in your hotel tonight. Is that going to be a problem, Señor Alex?"

"No, not a problem. I was just wondering."

"Do not worry about food, water, or accommodations. We have provisions for two days, and tents. It is not Acapulco, but there are villages in the area where we can take more food and drink if necessary. There are peasants living out there who are probably already at the site, checking it out. Unfortunately, there is not a lot we can do about that."

Gonzalez knew Alex wasn't prepared for the horrific things he was going to see.

This poor gringo isn't going to sleep tonight, Gonzalez thought, *and maybe not for many nights to come.*

CHAPTER 7

HANDS WAVING IN THE AIR, three peasants signaled to the lead Jeep that the convoy should go no further. The peasants had located the crash site, and from there the members of the investigating team had to leave the road and head up the mountain on foot. It had taken them two hours after leaving the main road to reach that point.

The two crash investigators, funeral directors, Alex, Gonzalez and most of the police left the Jeeps behind and followed the peasants along a narrow trail up the side of the mountain, through a thick forest. A few of the police stayed behind to watch over the Jeeps.

It was about an hour before they stopped. Stench and smoke filled the air. One of the investigators dropped back and took Gonzalez aside, chattering to him in rapid-fire Spanish for a minute or so. As he left, Gonzalez motioned to Alex to step to the side as the others continued on.

"What's going on?" Alex asked. "Why aren't we moving forward with the rest of them?"

"Protocol, Señor Alex," Gonzalez said. "We must give the lead investigator time to survey the situation before approaching the crash site. He will signal us by radio when we can move forward. We have to hold our position until he clears us to approach."

"So, what should I expect when we get up there?"

"To tell you the truth, Señor Alex, I cannot tell you for sure. Based on the reports of explosion and fire, my guess is that the remains will be rostizado—how do you say? roasted?— charred to such a point that you cannot recognize them.

Excuse my use of words, but that is the only way I can describe it. We really do not know if the explosion was first, which might have brought the plane down, or if the plane went down and the explosion was only upon impact. It will certainly be—how do you say in English—gutwrenching?"

Alex marveled at his choice of words. "Where do you get a chance to learn this type of word?"

"I read a lot in English, I think you would call it 'popular fiction.' What the investigator told me is that we should keep our distance. He expects there could be pieces of twisted metal just waiting to cut us, parts which could still be hot from the fire, and pools of fuel still burning. One thing is for sure: Whatever you are smelling right now will get much stronger as we approach; there will be a smell that will choke you. Here, cover your mouth and nose with this." Gonzalez handed Alex a red bandana, then put one on himself. "It is not a protective mask, but it may filter out some of the smoke and stench," he said, and Alex immediately tied his bandana around his head, covering his nose and mouth.

Forty-five minutes later, they received a signal over the walkie-talkie that they could advance. After twenty minutes of climbing over fallen trees and jumping from rock to rock to cross several streams, the plane came into view, in a partial clearing.

The fuselage was virtually intact but completely burned, with its nose dug into the hillside. Three body bags were laid out on the ground about ten feet from the plane, with three corpses laid out next to them—presumably the pilot, co-pilot, and passenger—their charred bodies burned beyond recognition, as Gonzalez had predicted.

Alex was about fifty yards back, his view partially obstructed by the team of police gathered around the funeral directors, who were working to put the blackened remains into the body bags. Dozens of peasants were also at the scene, but the police kept them off to the side. He tried to get closer, but Gonzalez held him back. He strained his eyes, and as the hot afternoon sun beat down on his head, the sweat dripped down his face and body. He wondered if it was the hike combined with the heat and humidity or the carnage in front of him that weakened his knees. He felt like he was going to heave but held it back.

Alex wasn't sure what he was seeing. Two corpses were full-sized, obviously large men, with head, arms and legs intact, though badly burned. The third, however, was truncated. No head, no hands; just a charred torso.

Alex pulled off his bandana.

"Señor Gonzalez, am I seeing right? How many corpses are out there on the ground?"

"Three people—pilot, co-pilot, and passenger," replied Gonzalez.

"I didn't ask who was on the manifest. Just tell me what you see, Señor Gonzalez; look out there, next to the body bags."

Gonzalez lifted his eyes and scanned the site again, from left to right and back again. The funeral directors were working quickly. It took them only a couple minutes to put the remains into the three body bags.

"To tell the truth, Señor Alex, I am not sure what I saw. I think there were three bodies, but the last one, the one on the right, was much shorter, and I do not know if I saw a head, and the arms were very short, like maybe there were no hands. Maybe the head and hands were blown off. You know, when all that is left is charred flesh, you really cannot be sure what you are seeing."

As bad a scene as it was, Alex was not at all prepared for one of the corpses to be mutilated. He wondered if his mind was playing tricks on him—but then Gonzalez seemed to agree that something wasn't right with one of the bodies.

After finding no personal identification papers on any of the corpses, the funeral directors closed the body bags and pulled them aside so the rest of the investigation could continue.

The investigators started taking photos of the site from several angles, then stretched a tape measure across the site and noted distances between the fuselage and all major parts. They found the wings on the ground about 100 yards away, apparently snapped off as the plane headed toward the ground and slashed through the forest. They took photos of the wings as well, then added their location to the site map.

They climbed inside the plane and looked for the flight recorder but returned empty-handed. Most of the instrumentation from the plane had been removed. They also found no personal identification papers anywhere in the plane.

The baggage compartment had the remains of a burned suitcase in it, but it was open and empty. Aside from the fuselage, major components, and corpses, there was fairly little from which to draw any conclusions. Most of whatever might provide clues had apparently been salvaged by the local community, perhaps as curiosities or for later sale as souvenirs.

The investigation lasted just over an hour. The lead investigator then came back to Alex and Gonzalez, wiped his brow, and related his tentative report in Spanish, which Gonzalez translated:

"The cause of the crash appears to be pilot error. Although the nose gear was destroyed, the investigator focused on the plane's flaps, or whatever remained of them. The flaps are used to permit the aircraft to make a steep descent just before landing without significantly increasing its speed. In this case, however, they appear to have been in a position for a steeper descent than the aircraft should have been making at the time. He concludes that the pilot's timing was off, which led him to descend too rapidly, just before making it over the top of the mountain.

"Given the remoteness of the crash site, he doubts they will bring back the parts of the aircraft for a fuller investigation. He will leave that to his superiors to decide, and that may depend on what the aircraft insurer wants to do and may require an additional trip. He suggests the American NTSB and the manufacturer may want to do their own investigations, but that will be up to them.

"He says that further work could be done if they could find the black box, but he expects it's now in the hands of someone who took it for salvage and may eventually put it up for sale in a village flea market. He offers the same comment on the missing instrument panel.

"He does not care to speculate on the purposes of the present flight; his job is merely to investigate the cause of the crash.

"As for the dead, based on the information in the flight plan and passenger manifest, and the bodily remains at the scene, he concludes that three people died in the crash: pilot and co-pilot, both Americans, and the passenger, one Ricardo Guttmann, of Argentine nationality."

"What happened to the head and hands of the third victim? asked Alex, probing. "Did we see correctly that there was only a charred torso going into the third body bag?"

"No way of telling," said the investigator through Gonzalez. "Maybe vandals or animals." He offers that all three bodies were already removed from the plane and lined up in a row when the investigating team arrived.

Alex continued to inquire. "But why aren't the two other bodies touched? Animals wouldn't be so picky as to focus on only one of three bodies. Which one was mutilated, and does the investigator have any idea why that one was chosen?"

"The third victim was the passenger," said Gonzalez, "because the other two wore the same belt, part of their official uniforms, with a heavy metal buckle which, even though melted, was still identifiable. The third had no such buckle on his belt, and thus was the passenger."

As to why the passenger's body was mutilated, the investigator doesn't know and doesn't really care, because he has identified the dead based on the passenger list.

Yes, the investigator had asked the peasants who were still around if they had any idea as to what might have happened to the third victim, what happened to the missing parts of the aircraft, and whether there was any money or drugs on the plane. They know nothing. They all say that by the time they got up to the crash site, everything was pretty much as it is now.

Gonzalez cautioned Alex to report the official investigation results and not make any mention of the fact that only the passenger's torso was found. No need to make any more of this than necessary. Small plane crashes aren't that unusual and, according to Gonzalez, there was no need to torment the family by telling them the head and hands were missing. They were going to cremate anyhow, and the funeral directors had been ordered to deliver the remains directly to the crematorium.

Given the expected condition of the body, the family had already been told none of them would be required to come to Mexico to make positive identification, and none would be present for the cremation. Only the cremains would be sent to them, in an urn, for a memorial service in Argentina.

AS THE CONVOY MADE ITS WAY back to Acapulco, images from the crash site flashed through Alex's mind, especially the mutilated body of the Argentine banker.

Why in God's name would someone want the head and hands of a corpse? Was there a bounty involved? Was this a set-up and attempt to avoid positive identification? Why weren't the Mexican authorities more concerned?

His nostrils held the stench of death and burning jet fuel.

Capitán Ramírez was kind enough to stop by the hotel so Alex could pick up his bag. Alex quickly changed into the clothes he'd worn to the beach, still carrying the odor of sweat, but at least they didn't smell like the horrible sight he'd just seen. They continued to the airport. Curiously, there was little discussion on the way back about the crash site, but Alex knew precisely what he could report. Gonzalez had been clear about that. After a polite goodbye and thank you, Alex raced through the terminal to catch the last flight of the day back to Mexico City, eager to return to his apartment to get working on the story.

AFTER BREWING A FRESH POT OF COFFEE, Alex started writing, then decided to call Jim Ferguson in Acapulco with an update. Jim picked up on the first ring.

"Hey, Jim, it's me, Alex. You been waiting by the phone for my call?"

"Actually, I'm just packing up my stuff to head back to Dallas tomorrow. How did you survive your guided tour of the outback?"

"I made it through. Quite a scene, actually, one I wouldn't want to have to see again. I suspect some real intrigue. The Mexicans are treating this as an accidental air crash—pilot error, they say—but I think there's something bigger."

"Should I be watching the newspaper for evidence of your literary talents?"

"This could be really huge. I told you the passenger, the Argentine banker, was a major player on the international banking scene. Something tells me an empire is about to collapse. A guy this important doesn't just drop out of the sky without other consequences. And I saw some weird things I'm not allowed to report—the Mexican Federal Police have essentially put a 'gag order' on me—I'm not supposed to write what I actually saw, just report 'the official story.' My boss is beholden to these guys, so if I go beyond, my job is probably at risk, and maybe more. But this is such a hot one, maybe my chance to break out of the mold—"

"Hey, there's more to life than a Pulitzer. Don't let your journalistic ambitions get the best of you! You're the new kid on the block—relatively new at the job, and new to Mexico. Go by the book and do exactly as you were told. If there are implications of this guy's demise, you can report them as they happen. And think about your boss: He got a heads-up on this story from the Mexican Federal Police, and if you screw up his relationship with them, there could be hell to pay."

"Thanks for the advice, counselor, and for a good time in Acapulco. But I'm still mulling over how to handle this one, and I've got some writing to do before I hit the sack. It's been a really long day. I'll fax you a copy of the story once it's out."

Alex had barely hung up when the phone rang.

"Yeah, I'm back at it, Hal. I should have something for you first thing in the morning. Gruesome scene, really."

McDonald spent a minute on chit-chat, then tried to get some of the details of what Alex saw, but Alex was determined to keep this his story.

"OK, whatever you say. I'll keep it brief, a couple hundred words, and we'll talk about developing it further over the coming days."

Alex resented McDonald's tight control not only over content, but also length and style, but he didn't feel he was in any position to challenge him directly. He knew he wouldn't budge and there was no negotiating with the Mexican Federal Police about what could be in the story.

Several drafts later, Alex turned out the lights and slipped into bed. It was after midnight.

CHAPTER 8

ALEX ARRIVED AT THE OFFICE at seven and took the elevator up to the fifth-floor offices of United Press International. He marched straight to McDonald's office at the end of the hall and, after hesitating briefly, left a draft of the release on his desk.

At around eight, he appeared at McDonald's open office door and knocked politely to announce his presence.

"So what do you think? Have I captured the essence of a twenty-four hour venture to hell and back?" Alex asked, somewhat sarcastically.

"Not bad, and I've taken the liberty to tighten it up a bit for you. Tell me what you think."

Hal picked up the draft with his handwritten changes, raised his eyeglasses into position, and read the text aloud:

"In the late evening hours of November 25, a private charter jet carrying Argentine banker Ricardo Guttmann crashed in a mountainous jungle area minutes prior to its scheduled landing in Acapulco, Mexico. Reported dead were Guttmann, along with a pilot and co-pilot from Executive Air, a New York air charter operator. Mexican authorities investigating the crash have determined the cause was pilot error. The aircraft was a Gates Learjet 24B, which has been in service for many years and has an excellent safety record. Guttmann has banking interests in Argentina, Belgium, Luxembourg, Israel, and New York. Telephone calls to his corporate headquarters in Buenos Aires have gone unanswered."

"To tell you the truth, I like your style, Alex. Clearly factual, no drama, and I only tweaked it a bit. Remember, this isn't literary stuff; it's financial journalism. Our readers don't want to smell the jet fuel and burning corpses; they just want to know how this calamity is going to affect the market, the banking and aircraft industries." McDonald seemed pleased that he'd been able to put his imprint on Alex's writing.

"Mind if I take this down to the copy room myself?" asked Alex. "I'm going that way anyhow and can save you a trip."

"That's fine. And by the way, I appreciate your keeping the gore out of it. I know it must be an incredible experience to see an air crash site, and you may even have your own ideas as to what actually happened down there. But the Mexican authorities really like to keep this stuff low profile, and if we're all going to keep our heads—if you know what I mean—we'd best follow their guidelines and not dramatize or cast any doubt on their ability to handle an investigation. Some of them just can't handle criticism."

Alex gulped and gave a straight reply, "Sure, no problem. We go by the book."

Book, bullshit. There was no way Alex was going to let this story get out without mentioning some of what he'd seen. It could go one of two ways, he thought: McDonald would either applaud him for having the courage to write it as he saw it or fire him for having broken the rules. At least the story would be out and, in the worst case, he could pursue it for someone else, maybe a news organization with a taste for the bizarre.

Alex took the draft from McDonald and folded it up and put it in his back pocket as he walked down the hall to the copy room. He then pulled another version out of his breast pocket and laid it on the desk of the lead copy editor, Jerry Melvoy, with a note:

"Jerry, get this one on the wires ASAP. It's hot. Hal McDonald has approved it. Alex Ginsberg."

The text read as follows:

In the late evening hours of November 25, a private charter jet carrying flamboyant Argentine banker Ricardo Guttmann crashed and burned in a mountainous jungle area minutes prior to its scheduled landing in Acapulco, Mexico. Reported dead were Guttmann, along with a pilot and co-pilot from Executive Air, a New York air charter operator. However, the remains of the three bodies found were burned beyond recognition, and there were only two heads and four hands; what was identified as Guttmann was only a charred torso.

Mexican authorities have determined after initial investigation that the cause was pilot error. Since the crash took place outside the USA, the NTSB will not investigate. The aircraft was a Gates Learjet 24B, a model that has been in service for many years and has an excellent safety record. Guttmann has banking interests in Argentina, Belgium, Luxembourg, Israel, and New York, and it is likely his disappearance will have significant repercussions on four continents. Guttmann is rumored to have connections with the left-wing Montonero guerillas, who oppose the current right-wing military dictatorship in Argentina. Telephone calls to his corporate headquarters in Buenos Aires have gone unanswered.

THE AFTERNOON EDITION of El Universal, along with hundreds of other newspapers worldwide, carried the rogue version of Alex's article. McDonald was reading the article when the phone rang. Predictably, it was Capitán Ramírez.

"Yes, I have seen it—actually, I'm just reading it now, Capitán Ramírez.

"I don't know how it happened, really, but this is not the article I saw, and I certainly did not approve it.

"You want to talk to Ginsberg? I can have him call you to apologize. His address? Let me look it up for you."

McDonald fumbled in the top drawer of his desk and found Alex's home address, then read it over the phone to Capitán Ramírez.

"Again, I want to say how sincerely sorry I am about Mr. Ginsberg's lack of sensitivity to your concerns, and I hope this does not reflect badly on our—"

Capitán Ramírez slammed down the phone on his end before McDonald could finish his sentence.

Visibly shaken, McDonald marched down to Alex's office and charged in without knocking. Startled, Alex stood up to meet his boss—now adversary—head-on.

"Alex, I don't know what got into you. I just had a call from Ramírez, and he is absolutely livid!"

"I'm sorry. I couldn't let you block the real story, and I hope I haven't done too much damage—"

"Damage?! Kid, would you classify an A-bomb as doing damage? It's a great story, except some very important people wanted it to blow over, and you've just opened up one helluva can of worms. I'm not sure if I'm more pissed off because you made a fool of me by publishing your 'special edition' or because you've just ruined my excellent relationship with the Mexican Federal Police."

"At this point, is there anything we can do for damage control?" Alex was beginning to realize he'd created a real firestorm.

"Kid, you are one naive journalism grad. You still don't get it! You're dead meat. Ramírez said he wanted to talk to you, but he didn't want your phone number. He didn't even ask if you were still in the office. He wanted your address, and I had to give it to him."

Alex now understood that journalistic freedom ended at the border. His body trembled as he imagined the kind of meeting in store for him. He'd often read about the brutality and torture for which the Mexican police were known.

"I don't see you have a lot of options, and neither do I. As of right now, you no longer work for UPI. Somehow, I'll get you a final paycheck. If you're smart, you'll head down the back stairs, exit the building by the rear door, and get a cab for the airport. If I were you, I'd grab a seat on the next plane for a U.S. destination and not look back."

Within minutes a police car, sirens blaring, screeched to a stop outside Alex's apartment building. Four officers charged up the stairs, burst into his apartment, and trashed the place. Nothing was left on the shelves or in the dresser drawers. Glassware was smashed, bookcases overturned, and his TV and stereo system destroyed.

At the airport, Alex eyed the departure board and spotted a flight in the boarding stage. He ran up to the ticket counter with only his briefcase under his arm and bought a one-way ticket to Los Angeles. He left behind all his worldly possessions and could only imagine the fate that had befallen them.

Exhausted, Alex collapsed into his seat. As the plane taxied away from the gate, he was relieved to be a step ahead of his pursuers, but he still didn't feel safe.

Had he seen too much at the crash scene to go unsilenced? What was at the bottom of the banker's disappearance, and were there others who would be interested in what he'd seen and might try to track him down?

As the plane made its way to cruising altitude, Alex ordered a Johnny Walker on the rocks to help him ponder the future.

WITHIN A WEEK, word of Alex Ginsberg's rogue journalism made it to the personnel offices of all the major news organizations. Alex instantly became a pariah; no one would touch him. It was obvious that neither a commitment to the news or the First Amendment were driving hiring policy; he was a liability. All this made it impossible for Alex to find a salaried job as a reporter with a major news service; he was relegated to freelance work, and under a pseudonym at that. For all practical purposes, Alex T. Ginsberg became Allen Gale.

In the days and weeks that followed the crash, the financial press was filled with stories, written by others, about failures of the banks in the Guttmann Group on four continents. He kept tabs on the Ricardo Guttmann story, but at a safe distance, waiting for the right moment to share what he'd seen.

But no auditor, government investigator, or reporter could get a handle on what had happened. What they learned was that there was a $200 million hole in the books, but it seemed the one person who would presumably have known how it was done had been reduced to ashes.

CHAPTER 9

December 2017

"E-M-M-A, I NEED YOUR HELP!" the attorney yelled from his corner office.

"I can't remember how to put an alternate message on my voicemail!"

He was nearly in a panic state. It was five o'clock on Thursday afternoon, the day before he was to leave on his first vacation in several years. He was clearly frazzled and had emptied his desk drawer in an attempt to find the written instructions, without success.

"No problem, David," Emma said in her usual helpful tone. Emma Campbell had worked for N. David Winkler, better known as "David," since he joined Kelly, Friedman & Green nearly forty years ago. In that time, he'd worked his way up the ladder from associate to top-level tax partner. His previous years of experience with a small international law firm in Europe had given him confidence and valuable problem-solving skills. When he returned stateside and made the switch to tax law from international deal-making, he thought he could succeed by working smarter, not harder. But law practice had become a business, and no matter what he did, he couldn't escape the billable hour rat race.

"It just takes a couple of buttons, and you'll be ready to record your alternate message," said Emma. She did her magic and passed the handset to her boss, who read from his computer screen in an upbeat tone:

"You've reached the voicemail of attorney N. David Winkler, of the Private Client Group of Kelly, Friedman, and Green. I'm out of the office but will return on Tuesday. Please leave a message and I'll call you back. If you require urgent assistance, please hit the pound key, dial zero for the operator, and ask for my assistant, Emma Campbell, who'll try to help you. Thanks for calling, and have a great day!"

"You're only taking a four-day weekend, David. Relax and enjoy it. You deserve a break. I don't know anyone more dedicated to this place than you."

"Thanks, Emma. Thanks for everything. You're a one-woman cheerleading squad, and I know you'll hold down the fort until I'm back. Just make sure they don't take my nameplate off the door while I'm gone. It's a funny feeling to leave, even for a couple of days."

There was a growing undercurrent of competition and dissatisfaction within the firm, which had become nastier over the years. "Blue shirt" personal injury lawyers, with their large contingent fees, were pitted against "white shirt" business lawyers, with their large corporate and banking clients and cyclical transactional work. The economy was on a serious downturn, and the white shirts were having a tough time keeping busy—except for the workout group, which was thriving.

Winkler's tax practice was mostly hourly-fee—not based on a percentage of any recovery or tax savings—and he often wondered if the stress between the various practice groups in the firm would one day cause it to split up.

Most recently, the Business Litigation Group had won a billion dollar contract case after three years of litigation, which brought in millions in fees. But as the case drew to a close, the Management Committee was struggling to fill the pipeline for the dozen lawyers and two dozen legal assistants who'd worked days, nights, and weekends on that lawsuit. Behind closed doors, they were hoping the other side would appeal, just so they could put some bodies to work for that client for another couple of years.

Winkler shut down his laptop, closed it up, and put it in its case as Emma watched, somewhat concerned.

"You're not taking your computer with you, are you?"

"No way," he said with a smile. "I wouldn't even think of it. I promised Eve a four-day second honeymoon in Aruba. No lawyer's yellow pad, no cell phone, no computer. I just want to stick this baby in the closet and go home before I think of something else I should do or the phone rings again. Tomorrow, we'll be sipping Margaritas around the pool in Aruba, thinking about where to go for a fabulous seafood dinner."

THE ALARM RANG ON HIS SIDE OF THE BED, and as the lawyer struggled in the dark to find the 'off' button, a second alarm went off on Eve's side. They always used a failsafe system in case one of them screwed up in setting the alarm.

It was three o'clock, an ungodly hour to wake up, but a necessary evil. They had twenty-five minutes before the airport driver would arrive. It would take half an hour to the airport at that time of night, giving them a full two hours before their six o'clock departure.

As they each washed in front of their respective sinks in the master bathroom, he looked over at Eve as she soaped her upper body. After more than forty years of marriage, he still reacted as strongly as the first time he saw her. He quietly stepped behind her, put his lips to the nape of her neck, and gently stroked her bare back with the tips of his fingers, down to her waist. She shuddered, turned, and they embraced; for a moment, they wished the driver was coming a few minutes later.

AS THEIR FLIGHT APPROACHED ARUBA, the pilot pointed out numerous islands and clear green and blue waters below. He gave an estimated arrival time of twenty minutes, "subject to traffic." Could he be serious? Could there really be congestion at the Aruba International Airport?

The landing was smooth, with a round of applause from the happy vacation-bound passengers. They grabbed their carry-on luggage and made their way down the stairs from the plane onto the tarmac.

They were told it would be hot and humid, but with a constant breeze. It was about two-thirty in the afternoon, and the weather was, indeed, extremely hot and humid. As they exited the plane, they felt like they were walking in front of jet engines that were still running, but they were shut down. Luckily, the breeze was a stiff fifteen to twenty miles per hour.

The Reina Beatrix International Airport in Oranjestad, Aruba, was relatively small, especially considering Aruba has over one million visitors a year. Expansion was in progress, but that day's visitors were still dealing with an overburdened airport.

Anxious to settle in at their hotel, the couple moved quickly through Immigration to the baggage claim area to find three conveyor lines. Five flights had landed within recent minutes, and one poor baggage handler was doing his best to rotate putting baggage on lines A, B, and C. They waited, and waited, and waited for any sign of the bags from their flight.

There were air conditioning ducts above the conveyor belts, but evidently they weren't working. The place was steaming, and Winkler's T-shirt was already stuck to his chest. Dozens of representatives from local hotels and travel agents were lined up outside the Arrival Hall, with placards bearing the names of clients. Winkler spotted an agent from Aruba Travel & Tours, with his name on a sign, and walked over to her as Eve continued to watch for their luggage.

"Welcome to Aruba, Mr. Winkler," she said. "I hope you had an easy flight."

"The flight was fine, but we've been waiting half an hour for our bag, and this place is a sauna."

"I am truly sorry for the delay, but you've arrived at peak time, and things here are just not as efficient as they should be."

At that moment, Eve spotted their bag and pulled it off the conveyor belt. She quickly walked to the Arrival Hall, passing right by the Customs Inspector, who didn't even take the time to wave her through and seemed to be looking only for locals bringing in merchandise.

"Nice to meet you, Mrs. Winkler," said the travel agent. "We have a bus waiting for you outside to take you to your hotel, but there's more congestion outside. This is a special day for Aruba. We have three hundred Arubian students leaving for the Netherlands to begin their university studies. They're all going on scholarships provided by the government since Aruba has no university. So today their parents, other family members, and friends have all turned out at the airport for an emotional goodbye, with a host of dignitaries and brass band as well."

They boarded the bus, which gradually filled with other travelers heading for various hotels around the island. As the last passenger was seated, a short, stocky, bald gentleman in his sixties stepped on, positioned himself next to the driver, and picked up a microphone.

"Good afternoon, ladies and gentlemen. I'm Mr. Tips, and on behalf of the Governor of Aruba, my job is to give every visitor a personal welcome. Welcome to our beautiful island! You're my twenty-ninth tourist bus leaving the airport today. I know you're eager to get to your hotels, but I'd like to take a few minutes to give you a brief introduction to the island, its people and languages."

After a short discourse on these topics, including the prevailing U.S. dollar exchange rate, he passed out fliers from the best restaurants and jewelry shops on the island, which he said would greatly appreciate our business.

"I should also tell you that today it's unusually hot and humid," he said as sweat poured off his brow and he did his best to mop it up with a handkerchief. "You'll forget all this, though, when you take a dip in our crystal clear, blue waters. Also, there's a tip box at the front of the bus. Your driver is the best of all the drivers on the island and would certainly appreciate a little something from each of you. Once again, have a pleasant stay!"

Mr. Tips then jumped off to greet the next bus, the bus driver closed the door behind him, and to everyone's delight, the air conditioning began to work.

As the bus began to make its way from the airport to their hotel, they passed dozens of cars parked along the airport fence adjacent to the runway, with family members of the scholarship students waving goodbye to the departing flight to Amsterdam. They saw police cars with flashing lights and the brass band and dignitaries lined up on the tarmac, next to the KLM plane. The students briefly looked back at their families as they entered the aircraft, bound for a life and country much different than they'd ever known in Aruba.

SONESTA SUITES WAS JUST MINUTES FROM THE AIRPORT. It was a brand spanking new first-class resort, highly recommended by one of Winkler's partners, who'd been scuba diving in Aruba for years.

The building was pale pink, with fresh white trim. There were two wings, each with five stories, surrounding a large central pool area, with a garden restaurant and bar. Two freshwater pools flanked the central pool, a beautiful free form pool with tropical garden islands in the middle. Palm trees of all types and sizes lined the pathways, as well as hundreds of different tropical flowers and bushes. It was a beautiful, idyllic setting.

A sand beach and swimming area lay beyond the pool, with a break wall and inlet to the sea. They had choices: Freshwater or salt water, sandy beach or cement deck. In each place there were lounge chairs and beach umbrellas, and palm trees provided shade.

Beyond the sandy beach was a walkway to the motor launch to Sonesta Island, a private island just a short ten-minute boat ride from the resort. The sign at the dock indicated the launch would leave every fifteen minutes throughout the day. The island was exclusively for guests at Sonesta Suites and the Sonesta Hotel and Beach Resort, across the street.

"DAVID, LET'S HIT THE POOL." Eve pulled her one-piece swimsuit out of their luggage and tossed him a pair of swimming trunks. "We can unpack later!"

Within minutes, they were swimming in the refreshing waters of the hotel's pool, surrounded by a tropical garden, as the heat, humidity, and frustrations of travel melted behind them.

Following a poolside nap, they had a light dinner at the hotel restaurant, then turned in early for a night of romance.

Neither had any idea how the events of the next day would change their lives.

CHAPTER 10

THE NEXT MORNING, Winkler and Eve leisurely ate a tropical breakfast on the terrace outside their room: Slices of ripe mango and pineapple and chunks of papaya and watermelon were all beautifully arranged on a plate. Yogurt and granola, croissants and jam, and a pot of freshly brewed coffee completed the meal.

By ten they were ready to venture out and decided to try the beach on the hotel's private island.

The hotel's shuttle boat carried only six passengers, and three women, two probably in their thirties, one who seemed a little older, all Spanish speaking, had already taken their seats. As the launch pulled away from the dock, the lawyer and his wife each silently began to create their own imaginary background for their co-passengers.

Eve noticed the cut of their bathing suits was relatively modest and their cover-ups were drop-dead gorgeous, definitely from top designers. The same for their leather trimmed straw beach bags and leather sandals. They wore tasteful jewelry, not overdone, and none of them had wedding bands. She imagined they were all single, upper class, probably professionals, living somewhere in Latin America, on a girls' vacation in Aruba.

Winkler, who knew some Spanish, tried to listen in on their conversation, but the noise of the engine made it almost impossible for him to understand. The younger ones, who were much darker than the third, seemed to be bantering on about the private island and a decision they had to make when they landed. The third seemed aloof and stared off into the blue sea ahead, letting the wind blow through her long black hair.

Each of them had an open beach bag stuffed with beach towels, bottles of water, suntan lotion, and reading material. The two younger ones had Spanish language magazines. The older, quiet one had a small book at the top of her bag.

Winkler leaned over to try to see the title of the book. Surprisingly, it was one he read decades ago: *Prisoner Without a Name, Cell Without a Number*, in the original Spanish version, *Preso Sin Nombre, Celda Sin Numero*. He was stymied. Why would anyone on vacation be reading a 1970s first-person account of torture in Argentina during that country's dark period, known as "The Dirty War"? Hardly a light read for the beach.

He imagined she was a university professor, teaching Latin American history and using this as course material. She couldn't possibly have any other reason for reading this sordid account of electroshock and other atrocities—or could she?

He gently tugged on Eve's arm and quietly pointed out the book as the boat pulled up to the dock and the three women stepped out first. Winkler and Eve followed them in the direction indicated by a sign marked "Beaches," which led to a path passing through a beautiful botanical garden. After walking two minutes there was a fork in the path with a sign in English: To the right, "Adult Beach." To the left, "Family Beach/Restaurant/Workout Room."

They stopped behind the women, who were chatting and laughing about which way to go.

Winkler decided to risk making a fool of himself and pulled together some basic Spanish. "*¿Saben ustedes cuál es la diferencia entre las dos playas*? Do you know the difference between the two beaches?" he asked.

"We theenk the playa para adultos—the beach for adults—ees a nude beach," said one of the younger women. "*Ustedes van par allá*? Are you going there?" she asked, smiling.

Eve squeezed her husband's hand, and they both agreed they were heading for the family beach. The three women likewise headed in that direction. Winkler would have to leave the adult beach to his imagination.

AS THEY LAID OUT THEIR TOWELS ON THE BEACH, Winkler and Eve compared notes on their observations of the three women.

"You know, Eve, we do this all the time, and we never know if we're right or one thousand percent wrong. The three of them could all be cops from Caracas, beauticians from Bogota, or pediatricians from Puerto Vallarta."

"Why are you so interested? The truth is probably a lot less fascinating than whatever our minds could conjure up," replied Eve. "Anyhow, what about that book you pointed out?"

"Did you notice what people were reading at the pool? Magazines. Novels. Generally easy stuff. But the book that woman had doesn't qualify as beach reading.

"I read it years ago, just after it was written, to get a feeling of what was going on in Argentina at the time. I had a client mixed up in that situation. You remember, the so-called 'Dirty War,' when the U.S. government supported a right-wing military dictatorship in opposing anyone who even smelled left-wing, like students, academics, and the intelligentsia.

"The book is a first-hand account by a newspaper publisher, Jacobo Timerman, who was held in captivity and tortured. If you want to know what it was like, just read that book.

Definitely not something I'd pick for the beach."

"David, I think that book has got you going. Why don't you be direct and ask her about it? I don't think she'll mind."

"Maybe later," said Winkler as a beach waiter clad in white shorts and a T-shirt stopped by their area.

"Ready for drinks, my friends?" said the waiter.

"Two piña coladas, please, with double rum," replied Winkler.

"David, it's not even eleven. I don't think I'm ready for that."

"Those are for me," he said, smiling at the waiter. "And a cappuccino for the lady."

THE RESTAURANT at the island beach was relatively small, and the tables were set quite close together.

Around noon, the three women got up to go to lunch at the restaurant, and Winkler and Eve decided to follow them, seating themselves at the next table. The woman with the book had brought it to lunch with her and continued to read intently while waiting to order.

Encouraged by Eve, Winkler decided to make his move and walked over to their table.

"Excuse me," he said, addressing the oldest of the three women, "but I couldn't help noticing the book you're reading. I read it many years ago, when all the disappearances and torture were going on in Argentina. It's a terrible part of history."

"Yes," she said. "Please excuse my bad English. I haven't spoken in many years, since the high school. I am just learning about this period for the first time. I grew up in Uruguay; we didn't learn about Argentine history."

"Your English is much better than my Spanish! So, I'm curious—why are you interested in it now? It's not your typical vacation reading...and you're not even from Argentina."

"Yes and no. Actually, it's a long story, and really strange. Maybe we should pull the two tables together, and I can tell you over lunch if you are really interested."

Winkler helped the women move their table over a few feet, making a combined table large enough for all of them. Introductions followed.

"I am Maria Theresa Romero, and these are my friends, Alejandra and Carmen."

"Pleased to meet you. My name is David Winkler, and this is my wife, Eve."

They agreed to order lunch first. Then, after a few minutes of small talk about the beauty of the island and laughing about the fact that they all chose the family beach, Maria Theresa continued.

"So I see that you have a particular interest in the period of Argentine history which I am just now learning about, David."

"Yes, while all that was going on, in the mid to late seventies, I had friends in Buenos Aires who would call each other at the end of each day to see if they were still there. Some of their friends were picked up by men driving Ford Falcons and never seen again. Something like 30,000 people disappeared during this time. I'm a lawyer and had an Argentine client at the time who was involved in a financial scandal, a rather complicated story. An Argentine lawyer I dealt with—the client's right-hand man—actually died under torture."

"Until recently, I had no idea that anything like that ever happened," said Maria Theresa. "I grew up in Montevideo, Uruguay, the only daughter of an Uruguayan businessman and his wife, a schoolteacher. My father died several years ago. My mother died two weeks ago."

"So what connection is there to Argentina?" asked Winkler.

"In my mother's papers, which I saw after she died, she told me that she was not really my mother...and that my father wasn't always an Uruguayan businessman. Both of them were Argentinians, and my father had been in the Argentine military during the Dirty War. My real mother was a prisoner and was pregnant with me at the time. I was taken from her by Caesarian section, and she was told that I died during the delivery. My parents—those people I knew as my parents my entire life—adopted me and left the country.

"Here, she says it all in this letter she left for me, to be found only after she died." Maria Theresa pulled out several sheets of folded paper from her purse, holding back tears. "As you can imagine, it was very hard for me to learn this, after so many years. I had absolutely no idea."

"It must have been a terrific shock. First, you lose your mother, then you find out she wasn't your mother and your parents had been living a lie all that time," said Winkler, shaking his head.

"So, now I am trying to understand a little about that period, to get some appreciation of my roots. That is why I bought this book," said Maria Theresa. "All the disappearances, torture, and killings. Anyone who opposed the regime was at risk. Even those who did not actively oppose but were merely suspected. It was a very frightening, terrible time."

Winkler asked if he could see the letter, and she passed it over to him. His eyes scanned the handwritten text, just a little over two pages for such a significant confession. Maria Theresa explained that most of it was her mother's regrets and apologies for not telling her the truth during her lifetime, but she was so ashamed of what had happened and hoped Maria Theresa would forgive her.

"There's something here at the very end. Do you know what she's saying here?" He pointed to the last paragraph and passed the letter back to her.

"She wasn't sure about my real mother's name. She says my father mentioned that there was a banking scandal in Argentina and a rich banker died in a plane crash and his banks failed with lots of money missing. The banker's wife was pregnant and was interrogated to find the money, and they took me from her. My mother had the impression that the banker was my father. The man I knew as my father was involved in the interrogation. My mother thought that the banker's wife—my real mother—was killed.

"At the very end, my mother says that she was always told that by adopting me, they were saving me, but I cannot see it as a good deed to steal a baby from its mother. This is all so terrible and confusing."

Winkler turned white, then clasped his hands tightly and looked at Eve, then at Maria Theresa.

"If your mother was right about this, you are the daughter of an infamous man, and our meeting is either an amazing coincidence or some sort of divine intervention."

THEY CONTINUED TO TALK THROUGH LUNCH, as Winkler described his connection to the banker, the man who may well have been Maria Theresa's father.

"I never actually met Ricardo Guttmann, but he and his organizations were clients of mine back in the seventies. I worked with his senior management and Argentine advisors. We were helping him buy banks around the world and set up companies for him. I even negotiated some of the bank deals.

"Then out of the blue one day, we got a telex saying his charter jet had crashed on a trip from New York City to Acapulco. And within a few weeks, all the banks in the group failed, and banking examiners on four continents were scratching their heads. Apparently, there were a number of phony transactions—something about which we were absolutely unaware—and hundreds of millions of dollars were missing!

"We weren't close enough to the situation to know what really happened. We learned mostly from the press that his body had been burned beyond recognition in the crash, then cremated. Yet some people speculated it wasn't really him. Lawsuits brought against him because of the bank failures were eventually dismissed because he'd been declared dead. And like Elvis, there were even reports that he'd been seen alive after the crash."

"So you really don't know if he survived or not, or whether he was responsible for the bank failures?" asked Maria Theresa.

"Personally, I don't know one way or the other. In the last articles I remember after his reported death, the Argentine government had confiscated millions of dollars of the family's properties. But that was decades ago, and I really don't know how the story ended."

"David, tell her about how you met the Brussels branch manager in the States a few years ago," said Eve.

"Right, that was bizarre. We were at a wedding reception, and a fellow came up to me and greeted me by name. I didn't have a clue who he was, and he introduced himself as Pierre de Neville, the former branch manager of the

Brussels bank Guttmann had owned. Back in the seventies, de Neville was my client, and I was his lawyer.

"That chance meeting was about five years ago. I asked him if he had any sense of what really happened—whether Guttmann really died in the crash, and whether he was responsible for the missing millions. He told me those were very strange times, that they often received a cable saying they should expect a courier to arrive with a briefcase full of cash, to be used to fund wire transfers to pay ransoms in Argentina.

"I then asked if he'd met Guttmann, because I always dealt through intermediaries and never met the man. I also pressed him as to whether he thought Guttmann was in the plane or not. I remember he didn't reply directly. Instead, he said something I'll never forget. He told me Guttmann was relatively short and stocky, with a very thick beard, and if he lost a lot of weight and shaved his beard, you'd never recognize him!

"I'm really sorry that I can't be more helpful," continued Winkler. "Actually, I know very little about this. I have a sort of fascination for this part of history, but no current information. For all I know, there could have been important developments right after I moved back to the States. So many years have passed."

"I understand, David, but I really need to have someone start where you left off, so to speak. I've been thinking about this, but do not know where to turn. At a minimum, I would like to know the final, official story and see if anyone has any theories that could be pursued. Assuming that my mother was correct—that Ricardo Guttmann was my real father—I would like to get a copy of the Mexican report on the crash. If his properties were taken by the Argentine government, I would like to know if they were ever returned. I would like to know for sure that my real mother did not survive. I am sure more questions will come up as we get into this. I do not have a lot of money to pay—"

"David, do you think your firm could take this on some kind of pro bono basis?" asked Eve.

"I seriously doubt it. Everyone is too busy looking at the bottom line," said Winkler. In his heart, he wanted to take the case, but his brain told him he'd get endless pushback from the Management Committee. And yet he felt a strange connection to Maria Theresa and her story.

"David, I don't know where else to turn." She was desperate and not about to take no for an answer. "I cannot fund your expenses without limit, but I inherited some money and could give you that to work with. It is about fifty thousand U.S. Dollars. What if you put that on the account, do what you can to find answers to these questions, and when the money is used up, you stop working? Would that make any sense?"

As tough as Winkler could be in a business negotiation, he was unable to resist her plea. "Maybe I can present it as contingent fee case," he replied, "where we only get paid out of a monetary recovery and take a percentage, with you bearing all the expenses. That might fly. And we'll keep it a very short-term engagement so we limit our own exposure in terms of hours. Let me see if the waiter has some paper, and I'll rough out an agreement to make sure there's no misunderstanding."

HALF AN HOUR LATER, Winkler had the essence of a contingent fee agreement handwritten on the back of several sheets of the resort's stationery, which he read aloud:

Contingent Fee Agreement
Legal/Investigative Services

1. Engagement and Scope of Services. Maria Theresa Romero (the "Client") hereby engages the law firm of Kelly, Friedman & Green ("KF&G") to undertake an investigation into the apparent death of Ricardo Guttmann ("Guttmann") in an air crash in Mexico in 1976, and the following related matters:

A. Locate copies of any reports of the crash prepared by Mexican or other governmental or non-governmental agencies;

B. Determine if Guttmann survived the crash and is still alive and, if so, his whereabouts;

C. Determine whether any cause of action exists against the charter air carrier or its employees, officers or directors, if Guttmann died in the crash and, if so, whether any applicable statutes of limitations have expired; and

D. Determine if any properties of Guttmann, members of his family, or business organizations owned by him seized by the government of Argentina were returned to the Guttmann family or the family's business organizations and, if so, whether those properties have since been sold or, if not, in whose name title currently appears.

2. Fee Agreement. In the event of any financial recovery as a result of the efforts of KF&G, the law firm will be entitled to a contingent fee equal to 40% of the net recovery, after expenses.

3. Expenses. The Client will bear all expenses, not to exceed $50,000 in total, which sum will be wired to the account of KF&G as a retainer, to be deposited to the firm's Client Trust Account, to be debited as expenses are incurred.

4. Nature of Commitment to Provide Services; No Guaranty of Success. KF&G agrees to exercise reasonable best efforts, without any guaranty of success, to investigate the matters outlined herein, either using its own staff or third parties selected by KF&G, in its discretion. Fees and expenses of third parties will be paid from the expense retainer. KF&G will provide the Client written status reports no less often than monthly. The Client understands that due to the complexity of this situation, the time which has passed since the incident, and the various governments involved, it may not be possible to fulfill this engagement within the agreed expense limit and, further, that it is possible that the retainer will be used without obtaining any positive results.

5. Publicity. KF&G is authorized to use whatever media sources it desires, in its discretion, to publicize the investigation, during the term of this engagement and at any time thereafter. The Client hereby releases KF&G from all normal obligations of confidentiality.

6. KF&G's Right to Terminate Services. KF&G is specifically authorized to stop providing services, at the firm's option, at the earlier of (a) 90 days after the retainer is received, or (b) at such time as the expense retainer is exhausted. Upon notice to the Client of its decision to provide no further services, KF&G shall provide a report of its progress to date, without any commitment to continue to provide additional services, which will be in the full discretion of the law firm. Should KF&G provide any additional services beyond the initial 90-day period or exhaustion of the expense retainer, that will not constitute a waiver of its right to terminate this engagement and will not in any event constitute an agreement by KF&G to provide additional services.

7. Client's Right to Terminate Agreement. The Client retains the right to terminate KF&G's services at any time, upon written notice, and to receive a refund of any unused expense retainer (less any accrued and unpaid expenses). However, should the Client thereafter receive any financial recovery based in whole or in part on any information provided to Client by KF&G, KF&G will be entitled to a fee based upon the reasonable value of its services. If the parties cannot agree on a fee, the matter shall be submitted to binding arbitration by three arbitrators, with each party selecting one arbitrator and the two arbitrators selecting the third arbitrator. The fees of the arbitrators shall be shared equally by the parties.

"I think that fairly captures what we'll try to do for you, and how we'll be paid. I threw in the possible wrongful death action, just in case there's no evidence that he survived and the crash report confirms pilot error. Maybe the charter airline did a bad job screening the pilot and he had a bad flying record; there could be some liability on the part of the officers and directors. The statute of limitations has probably expired, but we should check it anyhow."

"David, it all looks very clear, and very fair, to me. I understand that in ninety days you may just tell me that you have done what you can and my money has been spent, but I am very hopeful. Where do I wire the money for the expenses?" Maria Theresa asked.

"I'll have that information e-mailed to you Monday morning. Could you please fill in your home address, phone number, and e-mail address right here at the bottom? If we both sign this original, I'll make a copy for you back at the hotel later this afternoon and leave it for you at the front desk."

They both signed the agreement, then Winkler tucked it into his wallet and said, "If you need to get in touch with me before our first report, here's my business card. I hope we can find some useful information for you; we'll certainly do our best."

"I know you will. Something tells me you are the best person I could have asked to do this for me. But please be careful."

CHAPTER 11

THE MANAGEMENT COMMITTEE'S REGULAR MONTHLY MEETING was scheduled to take place the first day Winkler got back, and there was no way he could avoid it. The meetings started at nine in the morning, the first Tuesday of each month, in the large conference room.

Kelly, Friedman, and Green, the firm's founders, had broken off from one of the city's largest law firms some fifty years ago. Since those humble beginnings, the firm had grown from five attorneys to sixty, plus as many secretaries and support staff. As its size increased, the partners became acutely aware of the need for periodic reporting and monitoring of new cases, and progress on pending matters.

Though new matters were accepted by the firm on a daily basis, at the monthly meetings every major case was supposed to be reviewed by the Management Committee as to current status, resources required, and major strategy decisions. The meetings usually ran from one to two hours, depending on the depth of discussion. Each department head was supposed to present a brief written report on every new case and the status of every pending case.

Routine matters were skipped over in the oral discussion; large, complex cases were given most of the time. Contingent fee cases, which were rare, were supposed to be fully presented to the Management Committee, at a special session if necessary. The rules required a full review of likely resources required, source of disbursements for expenses, and probable outcome before any partner could agree to take the case.

Pro bono cases, on the other hand, were evaluated more superficially based upon the need for legal counsel, the inability of the individual or organization to pay legal fees, and potential public relations exposure for the firm. The firm annually committed to provide a certain number of hours of free legal work so it could remain on the State Bar's Pro Bono Honor Roll, a status symbol among the larger firms.

Rather recently, however, the meetings had begun to take a nasty turn: The firm's bottom line profitability had become the month-to-month focus. As the economy spiraled downward, major corporations had started to put their legal work out to bid, and many of them were demanding rollbacks of the firm's hourly billing rates. Some large companies refused to pay for expenses such as photocopying, faxing, and online legal research, which were previously a profit center.

Someone could be expected to mention the ever-increasing figure for accounts receivable, which had to be monitored closely to make sure cash receipts kept flowing. In the firm's nearly fifty-year history, there had never been a month where cash receipts didn't at least cover the monthly "nut" to pay the rent, keep the lights on and the associates and staff paid—and they wanted it to stay that way. The partners had represented too many younger law firms that had gone heavily into debt for expansion and to pay partner draws, and they didn't want to slip into oblivion as those firms had.

Representation of Maria Theresa Romero was certain to raise eyebrows, and Winkler wasn't really looking forward to what he expected would be a heated discussion. He knew he shouldn't have taken it as a contingent fee case without Management Committee approval. The prospects for recovery were so slim—they were probably negligible—he shouldn't even have considered it on that basis, even though there was a hefty retainer for out-of-pocket expenses.

Could he pass it off as a pro bono case? It didn't neatly fit into that category either. Where were the legal issues? Why were the services of a lawyer required at all?

Was the firm in the business of looking for dead people? Or missing ancestors? Or helping helpless maidens find their roots? He could anticipate a barrage of questions.

Ultimately, he expected it would come down to money. Since Winkler couldn't say there was even a faint hope of finding the banker alive, he'd be engaged in a fruitless search, with no likely upside. The retainer would simply come in and go out for computerized research and outside investigators. His time—and the time of any other attorneys and legal assistants he'd put on the case—would be written off. And all this while other billable files sat on the corner of his desk, gathering dust.

Word about the case had already gotten around the firm, as Winkler had faxed in the retainer agreement and the $50,000 retainer had already been wired into the firm's Client Trust Account. Also, during his call to the office for wire transfer instructions, he'd requested a conflict check. He hadn't thought about how his partners would react to the information on the conflict sheets that ended up in the mail slots of every attorney and legal assistant:

Client: Maria Theresa Romero

Address: Avenida de la Independencia 244, Montevideo, Uruguay

Nature of matter: Research into disappearance/death of father, Argentine banker, Ricardo Guttmann, believed killed in 1976 air crash in Mexico, connected with $200+ million banking irregularities and collapse of worldwide *banking group; research status of Argentine expropriation of Guttmann properties and current status of title; research possible wrongful death action against charter airline involved in air crash (name to be determined) and related statute of limitations.*

Adverse parties: Not yet determined. Possibly governments of Argentina, Belgium, Luxembourg, and Israel; charter airline owner/operator (name to be determined).

Fee arrangement: $50,000 retainer for out-of-pocket expenses only; contingent legal fee @ 40% of any financial recovery.

Damn! Even Yvonne, the always fashionably-dressed thirty-something receptionist, seemed aware of the hot water Winkler was in. As he dashed by her on the way to the conference room, she looked up from her switchboard and gave him a knowing smile. "David, you forgot your bulletproof vest!"

He opened the large French doors of the conference room and saw the six other members of the Management Committee seated around the twenty-foot long table. It was a minute before nine, and he was the last to arrive.

"Good morning, ladies and gentlemen."

Winkler always took a semi-formal approach to these meetings. He'd been a partner for more than thirty years, and a member of the Management Committee for more than twenty years, but he still felt a certain distance between him and the other members.

Tom Kelly, senior partner, always acted as chairman of the Management Committee meetings and could be expected to start the discussion on a matter of fact basis, but then open it up for pot shots by others.

"Pour yourself some coffee, David, and we'll get down to business. We've been chatting about this new case you took on—we saw a brief description in the conflict sheet, and the $50,000 retainer just hit the Client Trust Account yesterday. But since you were on vacation, none of us have had an opportunity to talk with you about it."

"Well, Tom, it's a fascinating case with some significant potential for the client, and the firm, but admittedly, it's a long shot. I certainly didn't intend to monopolize the meeting by a discussion of this case, but I'm open to all your questions and would be happy to start with an overview."

"That's fine, David, take a few minutes and fill us in." Kelly and the others were obviously interested, though Winkler knew their patience would last no more than ten minutes.

Ever since his fateful meeting with Maria Theresa Romero, Winkler had been thinking about how to summarize the facts, issues, and compelling reasons why the firm should take the case—which he'd already done—and why he shouldn't be given too much grief for doing it.

"In essence, it's an investigation into the death of Ricardo Guttmann, an Argentine banker who's believed to have died in the crash of a private charter jet on a flight from New York to Acapulco back in 1976. The client is Maria Theresa Romero, a citizen of Uruguay. Her mother died a few weeks ago, and Ms. Romero found evidence in her mother's personal papers that she was adopted and was told Guttmann was her birth father.

"She inherited some money and is willing to use $50,000 of that to fund the investigation. As you're aware, she's already wired that amount to our Client Trust Account as a retainer, for out-of-pocket expenses only. She doesn't have much, and since it's an extremely long shot, I agreed we would take the case on a 40% contingency."

"Why do you say Guttmann was 'believed' to have died in the crash?" Abe Friedman was the next to chime in.

His background as a trial lawyer included a dozen years in the Department of Justice, handling major white collar prosecutions.

"The press reported that he died in the crash, but there was speculation that he may not have been on the plane, that it was a set-up to make it look like he died. It's actually one of those 'small world' stories." Winkler felt uneasy providing all the details, since the coincidence of his prior relationship with Guttmann's empire and the chance meeting with Maria Theresa Romero were still bothering him. But he had no choice and continued.

"At the beginning of my career, I represented Guttmann when I practiced law in Europe. I never met him, but I was involved with his banking empire as European counsel. I followed the news stories and speculation after the crash. Within weeks after the crash, Guttmann's banks around the world all failed, and there was a lot of talk that maybe he wasn't on the plane, that he conveniently disappeared. There were even reports that he'd been seen alive in Spain and Cuba. Very quickly, however, interest waned, and frankly I got involved in other things and lost track of it.

"What I do recall is that the bodies on the plane were all charred beyond recognition, but Guttmann's family acknowledged his death and had his remains cremated immediately. It seemed strange to me at the time. I wondered how they could be so sure it was him, and so quickly. But it was done, and we just responded to inquiries about his companies after that.

"We're going back decades, but I clearly recall that after Guttmann's death—or disappearance, to leave the matter open for now—his banks on four continents all failed within short order. The auditors found 'holes in the books' representing over $200 million in questionable transactions; the money had been taken out of the banks to offshore entities about which there was little or no information. Gone. That's certainly what fueled the speculation that maybe he'd set up the crash to cover his tracks. It wouldn't be the first time someone had done something like that.

"The law firm I was with at the time had absolutely no idea what was going on. We just did the corporate work, formed holding companies, and negotiated acquisitions."

Abe Friedman jumped back in. "So, the speculation about his death or disappearance was connected to the $200 million in 'banking irregularities' you referred to in the conflict sheet?" Friedman's experience in financial crimes caused him to probe further into the monetary aspects of the case. He attempted to analyze the situation objectively but couldn't help taking on a sarcastic tone. He put his hands on his temples, looked down at the conference table, and closed his eyes in concentration. After a long pause, he continued.

"So here we are, several decades later, our little law firm, with its own financial challenges, getting into bed with the possible heiress to a huge illegal fortune. A fortune, even by today's standards—that much I will admit—which was allegedly stolen by a man who's conceivably alive but probably dead. A man who—if he is alive—has managed to keep a low profile all that time and evaded police and prosecutors on four continents for over four decades.

"And our law firm, with its clientele of blue-chip corporations and conservative individuals of wealth who prefer to stay off the front page of *The Wall Street Journal,* has agreed to look for him, for 40% of an amount which, if I were a betting man, I would give you ten-to-one odds— hell, let's make that a hundred-to-one—you'll never find." Friedman's voice rose, and his face turned red.

"And if you do find him, and if there is any money—which is really a separate issue—then it's highly doubtful the fortune will belong to him or, for that matter, to her—and remember that she's the client, because it wasn't his money in the first place! Do I have that right, David?"

Friedman could make even the Ten Commandments look foolish. His years of grilling witnesses on cross-examination gave him the ability to make you doubt anything. When you had him on your side, it was great, but God help you if he'd decided your case wasn't worth pursuing.

That goddamn Friedman, Winkler thought, *he's doing it to me again.*

It was alright for the litigators to pour a million bucks of time into a case, lose the case, and then write off the fees; nobody so much as raises a peep. It's okay if he puts a couple of associates onto a case defending a country club friend accused of skimming money from a public charity and considers that pro bono. But if someone else takes on a pro bono case and it's not for his favorite charity or one of his "good ol' boy" clients, then there's always hell to pay.

All eyes were on Winkler. Trickles of sweat dripped down his chest, anger swelled up inside him, and he was ever-so-close to speaking his mind—but then he remembered how he'd survived this long in the practice of law, and in this firm.

Calm down. Breathe deeply. Distinguish the chicken salad from the chicken shit.

He remembered this often-repeated admonition given to him over the years by Joshua Green, one of the founders of the firm, who was sitting at the other end of the table and thus far had been silent.

Forget your ego, and keep your eye on the ball.

It was as if Green was beaming this advice directly into Winkler's mind, without uttering a word.

Winkler knew his partners well enough to know the firm would be skeptical about his taking the case. His primary objective was to keep the Management Committee from forcing him to back out, and only secondarily to keep them from mocking his good judgment. He just had to deflect their attacks and hang on for the ride.

As he lifted his coffee cup to his lips and calmly took a sip, he remembered another of Green's negotiating admonitions:

Agree with your opponent no less than three times, then counterattack.

He put the coffee cup back on the table, then rose from his chair, stood behind it, made direct eye contact with Friedman, and smiled.

"Abe, I certainly see your point. It's definitely a long shot. Really long, I will agree. I thought about this when I first met Ms. Romero. It was an extremely tough case back in the seventies, and it's got to be harder now that so many years have passed.

"And on its face, it's really not a legal case, but an investigation into a missing person. In fact, it's probably only about closure: She wants to know what happened; what investigations were done; what the reports found. If there was a cause of action for wrongful death due to the plane crash, the statute of limitations probably expired years ago, and we'll just confirm that for her.

"She's not expecting to find any money, and frankly neither am I. The contingent fee aspect is merely an add-on. I felt if someone did collect something here, then we should be entitled to our cut. I really don't expect that we'll do much more than a due diligence investigation into the official story, kick the tires on some alternative theories, and report back that we've come to the end of our inquiry—"

A voice from the other side of the table interrupted any consideration of counterattack.

"And while you're doing that, David, you're writing off billable hours some other client would gladly pay for."

It was time for the youngest member of the Management Committee to take her turn. Silence was a sign of weakness. To gain respect, Marnie Chu, a highly regarded employment litigator and the first Asian-American member of the firm, had to jump on whatever bandwagon was being espoused by the senior members and voice concerns.

"Yes, Marnie, I assume we'll lose some billable time on this. But I contemplate putting an outside investigator on the case, using our legal talent only when absolutely necessary. I took the $50,000 retainer to fund these outside expenses, and possibly some air fare and online research into news articles and other sources we may not be able to get on the Internet for free."

"But isn't the amount of billable time you'll write off really an open issue? If you've taken the case on a contingent fee basis, how do you know when to stop?"

She wouldn't let go. He'd hoped to minimize the billable hour issue by focusing on the use of outside resources, but Marnie was always practical and direct in her questioning. She knew this type of case could be a bottomless pit.

"Yes, it's possible for it to get out of hand, except I have two controls, so to speak.

"The first is the amount of the retainer for expenses. When that's exhausted, we're done, that's for sure, unless she tops it up, which is highly doubtful, or we decide we want to continue. I think by that time, we'll have dug up enough to give her closure.

"The second is that we can stop working after ninety days, even if there are still funds in the retainer account.

I myself was thinking about how long it would take for an outside investigator to do a credible job, and although that's anyone's guess, I think ninety days should be enough. That's part of the engagement agreement. We have no obligation to do anything after ninety days from the time we receive the retainer for expenses, and we only have to give our reasonable best efforts during that time. On the other hand, ninety days seems kind of short to find the answer to a financial mystery that remains unsolved after many decades, but it's certainly enough time to spend $50,000 looking for one."

Winkler hoped that would shut her up. Everyone knew the firm's litigators could burn through $50,000 with experts in a couple of weeks. But being grilled by the Management Committee was like being attacked by a many-headed serpent, and Abe Friedman was waiting patiently to get in the last word:

"David, I admire how you've thought this through, but you can still rack up a lot of time in ninety days. How can you assure the firm that the number of dollars in billable time, which will undoubtedly be written off as a result of this 'venture,' won't shock us when all is said and done—and that we won't get a lot of complaints from billable hour clients whose work is put aside during this ninety-day period? Also, who were you thinking of as your outside investigator?"

Winkler had already been thinking about who to put on the team.

"As to the investigator, I had two thoughts," responded Winkler, fully prepared to lay out his game plan. "Our in-house computer network technician runs an Internet research service on the side. He's top notch and very reasonable. He can probably dig up a lot of material on this story at night and on the weekends. This will tell us what's been written in public sources—newspapers, magazines, court cases, and administrative proceedings.

"From there, I think we need a real criminal investigator. I was thinking of a fellow I've heard about who used to track down fugitives wanted on felony arrest warrants for the sheriff's office and has investigated a number of cold murder cases. Now he's a licensed private investigator with his own company. I believe he can tap into lots of official government sources, particularly if the fellow we're looking for was ever wanted on a charge that's still open."

The room was momentarily silent. Winkler had come up with answers to most of their challenges, except for the real issue: The case was still going to result in revenue lost to the firm, even in as short a period as ninety days. They hated to see that without any realistic upside potential. The fact that he had some control over the billable hours dedicated to this wild goose chase was no real answer.

Joshua Green, the sole African-American in the room, had been listening carefully. He took the floor and with the deep voice of a man in his eighties delivered each word with due deliberation in his usual slow and steady pattern.

"My friends, I think we're looking at this case all wrong. I've been sitting here thinking about why our partner, N. David Winkler, would have taken this case without the required approval of the Management Committee, when he himself knew there was no real potential for our firm to be appropriately compensated. We haven't seen a picture of Ms. Maria Theresa Romero, and though my guess is that she is probably very attractive, I won't even suggest that had anything to do with it."

The comment brought faint smiles from the other members around the table. Though several of the partners had been divorced for having affairs, they all knew Winkler was enamored with Eve as much as the day they were married and would never stray off the straight and narrow. He certainly would never take a case solely because the client was beautiful; in fact, he'd turned away a number of extremely wealthy, beautiful, grieving widows because of perceived conflicts of interest he could just as easily have overlooked. These high profile cases had been the talk of the office at the time.

"So, I'm going to assume there was some other appeal here. Some sense that 'justice' ought to be pursued on behalf of Ms. Romero.

"David, you haven't told us any details of how it came to pass that a woman born to an Argentinian banker happened to grow up the daughter of someone in Uruguay. Is there something deeper going on here, something more than just a mysterious disappearance or plane crash?"

Green was a lawyer from the old school who felt sometimes you just had to take a case, even if you couldn't see how you could make a buck. He also had an uncanny sense of a story within a story, probably from his early years as an investigative reporter.

"Well, as I said earlier, I was just giving you an overview. There is another aspect: The people who adopted Ms. Romero weren't your normal adoptive parents. Her adoptive father was an officer in the Argentine military, and she's been told her real mother was the wife of the banker. She also believes her real mother was a prisoner in Argentina during the period known as the Dirty War. She believes her adoptive father may have been involved in the killing of her real mother.

"Thirty thousand or more of these people vanished—disappeared—at the hands of the military, simply because they were suspected of being threats to the regime. Pregnant mothers lost their babies in C-sections performed in prison and were either killed or told their babies died in childbirth. There are several groups of people still trying to find out what happened to their relatives—the mothers, grandmothers, and children of the disappeared people. When I agreed to take on her case, I suppose I was sensitive to the fact that Ms. Romero was a child of one of those disappeared people."

"Tom, how much do we spend every year on that public relations company we always complain about, just to get our names and faces in an occasional newspaper article?"

Green knew where he was heading, and it didn't bother him a bit to put Kelly on the spot. He knew Kelly was the one pushing for PR exposure, and the firm's big problem was that, even though it did quality work, it was reluctant to go public with the results. The partners were always concerned about offending in-house counsel of its major corporate clients, whose bonuses depended on the perception that they, and not outside counsel, won their cases.

"I think our retainer agreement with Billings Ryan and Partners now provides for $50,000 a year, Joshua, if memory serves me," said Kelly.

Green continued. "So, what if we consider this a pro bono case, with disbursements paid, and take advantage of the tremendous PR potential? I'm sure if we let Billings Ryan have at it, they'll get us into *The New York Times*, *The Wall Street Journal*, and all the local and major national newspapers, prime time TV news, CNN—the whole nine yards! I'm afraid we've been so fixated on fees that we've lost sight of a real gold mine in terms of positive exposure for our firm.

"David, do you think Ms. Romero would have any objection?" asked Green.

"Not at all. In fact, I provided a publicity release in our engagement agreement. My only concern is that, if there is someone else interested in knowing about Ricardo Guttmann or the missing fortune, by saying too much we may be attracting them to her, or to us, but we'll be careful and keep that risk in mind."

"Well then, I think we've taken enough time on this case and should move on to other matters."

Green gave a friendly nod to Winkler, who heaved a sigh of relief. Kelly seemed satisfied with the grilling Winkler had received and was anxious to take up other matters.

"Next item on the agenda: Staffing issues in the public utility class action. You'll remember we recently took on several defendants in a mammoth consumer class action against hundreds of major electrical utilities, arising out of the recent series of power blackouts that swept the eastern half of the country. If we don't pull our clients out of this one, we may lose power ourselves!"

Winkler had hoped to handle the Romero case quietly, without major press exposure, but had now committed to exploit its public relations value for the firm's benefit. For now, he was glad to get off the hot seat. He hadn't given a thought to who else would be interested in the results of his investigation. He had to focus quickly on getting his team together; his ninety-day clock had begun to tick.

CHAPTER 12

SEATED AT HIS DESK in his large corner office, Winkler mapped out his preliminary game plan on a yellow pad. "Emma," he called, "I'm going to need some help on this one."

Emma had been his assistant for more than a dozen years and was the angel every lawyer needed and most could only dream of. She was his right hand, his confidant, and a beacon in every storm. Mid-fifties, extremely well-put together and well-spoken, she was at ease with everyone from the messengers to Winkler's multi-millionaire clients, whom she could identify by the sound of their voice over the phone and greeted by name. Officious when necessary, she could protect him from anyone, inside the firm or out. Able to find anything at a moment's notice, she kept his perpetual backlog moving.

Emma sat down in the chair across the desk from him, armed with her steno pad and a handful of pens. She was one of the last of the "old school" assistants who still took shorthand.

"Before we start, David, Joshua Green called and asked that you drop by his office when you have a moment."

"What's that about? I just left him a couple of minutes ago, at the Management Committee meeting. I suppose he wants to offer a post-mortem."

"He said it would just take a second, and there's no rush."

"Fine, but let me first tell you what's going on with that new case for Maria Theresa Romero. There's never a dull moment around here, Emma."

This was the first chance Winkler had to talk with Emma since he returned from Aruba. He briefly outlined the scope of the assignment, building on what she already knew from the conflict sheet and signed retainer agreement, which he'd left for her to open a file. He described the grilling by the Management Committee, sharing his frustration with how some of his partners reacted.

"I don't suppose any of that was a surprise to you, David, was it?" Emma asked with a knowing smile. This was certainly not the first case she'd seen him take because of the principle, regardless of fee potential.

"Probably not, except now we've got to treat this as a PR opportunity for the firm, which isn't a terrible notion, but I would have preferred just to go about our business. On second thought, maybe the publicity will bring some information out of the woodwork—and probably some wackos and gold diggers as well."

"Let's go over these names," Winkler said, running his finger down the list on his yellow pad.

"First, I'd like you to call our computer network guy. I don't know his first name, but we just call him by his last name, *Afzam*. He's been away for a while, for his brother's wedding in India, but I think he's back now. Tell him I'd like to meet tomorrow at noon in my office on a new case. I'd like him to be our main researcher, and my guess is, he'd like to earn a few bucks in the evening and on weekends. He's an absolute wizard on the Internet.

"We'll run that as a reimbursable expense, against the $50,000. His charges will be in addition to his normal salary for computer work for the firm. Make sure he keeps time records, and you can prepare pro forma invoices for him weekly. Get him an assumed name, *Afzam Information Services*."

"What address should I use on the registration?" Emma asked. She was always thinking a step ahead. "Doesn't he live across the river in Canada?"

The firm's offices in downtown Detroit attracted a few employees from Windsor, Ontario, which Winkler could see from his vantage point on the twenty-fifth floor of a high-rise one block from the Detroit River. Since 9/11, the number of terrorist attacks around the country had continued to grow; as a result, it had become difficult for them to make the daily commute, as security at the Windsor Tunnel and Ambassador Bridge often resulted in waits of an hour or more to cross. Most of the firm's Canadian employees couldn't put up with the long lines and had opted to leave the firm and find work in their own towns.

Afzam was an exception. Hard working, ambitious, and extremely talented, his U.S. dollar salary as computer guru for Kelly, Friedman & Green was much more than he could ever earn on the Canadian scale.

"Use our office address as his place of business. It should be fine; he's a Canadian citizen but has a permit to work here. And if that doesn't work, we'll just set up a limited liability company for him. Check with our Immigration Law Department to make sure we aren't breaking any laws. What's important is that we show the money going out to a third party, not to the firm.

"Next, please call Andrea Poppo, our Lexis-Nexis rep, and make sure Afzam gets an ID to use their services under our contract. Andrea will be happy to set that up for you, and make it operational immediately. Whatever Afzam can't find through general Internet searches, he'll find through Lexis-Nexis—news articles, as well as court cases and administrative proceedings. Afzam will be able to search an incredible universe of published articles through Nexis. It'll cost, but it's worth every penny, and the Lexis-Nexis charges will come out of the $50,000 as well. We'll start by reading every word that's been written in the press about Ricardo Guttmann since the mid-1970s."

"I'll get Andrea working on access for Afzam immediately," replied Emma. Once she said she was taking care of something, Winkler could take it off his mind completely.

"The other person I'd like at the meeting is a guy—a private investigator— who is, shall I say, an 'old friend' of my personal trainer, Frankie Zuccarrelli. I'm going to see Frankie at the gym on the way home tonight, and I can probably get his number then. I promised our new associate, Ray Adams, I would introduce him to my trainer."

Winkler ran his hand lightly over his stomach, trying briefly to hold it in.

"Vacations are great, Emma, but pigging out on three gourmet meals a day, sleeping, and lounging around for a long weekend on a tropical island sure doesn't help muscle tone." He sighed, then turned the conversation back to business.

"From what I've heard, this guy recently left the sheriff's office, where he hunted down fugitives wanted on felony warrants, and he may still have access to information that'll be useful to us. Emma, I sure hope I'm not going off the deep end here. Maybe it was stupid to take this case after all. Here I am, orchestrating a search for a man declared dead over fifty years ago, about to hire a P.I. I've never met, and it's virtually certain we're going to come up dry. Am I nuts or what?"

"Look at it this way, David. You only agreed to use your 'reasonable best efforts' to find out what happened, what investigations were done, and what the reports found. If you determine her father is officially dead, you tell her that, and if you find evidence that he may still be alive, you pass that along. You find out what happened to Guttmann's Argentine properties. You advise as to a possible wrongful death claim. That's what you told the Management Committee—and Ms. Romero—right?"

"Yeah, that's right, and no guarantees of any kind. You'll see I made that perfectly clear in the retainer agreement. I guess I'm just not accustomed to taking a case where I don't have some expectation of winning."

"Like you always say, David, let's take it a step at a time. First, let's see what Afzam comes up with, and what your P.I. can do on his end. I'll give Afzam a heads up about tomorrow's meeting, and you let me know if your P.I. will be joining you—"

Winkler interrupted her. "Not you, Emma—it's us. I'd like you to attend the meeting as well and be in on this one every step of the way. I have a feeling you'll be of tremendous assistance."

"That's fine with me, David, but in that case, I'm not ordering pizza for lunch—I think we'll all work better over salad!" Emma hardly ever ate lunch, but her girlish figure showed when she did eat, she made careful choices.

"Right. And don't forget the fresh-squeezed juices or mineral water instead of soda!" he added with a wink. "I think I'll go down to Joshua Green's office and see what he has on his mind."

CHAPTER 13

THE WALLS OF JOSHUA GREEN'S OFFICE were adorned with his Harvard Law School degree, State Bar and U.S. Supreme Court admission certificates, and commendations from everyone from the President of the United States down to the mayor. Photos pictured him with clients and celebrities, from politicians to movie stars. His long and illustrious career spanned over six decades, most of which was spent as a partner with Kelly, Friedman & Green, a firm he'd seen grow from a bunch of young upstarts to the legal powerhouse it had become.

"Joshua, is this a good time?" Winkler asked politely, standing at Green's door.

Green nodded affirmatively. "Come in, sit down, and close the door behind you, David."

Green always spoke behind closed doors. It was his way to assure there would be no interruptions. It also put the entire world outside the conversation. When the door was closed and calls shut off, it was as if the billable hour time clock stopped. He pushed the do-not-disturb button on his phone, a sign that the meeting wasn't going to be brief.

"I appreciate the lifeline you threw me in the Management Committee meeting, Joshua. I really do. I knew they wouldn't be happy about my taking the Romero case, but I guess I underestimated the degree of their concern. Frankly, I've seen more billable hours written off on our run-of-the mill pro bono case than we'll ever see here."

"I think you handled yourself well, under the circumstances. What you're not seeing is that they're desperate for fees. I say *they* because as you know, I'm on the way out, have been for a number of years. I just work on the few cases I want, cases that pique my interest, and I have a place to come every day. That suits me fine."

Green's tone was somber, almost morose. He'd been among the founders of a firm of which any lawyer would be proud to be a part, yet he'd acknowledged that the time had come to pass the mantle.

"David, I see panic in their eyes. We've always realized law practice has its ups and downs, but these are different times. Competition from the mega firms for the top law school grads has driven starting salaries to ridiculous levels, forcing us to boost our hourly billing rates sky-high. Yet these young attorneys don't know any more about drafting an interrogatory or taking a deposition than a new associate ten years ago earning one-half the salary." Winkler listened intently.

"So, our younger litigation partners—I don't suppose I have to name names—wake up one day to realize the only clients who can afford to hire them are the major corporations with extremely large cases, with huge dollars at stake. They call them 'bet the company' cases. Then those corporations, themselves feeling the profit squeeze, put the litigation out to bid. Our partners are offended that they have to spend countless non-billable hours preparing budgets, completing RFPs, and participating in beauty contests. Their self-image is that they're the best, yet they're being treated like vendors—no different than a software developer trying to sell an accounting package to a major corporation!"

"So, why don't they take a step back and ask themselves how they can compete in the twenty-first century, rather than beating their heads against the wall running the practice the way they always have?" Winkler had always been one to look for solutions, rather than stewing over what appeared to be an insurmountable problem.

"It's easy to say but hard to do. They're creatures of habit—we all are. For their entire professional careers, they've just racked up their billable hours and were paid for them. Now they're totally taken aback by the thought that they really have to compete for work, and in some cases they won't even get a chance."

"Why wouldn't a client want a firm with an excellent track record to handle its litigation?" Winkler was showing that he, too, was out of touch with the reality of law practice in major litigation.

"Let's call it the politics of corporate management. More and more general counsel at major corporations want a major national law firm, so they won't be criticized for a bad hiring decision. It reminds me of the mindset of corporate buyers in the early days of computers, who generally bought IBM computers with the official IBM blue logo, rather than less expensive IBM clones. It was all the same. The mantra was 'No one ever got fired for buying IBM.'"

"I get your point, but there has to be some solution," Winkler said. He wasn't one to take a defeatist position.

"Probably so, but they haven't found it, David. The bottom line is, because of our fee structure, we can only handle big cases, and those cases are getting harder to snag. Competition from large national firms is increasing daily, with local branches of those firms horning in on even our regular clients. Actually, the outlook for a firm of our size is rather grim."

It was the first time Green had ever spoken so openly with Winkler about the future of the firm. He continued.

"Usually, we have one or two major cases going on at any one time, and that keeps the armies of associates and legal assistants cranking out their billable hours. My guess is, with our senior rainmakers seriously cutting back, no one can figure out how to assure that the pipeline remains full. It's not a pretty picture.

"That's when the panic sets in. It's probably not a today or tomorrow situation, but if anyone looks at the business plan for the next two to five years—they'll realize there isn't one. That's when they'll seriously ask themselves how they're going to support their lifestyles over the balance of their careers. When you're used to having summer and winter vacation homes, fractional interests in jet aircraft, your kids are in the best private schools and expect to go to Ivy League schools for post-graduate or professional degrees, change is hard to imagine."

"There could be a couple of solutions, Joshua—"

Before he could even lay out some alternatives, Green stopped him. "David, I didn't really invite you here to discuss the future of the firm. It'll work out, or it won't. My guess is, we'll bring in some high-priced talent with a book of business, and that'll either be our salvation or a disaster. Or maybe we'll get gobbled up by another firm. In fact, rumor has it Kelly's been quietly exploring some merger options.

"My point is merely that you shouldn't take the grilling too personally; it was just your bad luck to come in with a case that reminded them of their serious concerns on the revenue side. Actually, I wanted to talk to you on a personal note." Green pursed his lips and drew a breath as he looked away from Winkler.

"I've got some health issues, David; some very serious ones. You probably know I've been dealing with various types of cancer over the years. I've told you about my chemo, haven't I?"

He looked back at Winkler, who immediately became flush, expecting to hear the worst.

"Well, let's just say I've probably used up my nine lives. This time, they tell me it's multiple myeloma. Bone cancer. Nasty stuff. If you looked at an X-ray of my bones, you'd see lots of little holes. It's eating away at me, and so far nothing they've given me has been able to stop it for very long."

Winkler wasn't sure what he was hearing. Was this the final word from a giant of his profession who never took "No" for an answer?

"I'm not one to be melancholy or ask for pity. Let's just say I'm being realistic, not optimistic. I'm going to try one more experimental drug before I hang up my gloves, so to speak. I'm telling you this because I'm going to be at University Hospital for treatment and don't know when I'll be back to the office. The stuff they want to use is poison, so either way, it won't be a vacation."

"I'm really sorry to hear that, Joshua. Does anyone else at the firm know?"

"Just the Management Committee. For now, I'd like to keep it between us. I've got other people involved in all my cases, so there won't be any problem with transition if I'm out for a while—or decide to take some time off after the treatments are over."

"Mind if I drop by while you're in the hospital?"

"Not at all. I'd look forward to the visit—and would certainly be interested to hear how you're doing on the Romero case."

Winkler felt a profound sense of sadness. Joshua Green had been his ally and mentor over the years and passed along many of his best clients. Professionally, Green had achieved whatever he aimed for, yet personally he was unfulfilled, and his life was a disaster. His series of three wives had each died young, the first in a tragic car accident, the last two of cancer. When his third wife died fifteen years ago, he vowed never to have another relationship. Though some thought he was kidding, he was deadly serious when he said being married to him was tantamount to a death sentence.

Green had one child, a son, who had a promising legal career ahead of him, got mixed up with the wrong people, and died of a crack cocaine overdose in his second year of law school. Green never talked about him, but it was clear his mentoring of the younger lawyers, including Winkler, was in some sense fulfilling his frustrated fatherly instincts. He treated each of them like the children he never had.

Green's eighty-some-odd years represented tremendous professional achievement, coupled with immeasurable personal tragedy. Now the last act would play, a man alone against a vengeful disease that had robbed him of his desire to live, and could ultimately take his life.

CHAPTER 14

"RAY, TIME FOR A BREAK."

Ray Adams looked up from his desk at Winkler.

"I told you I'd introduce you to my trainer, Frankie, and now's your chance. I don't have time for a full workout, but you can come with me to the gym for forty-five minutes and see what the place is like," Winkler said.

A recent law school grad, Adams had a tendency to stay late in the office and knew his energy would disappear soon if his routine didn't include an exercise program. But without a trainer, he knew he'd quickly fall off the wagon, as he had so many times before.

"I've been waiting for you to get the time," Adams said.

Adams left his computer on, grabbed his gym bag from the closet, and the two of them took the elevator to the parking garage, where Winkler's red BMW was parked on the executive level. Within minutes, they were in the elevator at the gym. Winkler pushed the button for the top floor with gym equipment for "Gold" members who paid a premium for the newest and best equipment.

"Your trainer—Frankie—he's not one of those macho men who's gonna work me 'til I'm dead, is he?" Adams had put on forty pounds in law school, and while he knew his body needed exercise, he didn't want to push it.

"Not a macho man at all, Ray. You'll see. Just a trainer who'll get you on a program and give you a reason to stick to a schedule so you don't stop going."

They stopped at the reception desk where Winkler got a visitor's pass for Adams, then swiped both of them in at the locker room door. Winkler then took his gear out of his locker, and they both changed into workout clothes.

Winkler glanced at his watch. "Right on time, six o'clock. My Monday - Wednesday - Friday appointment." The equipment room was filled with row upon row of exercise equipment. Though the place was packed, there were still a few machines available. "I start on the recumbent bike for a five-minute warm-up. Take the one next to me, and focus on what you're doing, not the gorgeous women in spandex on the other machines. Frankie'll be out in a couple of minutes."

Just as they started peddling, the trainer came out of the office.

"Ray, let me introduce you to my trainer—the best in the city—Francesca Zuccarelli. We call her Frankie," Winkler said.

The associate did a double take. Frankie was petite and trim, with her long blonde hair tied back in a neat ponytail and toned physique clearly the result of eight to ten hours of exercise a day.

Adams seemed pleased and relieved. "I thought David was taking me to slaughter, with one of those weightlifter type personal trainers whose motto would be 'No Pain, No Gain.'"

"Don't kid yourself, Ray," said Frankie. "We'll work you as hard as you can, and then some. You may feel a little pain, but it'll be good for you. You can quit any time you want, but David'll tell you he just keeps coming back for more! Once you get hooked, you'll feel something's missing in your routine if you skip a session."

After five minutes on the recumbent bikes, they moved over to the exercise benches, and Frankie ran them through two sets of ten abdominal crunches.

"This is just for starters, to get the blood flowing. Now let's move to the floor mats."

Frankie lay down on the mat between the two of them. Each of them had an exercise ball, and she worked along with them. For the next half-hour, she directed their movements as they did more crunches, lifted the ball off the floor between their legs, rounded their legs up over the ball, and arched their backs, taking her every order.

"Breathe out when you're exerting effort, gentlemen," Frankie said.

Winkler and Adams focused intently on their movements and breathing, sweat pouring down, while Frankie breezed along with no apparent effort.

"Time for a stretch," Frankie said, then took Winkler's left leg and put it up on her shoulder, to an almost vertical position. He winced, holding back a grunt.

Pain is good, he thought as she continued to stretch out his hamstrings.

"Frankie, I need a favor," Winkler said. "You were seeing that deputy sheriff who left the county to set up his own P.I. firm. I need a top-notch investigator for a special project. I was thinking he might be the one."

"I gave that guy eight years of my life, but he needed his space," she said.

Obviously aggravated at the thought of her ex, Frankie ratcheted up Winkler's leg another notch. He grimaced, pursed his lips, and closed his eyes as the pain in his hamstrings shot up from an eight to a ten. He held in a grunt, pressing both palms to the mat, digging his nails into the foam.

"Sorry to bring back bad memories, but I just thought he might be the right fit for a special assignment."

Sensing she'd gone a bit too far, Frankie eased off a bit. "It's not your fault, David. Probably mine. I let the relationship go too long when the signs were obvious from the get-go.

"Anyhow, you're not here for floor mat psychology. Luke Rollins is his name. From what his buddies have told me over the years, he's the best investigator there is, and he can certainly use the work. One of his problems was that he was paying alimony to two ex-wives and could never get ahead on a deputy sheriff's salary. Stop by the office on your way out, and I'll jot down his phone number. And make sure he knows where you got it. I'd like him to owe me."

Frankie released Winkler's leg and lowered it to the ground, looking over at Adams. "Ready to be stretched out, Ray, or have you had enough for today?"

"How about we take it a step at a time? Let's have a look at your schedule and see when you can fit me in, and we'll work up to it," he said.

"Fine. You fellows get changed, and we'll meet back in my office in five."

As they walked back to the locker room, Adams looked at Winkler with a grin. "Some trainer you have there. You were right, she's no macho man, but I'd hate to meet her on a wrestling mat. She practically had you in tears."

"Practically?" Winkler retorted.

CHAPTER 15

LUKE ROLLINS ARRIVED JUST BEFORE NOON, and Emma escorted him into Winkler's office, where he and Afzam were waiting.

Rollins was tall, maybe six-foot-eight, with a square jaw, broad shoulders, and military-style haircut. Although well over sixty, he appeared to be in excellent physical condition. He was a rugged type, wearing a brown suede sport coat, beige twill shirt, and no tie.

Emma had found Rollins' CV on his website. Military service, decades ago, with an honorable discharge, followed by a four-year college degree in criminal justice, then the sheriff's department, from which he retired. There was no mention of any achievements on his website, probably because he didn't want to attract the attention of the criminals he'd helped send to prison, or members of their family.

"Luke, I'm glad to meet you, and to have you aboard," Winkler said. "You've already met Emma, my assistant, who'll be keeping us all on the same page. This is Afzam, our computer research consultant for this project. Afzam's day job is to keep the computer system running for our law firm, which keeps him pretty busy, nine to five."

Afzam, originally from Kashmir, smiled modestly, knowing full well Winkler didn't have a clue how much work it really took to keep the network and more than a hundred users up and running seven days a week.

"We've ordered field green salad for everyone, dressing on the side, and freshly squeezed juice and mineral water are over there on the credenza, courtesy of Emma! She believes there's still time to make a healthy person out of me," Winkler said with a smile, casting a brief glance in Emma's direction. She'd been trying for years to get him to eat sensibly at lunch, and he finally seemed willing to follow her lead.

"You can start eating while I kick things off," Winkler continued.

"As I explained to Luke briefly on the phone last night, we're basically on a short-term 'due diligence' mission to flesh out the disappearance or death of one Ricardo Guttmann. He was an Argentine banker who allegedly died in the crash of a private charter jet. It was an otherwise routine flight from New York to Acapulco back in November '76. Guttmann happened to be a client of mine when I was in an international law practice in Europe back then."

"So what was the word on the street at the time? As his lawyer, you must have had an inside track." Rollins was definitely a bloodhound.

"It was very confusing," Winkler said. "We heard he died in the crash, and within a few weeks his banking empire collapsed. Banks in his group failed on four continents— in New York, Brussels, Luxembourg, Tel Aviv, and of course, Argentina, a result of what turned out to be a couple hundred million dollars in banking irregularities. Phony transactions, plain and simple, booked as loans. There were rumors galore. Some people reported having seen him alive in Spain or Cuba. Others said if he didn't die in the crash, someone certainly would have killed him—he stiffed so many people, including some very big-time Swiss bankers, who lost millions."

"What about his family?" asked Rollins. "Didn't he leave anyone behind? And do you recall if anyone watched to see if he reconnected with them?"

"That was the strange part. As far as I know, Luke, he left everyone—parents, brother, and wife—all to bear the wrath of the Argentine military inquisitors. There was a right-wing military dictatorship in power at the time, and they used every sadistic technique known to man to elicit information. Electroshock was one of their favorites.

"If you want some background, do a quick read of this book, *Prisoner Without a Name, Cell Without a Number*." Winkler pulled a copy off the bookshelf behind him and gave it to Rollins. "It's a very graphic, first-hand account written by an Argentine publisher, Jacobo Timerman, of how they tortured him in prison. Some of those former military fellows are still around, and that's one reason we're not just flying over to Buenos Aires and asking the Argentine government for an update."

"That's an interesting notion, David, and one I wouldn't totally reject," Rollins said. "My guess is, you'd probably run up against a bureaucratic stone wall, especially in Latin America. You said the assignment is to trace the official story, find out what investigations were done, and what the reports found. Am I right on that?"

"Essentially that's it, as a practical matter," said Winkler.

"Obviously, if something leads us to conclude Guttmann didn't die in the crash—"

"From your lips to God's ears, Luke. Let's cross that bridge if and when we come to it. The party line immediately after the crash was that he was among the dead. We followed the story for a short while, as things unwound. I left the law firm just a few months after Guttmann's—" Winkler hesitated. "Let's call it a *disappearance*."

"And what's the last information you had?" Rollins was starting to zero in.

"The last word I recall from Argentina—and I don't remember how I learned about it—was that the Argentine lawyer I dealt with, the inside counsel, died under torture during questioning. I imagined it was electroshock. He was in his fifties, and I knew he had a heart problem; he probably couldn't take it."

"What was his name?" asked Rollins, putting down his fork and picking up a pen to take notes.

"Sandoval. Miguel Sandoval. He was Guttmann's right-hand man. It didn't make sense that a fellow with Guttmann's wealth and power would fake his death and leave his family and inner circle to rot."

"I don't suppose you would have any reason to be in touch with anyone related to your former client since then?" Rollins was poking around, trying to determine if Winkler had any connections to the Guttmann organization or family that could be exploited.

"Only once, a real coincidence," Winkler said. "I ran into the former manager of Guttmann's Brussels bank, the Pan American Trade Bank, at a wedding. Pierre de Neville was his name. He was still living in Brussels. It really is a small world. He was the inside man at that bank, the fellow I worked with to set it up and get Banking Commission approval. He walked up to me at a wedding in the States and introduced himself like it was yesterday. But over twenty years had passed since I'd last seen him."

"Did you talk about Guttmann?" Rollins asked.

"Yes, briefly. I've always had a fascination with the case. I asked him if he thought Guttmann died in the crash, and what he looked like. Though Guttmann was my client, I never actually met the man. One time I was scheduled to have dinner with Guttmann and his wife, but Guttmann took sick at the last minute. So, I had dinner with his wife and some other people from the bank but never met Guttmann."

"And what did Pierre de Neville say about Guttmann?"

"He didn't know if Guttmann died in the crash or not. I guess he was like the rest of us, left to wonder what really happened. He said those were very strange times. He was frequently involved in arranging wire transfers of huge sums to pay ransoms. The kidnapping of wealthy individuals was rampant at the time."

"And what about Guttmann's appearance? Did he tell you what his boss looked like?"

"He certainly did. He told me Guttmann was short and stocky, with dark eyes and a black beard. He said he had a heavy Spanish accent but an excellent understanding of English, and if—" Winkler hesitated, as if trying to remember Pierre de Neville's exact words.

"And if what?" pressed Rollins.

"As I recall, his exact words were: 'If he shaved off the beard and lost some weight, you would never recognize him.' That's exactly what he said, and it made me feel like he had real doubts about whether Guttmann was really in that plane."

"Do you think de Neville would be cooperative if we went to him with some more questions?" asked Rollins.

"Cooperative, certainly, but I don't think he would have anything to add at this point," Winkler said. "He did mention that he kept his own file of news clippings and has some other documents, which I guess could lead you to other people. But the Belgian and Argentine authorities probably would have followed up on those leads long ago."

"I'm going to add him to the list, just the same," replied Rollins.

Afzam had been sitting quietly, taking it all in. Still, his curiosity was getting the best of him. "So why the sudden interest in your former client now, Mr. Vinkler, after so many years?" He had a heavy Indian accent and always addressed the attorneys in the firm very formally. His English was impeccable, but he could never get his 'W's right. "From what you are telling Mr. Rollins here, I don't get the feeling that you actually want to reopen the search for the missing banker," he said politely. Extremely deferential, he would do whatever he was asked – and do it well – but his inquisitive mind needed to know what was really going on.

"Good point, Afzam. The story gets more bizarre," Winkler said. "Currently, our client is Maria Theresa Romero, who believes she's Guttmann's daughter. I happened to meet her while I was on vacation in Aruba last week. Talk about a small world. She was reading the book I just gave Luke, *Prisoner Without a Name*, and we got to talking. Turns out Maria Theresa was born in prison after Guttmann died—or disappeared—when his wife was held in custody for months of questioning after the banks failed. Maria Theresa was adopted—stolen—by an Argentine military officer who later left the country and raised her in Uruguay. All these years, she thought her dad was an upstanding Uruguayan businessman."

"So, how did she find out about her birth parents?" asked Rollins.

"Her mother recently died and left her a letter outlining the real story. Although she raised Maria Theresa as her own, she wasn't comfortable that Maria Theresa didn't know her true parentage. Yet she didn't have the courage to tell her the truth during her lifetime."

"And Ms. Romero just happens to run into you, her father's former attorney from a prior life on another continent, decades ago, while you're on vacation in Aruba, and she hires you to kick the tires, as you say, on her father's death or disappearance? Have I got that right? I suppose you won the trip to Aruba in a charity raffle." Rollins shook his head incredulously. "David, I've heard some strange stories in my time, but this one takes the cake. Have you checked the retainer she paid you to see if the money's good? I assume you got a retainer?" Rollins said, with a devilish smile.

"Yes, a substantial retainer, wired in on Monday. Didn't even have to wait for a check to clear," Winkler said. "I agree there are some incredible coincidences here, but my life has been full of them. There's enough to fund a limited inquiry, for no more than ninety days. That's our deal. Our firm doesn't get paid a cent for professional services unless there's some financial recovery, which I'll agree is unlikely."

"The lawyers are working for nothing? That's a new twist. I should hire you guys for all my legal work!" Rollins quipped, with a light air of sarcasm.

Winkler smiled, having been the butt of lawyer jokes his entire professional career. "Essentially, it's a pro bono case. This woman is one of probably thousands of kids who lost their parents in Argentina in the mid-seventies to early eighties. Maybe we'll find some information on her birth mother during our search. Though Maria Theresa's mother didn't know the birth mother's name, I've already done some checking and determined Ricardo Guttmann's wife was Andrea Guttmann. She said her mother's letter was unclear as to what happened to her birth mother. Around five hundred babies were taken from their mothers by C-section. Most often, the mothers were killed. Sometimes they were spared and told the babies died in childbirth."

"Sounds like a grisly bit of the past," said Rollins.

"The past is not so far behind us," said Afzam.

Winkler had assumed he was just taking notes on his laptop, but in fact he'd already started his research and come up with a recent article. "May I just read from this one, it's very interesting—"

"Go ahead, Afzam. Let's see what you've found," said Winkler.

"It's rather long, so let me paraphrase—from a *New York Times* story of just a couple of months ago. It seems that the Argentine military men who had been tried and convicted of those atrocities so many years ago, and then were pardoned when there was a change in regime, can now be tried. The Argentine Congress revoked the amnesty law, and the Argentine Supreme Court ruled that the amnesty laws are unconstitutional. There are many people dissatisfied with the fact that the country has never come to terms with what happened back then. They want some sort of formal acknowledgment, with the hope that it will lead to national healing."

"Excellent segue into another important aspect of this case," said Winkler. "The firm has decided that, since we're unlikely to make any money off this engagement, we should at least benefit from the public relations value. I imagine our PR firm will get us some prime time based on the underlying story: *Child stolen from parents during 1970s Argentine military dictatorship searches for parents, aided by prominent U.S. law firm.*

"The fact that these criminals are finally being brought to justice should make our client's search for her roots even more newsworthy. I'll be in touch with our PR firm later this week to bring them on board."

"Her father's disappearance in a mysterious plane crash, leaving a trail of major bank failures behind him, ought to merit some attention as well. That part may even bring some people to us who may have information," added Rollins.

"That could happen as well, but let's step back a moment and map out a plan," said Winkler, trying to put some order into the process. "Afzam, I'd like you to take the next week to come up with whatever you can on Ricardo Guttmann. See what you can find on the Internet for free, but I'm also giving you full authorization to use Lexis-Nexis, as a client expense. Use whatever other databases you want."

"Unfortunately, I don't have any idea at all how long it will take to exhaust the sources, Mr. Vinkler, but are you saying I should see what I can find within a week's time?"

"That's right, Afzam, since we've got a ninety day time frame. As you'll only be doing this work at night and on weekends, you may need a week to gather and digest the information. It would be best if you can come up with a brief summary of what you find, keyed to the sources. Your objective will be to locate the 'official story' based on articles in the media and any court cases or administrative proceedings mentioning Guttmann. I seem to recall criminal charges were filed against him in various countries based on the bank failures. By the way, Emma, did you get Afzam a Lexis-Nexis password?"

"Sure did. Here it is, Afzam, on the outside of this folder, along with a comprehensive list of sources in their database."

Winkler continued. "So, a week from today—next Wednesday, or sooner if Afzam works faster than expected—we get together and review the results."

"And what will you be looking to me to do, David?" asked Rollins.

"Luke, my guess is there will be leads to sources Afzam won't be able to access. We'll have to see what develops and if you can get into them. I'm thinking about the Mexican government crash report, and whatever the NTSB—the National Transportation Safety Board— may have had to say about the crash. If Afzam can't get those on the Internet, he should advise you, and you can get them the old way. As Afzam's research turns up further leads, you can work them as well."

"So, basically you want me to refine the search after we see what Afzam finds? We peel the onion, layer by layer, so to speak," Rollins said. "How about having Afzam make three sets of anything worth reading, one for each of us?"

"Makes sense. And I would expect the documents may suggest people with further information. Luke, we may decide to work the interviews together, depending on who's involved, where they're located, and if we decide to meet them in person or do it by phone. Let me know who you think is worth interviewing and how you'd like to do it."

"You should also have a screening system for any calls that come in based on your media interviews," Rollins suggested. "You shouldn't have calls coming to your law firm directly, and you shouldn't handle the initial triage yourself. I've done lots of this stuff before—America's Most Wanted sort of thing—and I guarantee you'll get a thousand bogus calls for every one that might lead to something."

"What do you suggest, Luke? I don't know if we'll get any response at all from radio and TV interviews—and don't want to front any huge amount to deal with calls that may never happen—but I agree we need to be prepared."

"I can set up a call center for you at minimal cost," Rollins replied. "I'm guessing your PR agents will try to get you on CNN International—and if they don't, I would fire them! Since most interest in this story will likely come from outside the U.S., I'll get you an international toll-free number for both voice and fax messages, and a dedicated e-mail address."

"Are we going to need someone to man the phones? Remember, this is a low budget operation." Winkler was clearly concerned that miscellaneous expenses could eat into his budget.

"Nope, we'll get you free-standing voicemail; the calls won't even ring to a phone. We'll leave our message in English and Spanish for now and see if we have to add other languages later, depending on what comes in. Callers can leave a message, send a fax, or send e-mail. You'll also get caller ID, which can be handy in case the message is unclear. That way, anyone, anywhere can leave a message any way they want, and you're free to go about your business.

"Since all messages will either be recorded or in writing, we can deal with language translation on an as-needed basis. I can have an assistant sort through the calls and determine which are worth following up. That way, we can spend our time on credible callers. Anything else on the agenda for today, David?" asked Rollins.

"Just a couple of administrative details. Did you bring a copy of your standard contract for investigative services?"

"Yes, I put something together for you, short and sweet, basically just the hourly rate for myself and my assistant, plus out-of-pockets." Rollins pulled a two-page contract from his briefcase. "I left the scope of the assignment to be completed in an exhibit to be attached, which I thought we'd prepare after this meeting. As you'll see, I have a strict confidentiality clause. I can't divulge anything I learn to anyone else, and I can't use any of the information for myself. No time limits on either commitment. Mum's the word, forever."

"Sounds fine, though I'd like to take a few minutes to read it over," Winkler said. "You get us your statements weekly, and we'll cut you a check from our Client Trust Account. But before you incur any major out-of-pockets, say over a thousand bucks, make sure to get pre-approval. I think we'll be fine in terms of your hours, especially since we'll be looking at our cumulative commitment weekly, but I don't want the out-of-pockets to cause us a problem. We have only so much money to work with."

"That's fine, David. Take your time to look over the contract, and let me know if there's anything we need to discuss. You can put together the exhibit as well. Thanks for your confidence, and for the opportunity to be involved.

"I think that's as far as we can go today. Other than finalize the contract based on your input, David, the only thing I'll do between now and our next meeting is to set up the call center—and wait for Afzam to shoot me over copies of the Mexican crash report, and whatever the NTSB may be so kind as to share with us about what happened."

"Thanks for joining us, Luke. I look forward to having you on the team. Emma will show you out," Winkler said.

Emma then escorted Rollins back to the lobby and out to the elevator.

"Quite an interesting case, Emma, not like most I've seen in over thirty years as a fugitive hunter," Rollins said to Emma as they walked. "It's funny how the small-time crooks get caught, and the big-time crooks sometimes—"

"Disappear?" interjected Emma.

"Yep, that's what I was thinking," he said, with a grin.

"What's your take, Luke? Do you think Guttmann died in the crash? I know this has been on David's mind ever since it happened. It's really incredible how he just happened to meet Guttmann's daughter in Aruba."

"If you ask me, it's too much of a coincidence. But for now, it's moot because she's paid a retainer. We'll all do our jobs, my ex-wives will be happy—for a while—and we'll see where it takes us."

"Do you care to speculate on whether Guttmann is dead or alive?"

"Frankly, Emma, that's all it would be—pure conjecture. My guess is no better than yours. But if there's anybody who can find him, I'd like to think it would be me. Here, I forgot to give you my business card." He pulled a business card from his wallet with his color photo on it, bearing the following text:

Luke Rollins Investigations, LLC
Licensed Private Investigator
Three Decades of Experience in Finding People
We Use Biblical Methodology

"Flashy business card for a start-up, color photo and all." Emma held it up and read the byline. "What's 'biblical methodology' supposed to mean?"

"It's an ice-breaker. It refers to the expression, 'Seek and thou shalt find,'" Rollins said, with a smile. "It's actually in Luke 11:9."

EMMA RETURNED TO WINKLER'S OFFICE and related her conversation with Rollins.

"He makes a good point about the coincidence—you just happening to meet Guttmann's daughter, with your prior history and all." Her intuition was making her nervous.

"I'm not surprised he's skeptical about my meeting Maria Theresa. So am I," Winkler said. "But I just don't know what to do about it. The way I figure it, unless we can see a reason not to move forward, we treat this just like any other case. We do what we're asked to do, and if we become uncomfortable, we reassess."

"I suppose so," said Emma. "Coincidences do happen."

"Emma, if I told you the number of times I've bumped into people I knew halfway around the world, it would make your head spin. I ran into a client in a camera shop in Hong Kong, a high school buddy in an art museum in Zurich, and a cousin at Hyde Park in London. It's crazy, but it happens. And if you think about it, statistically it's even more likely to happen if you're not talking about someone you actually know, but someone who knows someone you know."

"Some people would even say that there is a higher power bringing you to this situation—that this is not purely coincidence, but that you have a particular and meaningful role to play in resolving this matter," said Afzam.

"Maybe so, Afzam, but for now I'm just the quarterback. We're not backing out, at least not right now, so we're not turning our back on destiny. Let's see what you come up with and take it from there."

"David, before Afzam leaves, you wanted me to make sure you spell out our firm's arrangement with him." Emma was always the one to keep her eye on the agenda.

"Thanks, Emma. I almost forgot."

Winkler explained to Afzam that he'd remain an employee of Kelly, Friedman & Green as concerns his general computer responsibilities, but the assignment would be billed hourly under a separate assumed name, Afzam Information Services, which Emma was prepared to register on his behalf. Afzam was to keep hourly time records, detailing each task, and Emma would prepare invoices. All disbursements that would normally be charged to a client would be charged to a separate account. He would be paid weekly, from the Client Trust Account, and there would be no income tax or Social Security withholdings; those would be his responsibility.

"If this is how the firm wants me to handle it, then it's fine with me," said Afzam. "I'm happy to be of help and earn a few extra dollars. This is all strictly legal, isn't it?"

"Should be no problem at all, but we'll make sure to run it by our immigration attorneys. If there's an issue, we'll restructure. Just sign the Assumed Name Registration form, and we'll get it filed. We've already made your letterhead for your reports and invoices," Winkler said.

He passed a folder over to Afzam, who signed the form, 'M. B. Afzam.' They then shook hands, and Afzam left the office.

"Emma, what else do we have on for this afternoon?" Winkler asked Emma, who was just starting to gather up the salad plates, plastic silverware, and glasses.

"I'd like to bring in some mail to review with you. Amazing how things pile up when you're out of the office for even a few days."

"OK, but let me shoot off a quick e-mail to Dan Duncan in our Immigration Law Department and make sure we're not getting Afzam into the soup. It'll just take a minute."

As Emma went to her desk to retrieve a stack of mail, he typed the following message:

Dan,

Afzam, our computer network administrator, is going to do some work on a special project. He's a resident and citizen of Canada. We need to have him bill our firm for these services separately, as an independent contractor, to get paid from Client Trust Account money as client disbursements. I am having him file an assumed name with the county clerk's office, using our office as his place of business, and his home address in Canada as his residence, all of which is accurate. If they won't accept that filing because he's not a resident of the county, then I propose to set up a limited liability company for him, again using our office address as the registered office. Any immigration law problems with this arrangement? If so, please advise immediately.

Thanks.

David

He hit the "send" button and immediately received the following reply:

I am out of the office at an immigration law conference. I will not be checking e-mail. I will reply to your e-mail upon my return.

Dan Duncan

That's an interesting way of making sure no one knows how long you'll be out of town, thought Winkler.

"Emma, let's tackle that pile of mail."

CHAPTER 16

"EMMA, THIS IS AFZAM. Please tell Mr. Vinkler that I've found a considerable amount of material over the past two evenings and I am in the process of analyzing it. Over one hundred seventy articles—more than five hundred pages of text. I'm going to be billing the firm extra for paper and laser toner," he quipped over the phone.

"Do you need any help to sift through this stuff?" Emma asked.

"Not just yet, Emma. Much of it is background history, and I would like to distill the information myself, to get some perspective. I was lucky enough to find the official Mexican government crash report, which was put on the Internet. There's also an article about the NTSB position—that they won't do their own investigation—so no use looking for an NTSB report.

"I do have NTSB crash reports on other incidents involving similar aircraft, so we can get an idea of what causes these planes to go down. Pilot error is often cited. I also have photos and specifications on our aircraft, the Gates Learjet 24B, and the safety record. I also found some top secret State Department material relating to the Argentine situation, which has been declassified."

"So no real smoking guns yet, Afzam?" asked Emma.

"Well, I also found what you might call 'relationship' software. It searches the web for names that appear to have a relationship with a given person. The more hits, the closer it puts the other people in relationship with the subject, in something like a spider web. No telling if this will be worth anything, but there are several people who are frequently mentioned in connection with Guttmann and the crash, other than direct family."

"Put together your list, and we'll discuss which ones to pursue with David and Luke. What kind of people are we talking about, Afzam?"

"The American reporter who covered the initial crash story, then seems to have dropped off the face of the planet. Alex Ginsberg. No other articles since the crash carry his byline. However, he was mentioned a couple of times in connection with a real estate finance attorney, James Ferguson, who was with a large firm back then. Maybe he's still in practice and would have some leads on Ginsberg.

"Then there's the poor fellow whose company owned the charter aircraft and never got paid for the trip. J.B. Winston. Seems he did his own investigation, which was mentioned in several news articles.

"Guttmann's right-hand man—Miguel Sandoval—appears in a prominent position, but I believe Mr. Vinkler said he was dead."

"That's right, Afzam, but maybe those other fellows are worth pursuing. When do you think you'll be ready for the next meeting?"

"If it's OK with you, I'll bring my materials tomorrow morning and leave binders for Mr. Vinkler and Mr. Rollins. Then we can decide what more needs to be done on my end.

"Also, Emma, I forgot to thank Mr. Vinkler for the book he loaned me on Detroit architecture. It shows the top twenty-five architectural treasures. And his wide angle lens for my 35mm camera. I had mentioned to him that I was putting together a little photo book for my family back home, and he was kind enough to loan me these things. Just thank him for me, and I'll give a proper thank you next time we meet."

"Sure. So, you'll be in the office tomorrow morning?" Emma asked.

"Yes, Emma, around nine, depending on the tunnel traffic. You know it's quite unpredictable."

TRAFFIC FROM WINDSOR via the Detroit-Windsor Tunnel that Friday morning was crawling. As Afzam waited patiently in one of a dozen lines of cars, the U.S. Customs & Border Protection officials seemed to be taking much more time than usual. Crossing into the U.S. had been very slow, even though many years had passed since 9/11, but this day the wait seemed interminable. Perhaps there was a heightened state of alert.

Everyone agreed that it made little sense to inspect inbound vehicles after they'd already passed through the tunnel to the U.S. But as long as no one had detonated a bomb inside the tunnel, the arguments seemed to fall on politicians' deaf ears on both sides of the border.

Finally, the car ahead of him cleared inspection. The CBP officer typed Afzam's license plate number into the computer, then motioned him to advance. Afzam rolled down his window and held out his Canadian passport. As a Canadian citizen, he didn't need a special visa to work in the U.S. He was a NAFTA Professional and had worked in the U.S. under this special status for years.

The agent flipped through his passport, then looked up at Afzam. "What is the purpose of your visit?"

"I work at a law firm in Detroit. Computer Network Administrator." Afzam handed the agent his business card.

"You do this trip every day?"

"Yes, sir."

"Your name is Mohammed Afzam, is that right?"

"Yes, sir."

"You were born in Kashmir, India, is that right?"

"Yes, sir."

"Pull your car over to the right, please. Just a routine inspection," said the agent.

As Afzam pulled away, the CBP agent picked up a phone. As if scrambling to meet a known enemy, three armed CBP agents raced out of their office to the carport to which Afzam had been directed for inspection.

The first agent engaged Afzam in further questions about his work and whether he had anything to declare, then asked him to open his trunk. The second agent then began going through the binders of Afzam's research material, while the third stood off at distance, with his hand on his sidearm.

The second agent shook his head as he saw photos of jet aircraft, NTSB crash reports, and declassified State Department memoranda. He then saw the book picturing Detroit buildings, a 35mm camera in a camera bag with a wide-angle and telephoto lens, and a pair of high-power binoculars.

Another agent yanked a memo off the bulletin board in the office, and walked it over to the other agents in the inspection area.

"Boys, I think we've got some trouble here. Ten days ago, one Mohammed Afzam, a Kashmiri Indian, was involved in a commando attack on the Indian Parliament and reportedly fled to Pakistan. Looks like a match to me, and look at this stamp in his passport from Pakistan just a few days ago. We may have ourselves an enemy combatant."

The first agent then pulled Afzam from the front seat and slammed him against the hood of the car, spread eagle, and slapped handcuffs on him. He patted him down for weapons, then had his technical support team go over the car with a fine-toothed comb. While they conducted their search, other agents took Afzam into the office and interrogated him. He explained the purpose of his visit to India, and the fact that he had to make a stop in Pakistan on the way back because of airline delays and flight rescheduling. Without revealing attorney-client confidences, he attempted to explain the items they strongly felt, taken together, were evidence of a threat to the national security of the United States of America.

Two grueling hours later, the agents still weren't convinced of his innocence. They did, however, allow him one phone call.

"Mr. Vinkler, this is Afzam, and I have a big problem!"

"No kidding, Afzam! We all do. The network has been down, your second-in-command is off at a technology conference, and the whole firm is at a standstill. You know our litigation team is in a state of paralysis when the network is down. Emma tells me you were going to be here at nine. Have they closed the borders for anthrax?"

"Not exactly, Mr. Vinkler, but there's been a snag, and I was hoping you could intercede. I apologize, but I haven't been allowed to make any outgoing calls until now." He then related what had happened.

"Will they let you pass the phone to me so I can explain what's going on?" Winkler asked.

"No, sir, they will not. They want to see a person over here right away, face-to-face, and they're not even sure that will convince them I'm not a terrorist. Seems there's a known terrorist with the same name, Mohammed Afzam. Kashmiri to boot."

"Afzam, I never knew you were Mohammed."

"As you can imagine, names sometimes can cause problems in relationships, so I normally use only my last name."

"Let me get Dan Duncan on this. If he can't get you out, we'll call the U.S. Attorney's office and pull some strings. Afzam, I apologize for what they've put you through!

"Emma," he shouted, "see if Dan Duncan is back from that conference, and get him on this ASAP. Call his cell phone if you have to. If you can't get him, get me a litigator with contacts in the U.S. Attorney's office."

This is one helluva way to keep a case low profile within the firm, Winkler thought.

Within a few minutes, the Management Committee would have yet another reason why he shouldn't have taken this case.

CHAPTER 17

"EMMA, WHAT'S THE LATEST ON AFZAM? I can't believe the Feds are so trigger happy, they'd jump on somebody who just happens to have the same name as a terrorist! Were you able to rouse Duncan, or are they going to ship Afzam down to Guantanamo?"

"I'm on top of it," said Emma. "Dan just got back this morning, and I was able to reach him at home. He went right over to the border as soon as I called him. He was able to talk some sense into the Homeland Security people. Seems the guy described in their security alert was ten years older than our Afzam—and they didn't even bother to check his birthdate."

"Damn, what a waste of time and energy! But I guess all that stuff in his trunk looked more than suspicious to someone who sees thousands of cars with empty trunks every day. Did he get all his research material back?"

"Yes—and no," replied Emma. "Dan told me Afzam had hard copies of some of it in binders, with PDF files of everything he found on a USB key. He had to agree to let them keep the binders a couple of days so they could review them more carefully. They still don't understand why someone would have NTSB crash reports, airplane specifications, and declassified State Department internal memoranda, and Dan didn't know how much he could say about your investigation, nor did Afzam. You can just imagine how this could raise eyebrows—even apart from the photos of major buildings, telephoto lens and binoculars.

"Dan initially refused to let them keep the material, claiming illegal search, but they were playing hardball and said they'd hold Afzam and refer the matter to counsel if he refused their demands. Since it was all public record, he thought it best to get Afzam out and let them keep the binders, especially since everything was on the USB key. They made copies of the files on the key. Afzam kept the original, and Dan had to agree on behalf of the firm to present Afzam for further questioning upon request."

"So much for keeping this thing under the radar," said Winkler. "How's Afzam holding up?"

"Really shaken up, but happy to be back over here. He's going to stay with friends on this side of the border for a week or so until things calm down. He's really afraid of something like this happening again."

"I understand," said Winkler. "Tell Afzam we'll pay to put him up for a while if he prefers. Let's hope the Feds get busy with other things and just stack the binders in the corner of an office to gather dust and forget about them. See if you can get Afzam to stick around, and get Rollins over here as well. I'd like to go over what Afzam found."

AFZAM SET UP SHOP in the large conference room, with a laptop and laser printer. When Winkler and Rollins arrived, he'd just started printing off his research material from the USB key.

"This is going to take a little while, but we can talk about what I found as it comes off the printer," said Afzam. As the printer started to hum and spew forth copies of the articles, Afzam pulled an extra ream of paper out of a cabinet.

"I started with the big picture, background on the Dirty War in Argentina, to see if there were websites that directly addressed the disappeared people and kept track of them. You already know that perhaps 30,000 people disappeared during that time. Numbers vary, depending on who is doing the reporting. There are websites giving the names of the disappeared, and also the names of the torturers. For the most part, it seems that the torturers who were convicted of their crimes were pardoned by the next administration.

"I found a CNN audio news clip of a high-ranking Argentine military officer who went public with his story a few years ago," Afzam continued. "He admitted that they had told many of the people they arrested that they were going to set them free in a remote area of Argentina, and that they needed vaccinations to stave off disease. But they drugged them, stripped them naked, took them up to 30,000 feet in airplanes, then dropped them into the ocean in the dead of night so their bodies would never be found. We can listen to that later if you want."

Winkler shuddered, picturing floating bodies.

Afzam pulled a short stack of paper from the printer output tray, shuffled through it briefly, and set it aside. "I found general background material, and stories on Mr. Guttmann and his role in the banking world, as he rose to prominence over a fairly short period of time. The last transaction I found was the pending purchase of a New York bank. He had applied to the New York State Banking Department for permission to own the bank. That all ended when the plane crashed and the file was closed.

"Then over here, I have the first article to appear in *The Wall Street Journal* after the crash, written by Alex Ginsberg," explained Afzam. "I wondered why he didn't write any more about it, when the financial press was filled with articles in the aftermath of Guttmann's supposed death."

Afzam continued. "Over here, I have something from a blog where a journalist asked about an old friend—Ginsberg. Someone mentioned that he was a pariah after writing that article and had to take on a pseudonym, and since then has been working freelance as Allen Gale. Apparently, he wasn't supposed to write the story he wrote. Something about offending the Mexican authorities. So, he was fired by UPI and couldn't get another news reporting job, at least not as Alex Ginsberg. I found some contact information on Allen Gale from articles over the years. He may have something for you.

"I also found something on his friend, the real estate finance attorney, James Ferguson. I think he's the right one," Afzam continued, while separating his research into packets for each of them to review. "I first linked him to Ginsberg through an article Ginsberg wrote about real estate financing in Mexico. Later, there was a press release about pending financing of a condo development in Acapulco. But unfortunately, I also found Ferguson's obituary and an article about his death. He was killed in his hotel room in Acapulco two days after the plane crash. Quite a coincidence. Suspected robbery, but it seems they never found out who did it."

"What about the official Mexican crash report?" asked Winkler.

"I have that as well, but it's not very informative," explained Afzam, locating the report in the stack of papers in front of him. "They determined it was pilot error and that Guttmann was killed in the crash. But you know that. I found no articles changing the official story; just lots of speculation."

Arms folded arms across his chest, Winkler announced his own conclusion. "I'll carefully review everything you've found, Afzam, but right now there's one person I'd like to talk to: Alex Ginsberg—or Allen Gale, whatever his name is—the reporter who was there when the Mexicans investigated the crash.

"Emma, see if you can track him down with the contact information Afzam found. A polite phone call from a charming female might set a nicer tone than if either I or Luke called him. He may still be on the run, if he took the trouble to change his name, but hopefully you can convince him to meet me and Luke wherever and whenever he wants. Tell him we're doing some follow-up work on the Guttmann air crash. Be honest, but vague. He's probably still scared if he thinks the murder of his friend Ferguson had anything to do with the crash."

"Sure, David. When would you be available to meet?" Emma asked.

"I guess that depends on where you find him. I'm available any time next week, even over the weekend. Eve's at a two-week yoga retreat in a remote area of upstate New York with some college girlfriends. If she likes the area, she may even add an extra week hiking. How's your schedule, Luke?"

"Whatever you say, David. I've got no one waiting at home for me," Rollins said.

"Emma, no need for you to stick around. You can wait until Monday to start working on this. We've got a lot of reading ahead of us."

MONDAY MORNING, Emma arrived at the office early and began her search for Allen Gale, formerly known as Alex Ginsberg. Winkler arrived at the office at nine, relatively early for having spent most of the weekend into the wee hours of Monday morning pouring over Afzam's research. Emma reported that the phone numbers Afzam had found for Gale were stale, and he wasn't listed in any online phone directories; however, one of his freelance articles carried an e-mail address, which was still live.

"I sent Gale an e-mail early this morning, asking if he'd be willing to meet a couple of people who are revisiting the Ricardo Guttmann story and want to talk to Alex Ginsberg," said Emma. "I asked if Mr. Ginsberg would be willing to share his observations for a reasonable charge. I thought that would encourage him."

"I hope you didn't commit to our paying a huge fee, Emma. We don't know if the guy has much to add at this point." Winkler always had an eye on the budget.

"He replied in a matter of minutes and didn't even question how we linked him to Ginsberg. He didn't say how much he would charge, so you've committed to nothing," Emma said. "If you ask me, I think you've hooked a live one. For a person who wanted to 'disappear,' he was almost too eager to meet. To his credit, he insisted on meeting in a public place and suggested the Iron Horse Bar, on Cliff Street, in Manhattan's Financial District. But don't be fooled by the location. From what I've found, it's a dive bar, with a swing and all. He said to ask the bartender for Mr. Allen.

"Oh, on the question of fees, he said, 'Remind your handlers that I don't take credit cards.' Seems like quite a character. I suggest you bring some cash and play it by ear. I set up a meeting for two o'clock tomorrow afternoon. You have a meeting at two today with a Mr. Trevor Banks, from Tricontinental Research. I booked a conference room for you. He said it had to do with Ricardo Guttmann and asked for you personally. If you want, I can have Luke meet him alone, but since he said it was a legal matter and asked for you, I thought you and Luke should meet him together. He may be trying to sell you something, but I tried to get more information, and he just said he needed to meet. What do you think?"

"Fine. If he wants a lot of money to bring us to Guttmann, like some of the whackos calling the toll-free number, the meeting will be very short. But make sure Luke's there," said Winkler.

"Other than that, David, I cleared your schedule for the next two days, and I've booked you and Luke on a flight to New York tomorrow for your meeting with Mr. Gale."

CHAPTER 18

TREVOR BANKS ARRIVED fifteen minutes ahead of schedule, accompanied by two associates, each carrying a briefcase. He picked up one of Winkler's business cards from the collection at the receptionist's desk and asked if they could wait for him in the conference room. The receptionist ushered them in and offered coffee, which they politely declined.

Banks was in his sixties, with gray hair along the temples and mostly bald. He was clean-shaven and wore wire-rimmed bifocals. His associates were considerably younger, had close-cropped hair, and wore gray suits and white button-down shirts with nondescript ties.

Once alone in the conference room, they quickly opened their briefcases and swept the room for electronic eavesdropping and recording devices. Without a word, they gave Banks a "thumbs up," packed away their equipment, and took their seats at the conference room table, one to each side of Banks.

Winkler and Rollins entered the conference room promptly at two o'clock, and Winkler greeted the visitors.

"Afternoon, Mr. Banks. I'm N. David Winkler—you can call me 'David.' I'm very pleased to meet you. This is Luke Rollins, an outside investigator assisting us in the Ricardo Guttmann matter." Winkler assumed the older of the three was Trevor Banks. "Have you been offered coffee?"

"Yes, thanks, but we don't care for any," replied Banks.

Winkler poured ice water for himself and Rollins. "May I pour you gentlemen some?" he asked.

Banks nodded. "We're delighted you could see us on such short notice. Let me introduce my associates, Eric Fox and Kal Benson."

"Before we start, I'd like your assurances, and from Mr. Rollins as well, that everything we say here today will be kept strictly confidential. If you don't take the assignment, then it should be as if we were never here—even my name will be eliminated from your appointment book, and the names of all three of us will be pulled from the visitors' log at your receptionist's desk. Do I have your word on that?"

"Certainly," said Winkler.

He knew they'd come about the Ricardo Guttmann matter and had no idea why secrecy would be so important, but the request itself piqued his interest. Sometimes prospective clients would disclose confidential information to a law firm, then not hire the firm, with the intent to disqualify it from representing an adverse party in the same matter.

"But since it's my understanding that you're here about the Ricardo Guttmann matter—and you obviously know we've already been engaged to look into his death or disappearance—I don't want you to tell us anything that could, by any stretch of the imagination, create a conflict of interest with that representation. If we don't take your case, then you weren't here and you told us nothing. Is that acceptable to you?"

"Certainly," said Banks. "But if you do agree to help us, I must have complete confidentiality. Not only can't you disclose your representation to third parties, we must also have complete confidentiality *within your law firm*. Absent my specific written approval, the only people to know anything about this will be those who are working on the case and have an actual need to know the information—plus any outside consultants you may decide to bring in—

and obviously, you'll subject them to the same obligation of confidentiality as you will have undertaken."

"So, if I understand you correctly, you're asking for a Chinese wall, is that right?" asked Winkler.

"Exactly," replied Banks, "and all files are to be segregated in a separate, locked file cabinet and any e-mail between us sent via a separate e-mail address through a secure service we'll provide you. You will not use your regular e-mail for this assignment, nor your fax machines. If we send you a fax, it will be routed to your special e-mail address. No land line phone calls. No standard cell phones. We will give you a secure smart phone."

"I get the picture, Mr. Banks." Winkler had rarely had a client so paranoid about confidentiality. Most just assumed everything about their case would be confidential, but he didn't minimize Banks' concerns. "'Loose lips sink ships,' as they say." This was one of Winkler's favorite admonitions, passed down from one of the senior members of the firm. "But I do have to send a conflict sheet to all our attorneys and administrative staff before I can take on a new matter. That could cause you a problem."

"Look, David, you're going to have to be creative on that score. If you decide not to take the case, you won't have to worry about the conflict sheet. And if you decide to take the case, I'm sure a clever lawyer such as yourself will figure out how to honor your confidentiality commitment."

"You're absolutely right, Mr. Banks. Please go on. I'm very interested to hear what this is all about," said Winkler.

"I'll try to be brief, but please bear with me, David, as this is a fairly complex situation. Here's my business card. I'm going to be totally candid with you today because I feel you need to know the importance of what you're being asked to do, and we have no time to waste.

"Tricontinental Research is a U.S. government entity that engages in special projects from time to time, where no direct government linkage is desired. It was set up by the Department of Homeland Security, under the radar of the FBI and CIA. Too small for them to worry about, or maybe it's a way of avoiding turf issues on certain projects. Don't bother to pull a D&B report or search for a company website. You'll find nothing except Delaware incorporation papers, with a corporate address at a company that serves as resident agent for thousands of other companies. We have no physical presence anywhere; just a virtual office."

"So, in essence, your company is just a shell?" asked Winkler. "When we have to list owners of Tricontinental in our conflict system, we just leave it blank, right?"

"I'd prefer to say it's essentially a bank account that allows us to keep a low profile while engaging in very important special projects with government funds," explained Banks. "Tricontinental Research would be your client, so neither your partners, your associates, nor your bookkeeping staff—not even your outside CPAs—will know the government is involved."

"So, if I may ask, why did you even bother to tell me you're a government entity? Why not just have Tricontinental Research hire us and say nothing about who you really are?" asked Winkler.

Banks stood, as if preparing to give a lecture. "That's how we'd usually proceed, but in this case I feel it's important you know what's really at stake. So, here's our situation: The U.S. government is concerned about the economic situation in Argentina. Based on our intel, there are credible signs of an imminent repeat of what happened in its last major economic crisis.

"You may recall some years ago that country defaulted on its national debt to the tune of over $100 billion, and it was on the verge of collapse. This was their Great Depression of 1998-2002. They got out of it— I won't bore you with the details of how they did it— but during the crisis, there was tremendous suffering. Bank accounts were frozen, limits on withdrawals of $250 per week were imposed, there was rioting in the streets, and dozens were killed.

"The streets of Buenos Aires looked like a battleground. Clouds of smoke hung over the Plaza de Mayo, outside the pink government palace, where thousands of protesters vented their anger over the economic crisis and called for the President to step down. Police officers in black uniforms, swinging clubs, fired rubber bullets at citizens. They even used water cannons on the raging crowds of demonstrators, who threw brick pavers back at the police line.

"The President of Argentina ultimately resigned and fled the Presidential residence in a helicopter. He was driven out of office after days of rioting that led to twenty-two deaths and homes and supermarkets around the country ransacked. More than 200 people were injured nationwide."

"I don't understand, Mr. Banks. What does that have to do with the United States today? How does this relate to Ricardo Guttmann?" Winkler was confused.

"We have information that another crisis is looming. What's worse is that the rioters back then, and those behind the unrest today, aren't entirely home-grown. There are indications that Al Qaeda was financing some of them and is continuing to do so. Known Qaeda operatives have been identified as part of a larger plot to destabilize Argentina. Al Qaeda has training camps in a lawless area called 'The Triple Frontier,' where the borders of Argentina, Paraguay, and Brazil meet. Ciudad del Este, in Paraguay, is an operational epicenter for terrorist groups.

"The bottom line is, if anarchy comes to Argentina, the rest of Latin America will likely be affected. And there's no question another economic collapse of Argentina will have a direct effect on many major multinational corporate and banking interests, just as it did before. The last time, multinationals in France, Italy, Canada, as well as the U.S. were severely affected. In the United States, companies like Metropolitan Life and banking behemoths such as Citigroup and FleetBoston Financial suffered huge losses. We saw a tremendous ripple effect."

"So, what would you like from us, and how does this relate to Guttmann?" asked Winkler.

"Let me get straight to the point," said Banks. "The U.S. government would very much like to shore up Argentina's financial situation for obvious reasons. But frankly, we don't have the billions it may take. Our people were rummaging through old files, trying to find a way to come up with a significant amount of cash, just as your story about revisiting the Guttmann affair hit the press. We identified you as one of the people who had connections to Guttmann—one of his last known legal advisors. We've attempted to locate several others, and you're the first one on the list who's still alive."

"But that was decades ago. What makes you think I would know more than governmental authorities on four continents who've been unable to find him despite years of searching?" asked Winkler.

"You're probably right," replied Banks. "We don't expect you'll be able to find him, though it could happen. But our bean counters are intrigued with the possibility that the missing money may still be out there somewhere, and if it is, maybe it's grown and could provide a way to prop up Argentina without costing the U.S. government. They've done the math. Over forty years, a couple of hundred million at 10% could easily become $10 billion, maybe more."

"With all due respect, Mr. Banks, I honestly think you're dreaming. I'd like to believe it could be true, but I would never tell anyone I have any realistic possibility of finding that money. Whatever you pay me would be wasting taxpayer dollars. Why don't you just wait and see what comes of our investigation for Ms. Romero?" Winkler asked.

"Frankly, we don't think that's going to take you anywhere," Banks replied. "From what we heard on the news reports, your work for Ms. Romero will be a short-term, small budget affair. We expect you'll shut it down in a couple of months without knowing much more than what's been reported in the press over the years. You'll get some positive press for being a do-gooder, and she'll get the feeling she's done something, but no definitive answers. You need to put some firepower into this, and that takes money, which she doesn't have."

"What are you proposing?" asked Winkler.

"Tricontinental Research will hire you for a nonrefundable retainer of $500,000 to investigate the death or disappearance of Ricardo Guttmann, and to trace the missing funds. You'll be free to share information about Guttmann with Ms. Romero."

"And what about the money, on the off-chance I find it?"

"If you find the funds, and if we can't come to an agreement about how they should be disbursed, we throw them into an interpleader action in Federal District Court, if we can get jurisdiction in the United States, and let the court decide who's entitled to the funds. If they're offshore, which is more likely, we'll deal with them in whatever legal system we find ourselves. My guess is that we'll have lots of folks pressing claims, primarily the Argentine government, which is how it ought to be. But the banking authorities in several other countries are likely to become involved as well."

"You know this is more than a long shot. Does Congress know its funds are being wasted in this way?" asked Winkler.

"Probably not," Banks said. "Your duly elected representatives vote on allocations in broad categories. I can't say whether this one fell into a multi-billion dollar figure for national defense or intelligence, but a small amount eventually trickled down into Tricontinental Research. If you asked your Congressman about it, he wouldn't have a clue."

"How do I deal with the potential conflict of interest with Ms. Romero?" asked Winkler.

"You're the lawyer, not me," replied Banks. "Frankly, I don't see any conflict. You maintain our confidentiality, which means you don't tell her or anyone else what you're doing for us without our written agreement. I don't expect your work for us will in any way prejudice what you're doing for her. In fact, it'll probably be enhanced by the fact that you'll have more funds to work with. You can share with her whatever you learn about her parents. If and when you find the pot of gold at the end of the rainbow, it goes to its rightful owners. I don't know if you could change that result, regardless of whatever your deal with her on that score is, and I'm not going to ask. That's strictly between your firm and Ms. Romero."

Winkler couldn't mention his contingent fee arrangement to Banks, and he wondered if he should be concerned about it anyhow. It all seemed so far-fetched. Why should he turn down a cool $500,000 because there was a one-in-two hundred million chance he could have a conflict fighting over the missing funds? As Abe Friedman had pointed out at the Management Committee meeting, even if he established that Maria Theresa Romero was the heiress to Ricardo Guttmann's fortune, it certainly wouldn't include any ill-gotten gains.

"So tell me, Mr. Banks, if we take your case, I would assume the same people in our firm as are working for Ms. Romero would be billing time to your case. Do you have any problem with that?"

"David, let me be perfectly candid. We're proposing to pay you a nonrefundable retainer. We ask only for your 'best efforts' to achieve the objectives I've laid out and weekly updates on your progress. If you want to put all your time down on the account of Tricontinental Research, except that relating to direct contacts with Ms. Romero, that would be fine with us. It seems to me the only reason you're keeping time is because there's a chance we may replenish the retainer if you run through it and are making some real progress.

"I hate to pressure you, but I need to know today if you'll take this on. Otherwise, I have to explore other possible connections with Guttmann. Other lawyers. High-level executives in his companies. People who were close to him and vouched for him on his applications for banking commission approvals—"

"I can imagine the pressure you're under, Mr. Banks, to see if this will pan out. Can I have until the end of the day? I need a little time to make sure we're not going to shoot ourselves in the foot."

"That's fine, David. Let me know by the close of business today if we're good to go. If it's affirmative, you can e-mail me your retainer agreement, and I'll get it back to you immediately. Here are instructions to get a secure e-mail address if you decide to go forward." Banks jotted down some notes on a pad of paper, ripped out the sheet, and handed it to Winkler.

"Let me know, one way or the other, by phone. You can use the cell phone number on my business card. Just a 'yes' or 'no' will be fine. I won't be offended if you decide you can't take the case, but I really can't imagine why you'd turn it down. It looks to me like a win-win for your firm, Ms. Romero, and conceivably the governments of the United States and Argentina."

Winkler led Banks and his associates to the elevator, then returned to the conference room, where Rollins was waiting.

"DAMN, IF THAT WASN'T THE STRANGEST MEETING I'VE EVER HAD," said Winkler. "Luke, what do you make of all that?"

Winkler started toward the water glasses on the table, intending to move them off to the sideboard, but Rollins stepped in front of him, blocking his path.

"David, let's just think about this for a minute. First of all, I don't necessarily buy this business about a special-purpose U.S. government front entity to fund a special investigation. I suppose it could be true, but I'm not ready to take it at face value. I'd like to know who these guys really are, and I want to have those water glasses checked for prints and see if we're dealing with someone known to law enforcement. Do you have some plastic bags around here so I can preserve whatever they may have left on them?"

"Sure, Luke. Emma can bring you some from the kitchen. What are you thinking?"

"I don't know what to think. A guy shows up with a couple of young sidekicks with briefcases they don't open and who don't say a word—the only thing they're missing is dark glasses—and offers you 500,000 bucks to run a search the government—if it really is the government funding this—could do on its own if they wanted to. He gives you a couple of hours to make a decision. He promises to wire you the money up front, as a non-refundable retainer. He tells you in advance you shouldn't waste your time trying to confirm his bona fides, because you won't find anything. He tells you he's funded by Congress, but don't bother to ask your duly elected representative, because he won't know. Don't bother to ask the FBI or CIA. Sounds fishy to me, but on the other hand, isn't this how big government sometimes works?

"Frankly, if the money is good—and what can be the problem with funds transferred to the firm's account by wire?—and if you can deal with the potential conflicts of interest, I wonder why you wouldn't just take it and see what happens down the road if you come up with new information."

Winkler paused a moment to think. "Assuming Tricontinental Research is a front for someone—and it's not the U.S. government—if we don't know who our client really is, I suppose we could be technically violating the Patriot Act or something like that. But why should we have to look behind what's presented to us as a Delaware corporation, owned by the U.S. government? So, let's just take things at face value for right now.

"I think my first problem will be with the Management Committee, in light of the apparent conflict of interest. I don't have the time—or frankly, the inclination—to assemble the entire committee and run all this by them. I think I have to be more strategic. They'll be most interested in the $500,000 nonrefundable retainer. I'm going to run this by Tom Kelly, Chairman of the Management Committee, to get his buy-in. The others will fall into line. But before we can open a billing account and accept the retainer, I need to circulate a conflict of interest sheet. I'll recommend to Kelly that I simply name the client, Tricontinental Research, indicate 'consulting on special project' as the nature of the services, and omit any reference at all to Ms. Romero or Ricardo Guttmann. Keep it simple and extremely low profile. I'll tell him anyone else who has a need to know can have as much information as I can provide within the limits of the Chinese wall concept."

Winkler asked Emma to see if Tom Kelly was available for a short visit. He'd just finished a long meeting, was about to start another and was running late, with clients waiting. But Emma said it was important, so he agreed to meet for no more than five minutes.

Winkler gave Kelly an overview of the meeting with Banks from 30,000 feet: The U.S. government, through a special-purpose entity, wants to fund some research on the missing Argentine banker, and the missing funds. It's a matter of national security, and no, we aren't sure if this is the real McCoy or someone who wants us to believe they're hiring us on behalf of the government. No, we can't do much to check them out; it's a question of turf, and we've been told it wouldn't do any good anyhow.

Yes, they'll pay, and they've offered a $500,000 retainer—to be wired to the firm's Client Trust Account as soon as we accept the engagement. No, there would be no real conflict with the Romero case, because we'd be free to share any information we learn in this case with her. At the same time, during the investigation we need to be very careful about confidentiality, even within the firm.

Kelly soaked it all up, stroked his chin, and thought for a moment. "This guy, Banks, from Tricontinental Research, is actually going to pay us a $500,000 *nonrefundable retainer* for your best efforts to find the banker and/or the money? The entire fee will actually be earned even if you strike out, and regardless of whether you reach that conclusion after a few days, even if you don't rack up enough time to equal the retainer?"

"Absolutely," replied Winkler, "that's the deal, and I'll get it in writing before he transfers the funds. It'll be crystal clear."

"Sounds crazy," said Kelly, "but this whole thing is bizarre if you ask me. At least this guy apparently has some resources."

Kelly looked into the glass on a picture on his office wall and straightened his tie in preparation for his next meeting, then started to walk out of his office with Winkler—but suddenly stopped.

"David, make damn sure the engagement agreement says the retainer is fully earned when received. That way, we can take it into fees immediately. It'll certainly help cover this month's expenses!"

Winkler shook Kelly's hand and smiled. He knew the nonrefundable retainer would overcome any other concerns.

Kelly gripped his hand firmly and pursed his lips. "And David, in the event you actually find the money—watch your back!"

CHAPTER 19

WINKLER AND ROLLINS arrived at the Iron Horse Bar a few minutes before two in the afternoon the next day and were surprised to see it was packed. They glanced around the main seating area, looking for a man sitting alone who might be the reporter whose career had gone off the tracks several decades before. They then decided to ask the bartender for Mr. Allen, as they'd been told to do.

"Mr. Allen? Sure, right over there," said the heavyset, red-cheeked bartender, smiling and pointing to a booth in the far corner of the room. Allen Gale was looking right in their direction. A half-finished glass of bourbon on the rocks in his right hand, he motioned them over.

"Welcome to New York City, gentlemen," said Gale in a hushed tone. "If you don't mind, I'd like us to keep our voices kind of low. No need to broadcast, if you know what I mean." Either Gale was paranoid, or there really were people out to get him.

"I apologize for any confusion about the name, Mr. Allen, I mean, but that's how I'm known around here. I try to keep a low profile. I'd prefer to keep Allen Gale, and certainly Alex Ginsberg, out of the spotlight. How did you put it all together, if I may ask?"

Gale looked well-fed but worn. His grey hair was long and frizzy, and he had a ruddy complexion, with dark, puffy bags under his eyes. Clearly a serious drinker, he held his glass of bourbon like a longtime friend as he savored every sip.

"Good stuff, Pappy Van Winkle. Thank you, by the way! But I forgot to ask what you fellows would like to drink." He motioned the waiter over to the table, and Winkler and Rollins each ordered a beer.

"Actually, we first ran into a brick wall after your initial article on the '76 crash in Mexico," said Winkler. "We couldn't find anything more by Alex Ginsberg. It looked like you'd either retired or gone underground. When we found a story about the murder of your friend, Jim Ferguson, just a few days after the crash, we wondered if the two were connected. There was some speculation about this on a blog, years later, and the blogger mentioned you were doing freelance under the name Allen Gale. It's amazing how things turn up."

"Yeah, you have a couple too many drinks, mention something in confidence to a friend, and to them that means label it 'confidential' on your blog!"

Gale was obviously ticked the connection could be made by anyone intent on pursuing it, but he still held some hope that he wasn't front page news. He was also aware his drinking excesses sometimes put him at risk. At the same time, however, he motioned for the waiter to bring him another bourbon on the rocks.

The waiter brought the next round of drinks, and Gale reluctantly gave up his glass for another.

"So, let me be brutally honest with you gentlemen. I eke out a meager living as a freelance reporter. It pays the rent, and occasionally a meal and a drink. Maybe more drinks than meals. So, in order for you to get the information flowing here today—to prime the pump, so to speak—I'll ask you for some cash, say $100 to start the discussion. And obviously, you're picking up the bar tab as well."

"No problem, we'll pay as we go, and let's see where this takes us." Winkler reached into the inside breast pocket of his sport coat and took a crisp $100 bill from his wallet. "But I have to tell you, we're on a limited budget, so this may not be a very long meeting. And do you mind if I record our discussion?" he asked as he put down his recorder on the table.

"Fair enough," replied Gale. "Let me first ask you fellows why you want to revisit an affair on which everyone else has simply closed the books?"

"That's an easy one. A client who thinks she may be related to Ricardo Guttmann hired us to dust off a cold case, confirm the official story, and see if there were any loose ends that could be explored further. For her, it's mostly a question of closure. For us, it's probably a wild goose chase without any real prospect of getting paid a nickel. I did some work for Guttmann's organizations years ago, but that's not really relevant. You seemed like a guy who might have some insights, having been with the Mexican crash investigation team. And since your take on the story seemed to have been lost in later reports, we thought you might be able to provide a different perspective, out of journalistic pride, if nothing else." Winkler was hoping to get Gale to open up.

"Let's start with the basics," said Gale, "and I know I'm in the minority here, but there's no way anyone can say with 100% certainty that Guttmann died in that crash. It's all circumstantial evidence. Three people died—pilot, co-pilot, and passenger—that much I'll give you. And we also know Guttmann's name was on the passenger list as the only passenger."

"So, why don't you think Guttmann died in the crash?" asked Rollins. He knew what Gale's initial news report said but wanted to hear it from his own mouth.

"It may well have been Guttmann. But what I'm telling you is that no one—not his father or mother, not his wife, who knew every inch of his body— could have identified that charred piece of flesh as Ricardo Guttmann. You must have read my article, right? What was identified as Guttmann's remains was just a goddamn torso—no hands, no head— just a trunk. It was bizarre. Two other bodies neatly beside him, charred to be sure, but no parts missing, and then this chunk of flesh – and they conclude it's Guttmann just because his name is on the passenger list. If it was Joe Blow, I wouldn't question it. But then the shit hits the fan, and it makes you wonder, that's all."

"So put the pieces together for us, would you?" asked Rollins.

Gale finished off his glass and motioned to the waiter to bring him another. The $100 bill was still on the table, and he tapped his index finger on it, looking Winkler in the eyes, smiling. Winkler got the message and took another $100 bill from his wallet. It was worth the price to hear this piece of history from the lips of someone who was there at the time.

"What got me ticked off at first was the fact that the Mexican authorities were so quick to conclude it was Guttmann. There was no discussion. No concern that the head and hands were missing or why they were missing. It was just a file to open and close, and watch out if you even suggested they weren't correct in their conclusions. That was my problem. I asked too many questions and reported what I saw, against direct orders, and the wrath of the Mexican Federal Police rained down on me.

"Then the family wasn't even asked to identify the remains. Maybe a pointless exercise, but they could have been asked anyhow. No, they'd decided to cremate, so they just directed the funeral directors to take the charred torso represented to them to be Ricardo Guttmann, cremate it, and deliver the cremains to the family. I don't know if DNA testing was around at the time, but it wasn't even considered. I suppose someone could even do DNA testing now on the cremains, if they had them, and if they had a verified source of DNA against which to compare, but that's neither here nor there. The file was closed as soon as it was opened.

"Also, there was no real investigation into the cause of the crash. Pilot error, they said, but that's too easy. Why would a first-class aircraft with a solid maintenance log and experienced pilot with a clean record go down? They didn't even interview the controller in the tower that night. There are usually two on duty, but when that plane went down, there was only one. The crash investigator's report says the plane descended too steeply, but the controller who gave the instructions to descend wasn't even asked for an explanation.

"The Mexicans didn't seem to care, and the American NTSB didn't investigate."

"Mr. Gale, you've got an incredible memory. It seems like you've been re-living this story all those years," said Winkler.

"You haven't heard the half of it," said Gale. "My place in Mexico City was trashed by the Mexican Federal Police immediately after my story hit the papers. At least that's what my building manager told me. I was on my way out of the country, at the recommendation of my then boss at UPI, Hal McDonald. Was this just a matter of their professional pride, or an effort to send a message that if I continued, I could expect more reprisals?

"And a couple of days later, my good friend, Jim Ferguson, an attorney down in Acapulco on business—and with whom I shared my observations on the crash—was murdered in his hotel room, right before he was supposed to head back to the States. Do you think they investigated it? Hell no. Why should they? His cash and computer were taken, so they write it up as a robbery. Did they even interview any of the hotel staff or review the security videos? What do you think? Of course not. If they even checked the ballistics on the bullet that killed him, they might have learned something, but they couldn't find any bullets or casings. They offered no explanation other than the fact that the bullet went right through the body and the killer must have cleaned up after himself!

"Then I hear Hal McDonald quit his job at UPI—after eighteen years, just a couple years short of retirement—and doesn't want to talk to anyone about why, least of all me. Maybe he read about Ferguson. Maybe he got a late night phone call from his friends at the Mexican Federal Police.

"And who says it was Guttmann who got on the plane in the first place? It could have been someone else with a fake ID. Even better, maybe it was Guttmann who got on the plane in New York, but then got off and had someone else take his place at one of the two stops on the way. You know the plane stopped in Memphis and Dallas on the way down, don't you? God knows why Guttmann would have wanted to substitute someone else—could be he didn't know the plane was going down, or maybe he did. The whole thing is ripe for speculation, and that's all we've had—lots of speculation, but no real investigation."

Gale was still livid, after all these years. "Waiter, another one for me, and another round of beer for my guests." He tapped lightly on the hundred dollar bills, and Winkler whipped another one from his wallet and laid it on top of the pile.

"So, we have a very curious air crash and superficial investigation, the police trash my apartment, and then the guy I stayed with in Acapulco, who everyone would assume I told what I saw at the crash site—which is true—is murdered in his room in a ritzy hotel and the murder investigation is half-hearted, or bungled at best.

"But then Guttmann's banking empire collapses on four continents, and a goddamn fortune is missing. A couple hundred million dollars as I recall. The financial press around the world is buzzing. Everyone speculates it could be a set-up, that Guttmann could have taken the money and engineered his own 'disappearance' to cover it up. But no, he's officially dead—and so, after a relatively brief inquiry, the matter is closed.

"Follow the money, I say, gentlemen, and you may find out what really happened to Ricardo Guttmann—if you don't get killed first!"

"So where do we go from here?" asked Rollins. "For the whole world, aside from our client, the case is closed. Is there anyone else we should talk to who also questioned the official story?"

Gale tapped on the stack of $100 bills again, then held up two fingers. He was looking for an even $500 for his interview. Winkler pulled out two more $100 bills, added them to the three on the table, and rolled all five bills together. He then put them in the palm of Gale's hand.

"Allen, or Alex, whatever your name is, we've just maxed out our expense account for today. After we pay the bar tab, we're gonna be taking the subway, not cabs!"

"Fine, I think we're almost done. But I've been thinking about this mess for a long time, and it seems to me there's a person who could have some information for you, stateside at least. I don't have any leads in Mexico or Argentina.

"If I were following up on this, I'd be very interested to hear what the owner of the charter aircraft has to say. For some reason, his name sticks with me: J.B. Winston.

He was the owner of Executive Air. I don't know if the company's still around, or if he's even alive, but I read he was a former FBI agent and wasn't happy that he didn't get paid for the charter, so he went down to Mexico and did his own investigation. If you can find him, he may have some information for you."

"We came across Winston's name in our research," said Winkler. "We'll try to locate him next. What else do you have?"

"Waiter, another bourbon here." Gale was trying to stretch the bar tab as far as he could. "Nothing else right now, but you never can tell where Winston may lead you."

"If you think of anything else, just give us a call," said Rollins, handing Gale his card, then motioning to the waiter to give him the bill.

CHAPTER 20

EMMA DID HER MAGIC researching Executive Air and determined it had gone bankrupt shortly after the crash in 1976, but another company, Executive Air East, continued to operate. J.B. Winston was the owner. Emma had no problem scheduling a meeting with him for four o'clock that afternoon.

After a stop at their hotel, Winkler and Rollins took a town car from Manhattan to the Westchester County Airport, in White Plains, New York. The company was headquartered in Suite 150 of Hangar B in the general aviation section. The airport was a favorite of the moneyed population of Westchester County. It was small, efficient, and far from the tumult of LaGuardia and JFK.

Hangar B housed the offices of several small air charter companies, a medevac service, an aircraft maintenance company, and a limousine service. As there was no walk-by traffic, the companies were identified by simple signage on each door. The sign for Executive Air East bore bold blue letters on stark white background.

Winkler knocked on the door.

A man in his seventies opened it and invited them in. Six-foot-two, trim, with grey hair in a military style cut, it was J.B. Winston himself. The small, tidy office held two desks, and he explained that his secretary—the brains of the operation—had some personal business to attend to and wouldn't be in until the next day.

"So, your secretary tells me you're researching the crash of our Flight 83 to Acapulco back in 1976," said Winston. "After all these years, I'd have to say I'm a little surprised—but at the same time, I've been waiting a long time for someone to take an interest."

Winkler explained in general terms how his firm had been engaged by someone who could be a family member of Ricardo Guttmann—and said nothing about Tricontinental Research.

"In our business, you deal with safety and risk every day," said Winston. "You do the best you can. You hire the best people, you follow all the rules. But you can't eliminate all the risks—the other guy, the weather, unforeseen technical problems, miscommunication in foreign travel. With all the technological innovation—and our jets are marvels of technology, don't get me wrong—once in a great while something bad is going to happen."

"We understand you did your own investigation. Do you remember what you found?" asked Rollins.

"Remember? Hell, I've got everything right here," Winston replied, walking over to a file cabinet, opening the top drawer, and pulling out a series of manila folders. "The top two drawers house my archives on this mess." He emptied the first drawer, then the second, and laid the folders on his desk, fanning them out like a deck of cards so the labels on the folders were all visible. "Charter contract with Guttmann's Belgian bank. He'd used our services many times before, and we never had problems with payment, so we invoiced them after each flight, and they usually paid within thirty days. Not this time. They stiffed us for thousands, not that anyone would ever pay for a flight that ends up in flames, but on top of it, the bank then went bankrupt.

"I couldn't figure it out—pilot error! I knew the pilot my whole life—he was my younger brother, for God's sake! But don't take my word for it; he was a Navy pilot, a Vietnam vet, best in his class." Winston pointed to a wall covered with certificates and photos. "That's him, the good-looking guy in the upper right. He had it all going for him—great skills, terrific personality, beautiful wife, and two great kids. And then a simple charter to Acapulco goes wrong." Winston started to choke up and was visibly shaken.

"So, I wasn't about to take the Mexicans' word for it, that it was pilot error—and I went down there and did my own investigation. I started out in law enforcement—ten years with the FBI—and wasn't about to let some half-assed Mexican inquiry sully my brother's good name and our family's reputation in this business—not without turning over some stones myself. Here's a folder with my notes of my investigation. I made three trips to Mexico and met everyone from local villagers to the funeral director who retrieved the remains from the crash site." Again, Winston swelled up with emotion.

"The big deal at the time was whether Guttmann was really the passenger who died in the crash. There was lots of speculation. But no one gave a hoot about the pilot and co-pilot. There's no question that it was my brother, Larry, and our co-pilot, Jeff Simpson, who went down that day.

"I hired a guide-interpreter to take us to the crash site and took an aviation crash expert with me. We spent a day there but really couldn't make any more of it than what they put into the Mexican crash report. Couldn't find any indication of an explosion that might have brought the aircraft down. But the plane was so badly damaged, my crash expert said it would have been hard to distinguish the effect of a small explosive that could have been triggered by a timer, or decrease in altitude, from crash damage and subsequent explosion and jet fuel fire. Here's my expert's report—inconclusive as to the ultimate cause.

"I tried to locate the UPI reporter—Alex Ginsberg—who accompanied the Mexican investigators, but he left UPI shortly after his first, and only, story on the crash appeared. His boss at UPI—Hal MacDonald—left a little while later, but I did manage to track him down. He said he had nothing to add to Ginsberg's story. The conversation was very brief. The guy sounded like he was scared to say too much, really nervous.

"Since our people were involved, the funeral director—a Mr. Rodriguez—was very willing to talk. He was most sympathetic, really emotional when I told him my brother was the pilot. I remember that interview distinctly. He told me neither his people nor the Mexican investigators removed the bodies from the plane. They found them all lined up outside the aircraft when they arrived at the scene.

"But the real kicker—confirming Ginsberg's UPI story—was that what was identified as the remains of Ricardo Guttmann was just a charred torso—no head, no hands—just a trunk of a body. He said he couldn't have identified it if it had been his own son, but he was told it was Guttmann because the other two were clearly crew. So, he tagged it Guttmann."

"There was no flight attendant on this flight?" asked Rollins.

"Not on this one. It was rather unusual, but the flight attendant called in sick at the last minute, and we couldn't get a replacement in time. Guttmann didn't care. He'd made the flight many times before, and I guess he knew where the bar was."

Winkler was impressed by the work Winston had done to investigate the crash. "Did you interview the air traffic controllers from the tower in Acapulco?" he asked.

"There were two on duty that night. One left the tower temporarily just before our flight asked for instructions. The controller who guided them down wrote a report, which shows nothing irregular until the plane dropped off the radar. The aviation authority refused an interview, said I should rely on the written report. Since I was asking only on behalf of our company, not part of an official investigation, they were able to blow me off. For some reason, the recorder in the tower wasn't functioning, so we don't really have independent evidence as to the exchange between the tower and the aircraft. As you may know, the aircraft's black box was missing."

"Sure sounds suspicious to me. Did you interview anybody else?" asked Winkler.

"There's one fellow who was very close to Guttmann. An American rabbi. I interviewed him about a year after the crash, when I somehow became aware that he'd moved back to the States. Here's my file on him: His name is Jonah Weinman. He'd gone to Argentina after finishing his rabbinical studies, stayed there a few years, got to know Guttmann's family real well. Some said he was Guttmann's confidant. That's why I thought it would be worthwhile to ask him a few questions."

"I assume he couldn't shed any light on what happened?" asked Rollins.

"He was a very nice fellow. We talked for about an hour about Guttmann, the family, their business interests, and Argentine politics. But you're right, he had nothing to add—although for some reason I had a feeling he wasn't being totally candid, that he was holding back. You know how it is, a person tells you he wants to be helpful and says he's sharing whatever he knows, but you still get the feeling there's something important he's not telling. Maybe it's the cloak of the clergy, stuff learned in confidence has to stay confidential."

"Do you think it would be worth contacting him again, after all this time?" asked Winkler.

"Couldn't hurt. Probably won't get you anywhere, but you never can tell. Maybe the passage of time will have changed his attitude. Mind you, I can't say for sure that he was holding back, but for someone who was presumably so close to Guttmann as this fellow was—well, let's just say it wouldn't surprise me if he knew more than he was willing to tell me.

"And just maybe you'll be able to get through to him since you're inquiring on behalf of a member of Guttmann's family. What I mean is, you're not looking to collect payment for a charter flight or put Guttmann in prison for lining his pockets at the expense of his depositors. Possibly because of the rabbi's relationship with the family, he may be willing to open up to someone new who comes with a different agenda."

"Makes sense," said Winkler. "Any idea where he might be now?"

"Let me see if we can find him online." Winston swung around on his chair so he could reach his computer mouse and went to Switchboard. "When I spoke to him, must have been 1977 or 1978, he lived in Queens. Let's see…yep, he must like the area…he's still listed there. Rabbi Jonah B. Weinman, 84 West 119th Street, in Forest Hills, Queens. Let me print this for you. And while we're at it, let's see if he's affiliated with a temple or synagogue so if you can't get him at home, you can try him at work, so to speak.

"Here he is, Rabbi of Congregation Beth Tefilo, in Forest Hills. I'll print the temple's home page for you also."

"Great! We'll see if we can meet with him on this trip, maybe even this evening. Anything else you can think of?" asked Winkler.

"No, but if you want to have a closer look at all my files, back at your office, maybe something will occur to you. Some years ago, I made a backup of all this paperwork on CD, which I've kept in a fireproof safe over here. You can have a copy of the CD if you want."

"That would be great," said Winkler.

Winston walked over to the safe, bent down, spun the dial, then took out a CD and handed it to Winkler. "I really hope you find something I missed. Or maybe after all these years, someone will open up. I'd rest a lot easier if I knew the crash wasn't pilot error.

"And one more thing: If it would make your work any easier, I'd be happy to make one of our executive jets available to you. I really want you to get to the bottom of this."

"That's incredibly generous of you, J.B. Having a jet will certainly give us some flexibility, but we won't take you up on it unless we really need it," said Winkler.

"It's been a burden on me, my family, and all our pilots for too many years. Guttmann's estate even got a huge wrongful death judgment against Executive Air based on the alleged pilot error, so we filed for bankruptcy and set up our new company, Executive Air East.

"Just call our toll-free number for scheduling, anytime, 24/7, and we'll be there," said Winston.

THE TOWN CAR AND DRIVER WERE WAITING, and as soon as Winkler and Rollins got in, Winkler called Emma to see if she could reach Rabbi Weinman and set up a meeting in Queens that evening. Emma called back within a few minutes and confirmed the rabbi's home address. He wasn't available, but they were welcome to stop by at eight in the evening. Mrs. Sarah Weinman would be expecting them.

CHAPTER 21

TRAFFIC WAS MOVING AT A CRAWL that evening. The town car driver, a Russian immigrant in his sixties, did his best to consider alternate routes, but rush hour, combined with the pouring rain that started a few minutes after they left White Plains, only made matters worse. What could have been a forty-five-minute ride on a good night was likely to take almost two hours.

The driver was a jovial sort, the type who bantered with his passengers in-between personal phone calls in Russian.

"I am Igor," he said, turning his head a bit to address them in the rear seat as he drove, "and if you gentlemen have some time, maybe you stop for dinner in my favorite Russian restaurant. I live in Queens, and it's very close by where we going."

They were strangers in a foreign land, it seemed, and the real foreigner, Russian accent and all, knew the territory much better than they did. They were hungry, and it sounded like a good idea to stop for a quick meal.

"We going to 84 West 119th, and the restaurant is in Forest Hills, not out of way at all," he said.

Despite the rain and traffic, they managed to arrive there in time for a meal of Bukharian specialties. Winkler invited Igor to join them, but he politely refused and waited in the car, keeping very busy with his cell phone. After they ate, they proceeded directly to the Weinman residence, arriving just at eight o'clock.

The men made their way up the long set of concrete steps leading to the front door of the tidy brownstone. The door was ajar, and when Winkler knocked, it slowly swung open. They saw a dozen people inside, saying their goodbyes and hugging a woman wearing a black dress with long sleeves; they assumed she was Mrs. Weinman.

Winkler and Rollins entered, standing off to the side while the others passed through the narrow foyer and left. After a couple of minutes they were alone, and the woman welcomed them warmly and invited them into the front room.

"Mr. Winkler, I'm sorry you're about a week too late. My husband, Rabbi Weinman—may he rest in peace—died eight days ago, after a rather short bout with cancer. This evening was the end of our shiva period—seven days of mourning."

Winkler gulped and turned pale; he'd come all this way, and the man he was to meet was no more.

"You look shocked, but I told your secretary. I guess I was a little ambiguous. I suppose I still can't admit that he's no longer alive."

"Please accept our sincere condolences," said Winkler, disappointed that he had missed meeting the rabbi by a few days. "How long had you and the rabbi been married?"

"Ten years, almost to the day. I was his second wife. His first wife, Rivka, died, and we married a year later. But we'd known each other for many years. He was such a kind man, a good man. He was a few years older than me, but not old, no, not at all. He loved to talk, to go out, to be with people, to travel. You wouldn't believe how many people were at the funeral, maybe a thousand, and the visits have been nonstop all this past week. He touched so many people, and they don't know how they'll get along without him. Neither do I, but in these things, we have no choice; we must go on, and with God's help we will."

"Mrs. Weinman, we appreciate your willingness to see us, but you must be exhausted. If you weren't with your husband in Argentina back in the seventies, then should we assume you don't have anything you can share with us about the Guttmann affair—or perhaps the rabbi spoke to you about this?" Winkler asked.

"You're correct. I wasn't with Jonah in Argentina, and the whole thing was past history that only came up a few times in conversations. Whenever he would see an article in *The New York Times* about something going on in Argentina, he would recall his years down there and the terrible things that happened—the killings, the disappearances."

"Then he never specifically mentioned Ricardo Guttmann or any of his family?"

"No—not until about two weeks ago. Just before they put him on morphine. He was in such pain. Then one night out of the blue he said, 'Sarah, there's something important I need you to get in the vault.' The key was in his desk drawer. I knew he had a safe deposit box down at First Independence Bank, about a mile from here—he deducted the safe deposit box rent on our tax return—but I never went there.

"So, first thing the next morning I went to the bank, and they let me in the safe deposit box. Both our names were on it. To tell you the truth, I don't remember ever signing anything about it, but sure enough, they had my signature on a card, and they let me in.

"I couldn't imagine what he would keep in a safe deposit box. We were not rich people, Mr. Winkler. A rabbi can make a decent living, but it's certainly not a fortune. The rewards come in personal satisfaction from helping people, in teaching, and celebrating the holidays and life cycle events, the good times and the bad times, with the members of the congregation. Doing God's work."

"So what did you find, Mrs. Weinman?" Winkler was more than curious and becoming impatient.

"Just two envelopes. One contained a certificate showing ownership of two burial plots, one for Jonah, next to Rivka, and the other he said was for me, next to him. Always a thoughtful gentleman, wanting to have his ladies, one to each side of him."

"And the other envelope, Mrs. Weinman? Did that have something to do with Ricardo Guttmann?" Winkler couldn't stand the suspense anymore.

"The other envelope was large—you know, the big manila type—and it was sealed. Jonah said I should never open it and should only give it to Ricardo Guttmann or a member of his family—or their representative. He said there was a letter from Ricardo Guttmann."

For the next fifteen minutes, Winkler briefed the rabbi's widow on his assignment for Maria Theresa Romero. He told her about the charter jet crash that reportedly took Guttmann's life, how Ms. Romero came to believe she was Guttmann's daughter, and how he met her in Aruba after the death of the woman she always believed was her mother. Mrs. Weinman seemed to know a fair amount about the disappearances in Argentina but hadn't ever linked them to the Guttmann affair. She had many questions.

"You know, it's different when you hear about atrocities happening to so many people, and then you know, or hear about, someone who's directly affected, like your client. Like the Holocaust, a mind-numbing event in history, which has so much more meaning when you meet a survivor," she said.

"This is an incredible story—it's *bashert*, we would say in Yiddish, it's fate—you being Guttmann's former lawyer, then meeting his daughter decades later. And how did you come to the rabbi?"

"J.B. Winston, the owner of the charter aircraft that went down. We met him earlier today, and he said he'd met your husband years ago and felt there might be more to learn. He suggested we pay him a visit."

The rabbi's widow was beginning to warm up to Winkler, and she was clearly sympathetic to the plight of Maria Theresa Romero. "What a terrible thing to believe you knew your parents your whole life, then to find out you were stolen from your real parents and don't know if they're dead or alive." Mrs. Weinman sighed and shook her head.

"Mr. Winkler, for over fifty years no one has contacted my husband to claim the letter. I guess this must be so, because my husband still had it. How long am I going to live? No one knows. I have no one to give it to. You say you represent the daughter of Ricardo Guttmann and you used to be his lawyer. I'm thinking maybe you're the one, Mr. Winkler, the emissary who was sent to pick it up. What do you think?"

"Mrs. Weinman, I assure you, your husband would have wanted me to have that letter." Winkler's heart was pounding, and his palms were sweating. It was as if someone was about to give him the key to a box containing the Holy Grail. "Should we go to the vault with you tomorrow to pick it up?" he asked.

"That won't be necessary," she said. She walked over to the other side of the room and opened the sliding glass door of a breakfront, home to generations of silver wine cups, candlesticks, and trays. Wedged in-between two worn leather-covered prayer books was the manila envelope.

The flap was sealed with red sealing wax and the rabbi's personal seal. The front bore these words:

"Only to be given to Ricardo Guttmann, a member of his family or their representative."

It was signed Rabbi Jonah B. Weinman, and under the signature it was dated December 23, 1976.

"Mr. Winkler, please, take the envelope. By the time I brought it back from the vault, my husband was in no condition to speak about it, so I don't know what the letter says, just that there's a letter from Ricardo Guttmann. I hope it helps you in your search, but since Jonah never discussed the contents with me, please don't open it here, and don't tell me what you find out. For some reason, this envelope frightens me. For you, maybe it will lead to something good. But for me, it reminds me of the terrible things Jonah told me about what happened in Argentina— and his pain when he asked me to get it from the vault."

"Certainly, Mrs. Weinman. If the letter leads to any major discoveries, I'm sure you'll hear about it on the news. But we'll respect your wishes and not involve you any further. And thank you so much for seeing us at this most difficult time."

"I know Jonah would have wanted me to see you. Go and be well, Mr. Winkler. You and your friend should both go and be well." Mrs. Weinman showed them to the door. "I have an early flight to Ft. Lauderdale tomorrow. I'm going to stay a while with my sister-in-law. She hasn't been doing too well."

"Thanks again, Mrs. Weinman. Here's my card, just in case you think of something," said Winkler.

CHAPTER 22

"WHERE TO NOW, GENTLEMEN? Time to relax?" Igor said to them once they were back inside the town car.

Winkler and Rollins looked at each other in amazement, then Winkler said, "What do you think, Luke? Do we open it right now, or wait until we get back to the office? I think we still have time to catch the last flight out this evening."

"David, I don't know about you, but I certainly wouldn't be able to sleep if we really did have a letter from Ricardo Guttmann. Did you see the date of the rabbi's signature? December 23, 1976. That's about a month after the crash. That letter could be nothing, or it could hold the answers to a whole lot of questions."

"Should we open it here?" asked Rollins.

"No," replied Winkler. "This is too important."

"You fellows like to go back to Russian restaurant for a little while?" said Igor, turning his head a bit as he kept one eye on the road. "They stay open late, close after midnight."

"Sure, good idea. We've got time. Let's spend a few minutes and see what this envelope is all about," said Winkler. "It may well hold the key to a missing fortune."

Within minutes the town car pulled up in front of the restaurant, and Winkler and Rollins got out, leaving Igor in the car. It was dark, and the off-again, on-again rain was on-again, pouring hard.

"We're just going to have a drink and be out within half an hour," said Winkler.

As soon as they stepped out of the car the driver made a phone call in Russian.

Once inside, they asked the hostess to seat them at a table in the back, in a relatively quiet section away from the main dining area. Though it was late, the restaurant was still full of patrons, mostly Russian. They each ordered a drink, which was delivered promptly, then turned their attention to the manila envelope and its contents.

"David, before you open it, let's take some precautions. Let me slice through the envelope rather than breaking the wax seal. We may need to authenticate it. I've got a sharp pen knife." Rollins pulled a small knife from his pocket, then put on rubber gloves.

"Rubber gloves, Luke? You certainly come prepared! But in a restaurant?"

"Second nature, I guess. You can never tell if we're going to be dealing with evidence. I don't want to contaminate whatever's inside with our own fingerprints."

Winkler looked on as Rollins neatly cut through the top of the manila envelope, pulling a smaller white envelope from the inside. The flap was unsealed, and the outside of the white envelope bore the rabbi's name and address. There was no return address.

"Can you make out the postmark?" asked Winkler.

"Nope, it's blurred. Let's take a look at the letter."

Rollins took the letter out of the envelope, three pages, single sided, in handwriting, with a separate sheet attached. Four pages total.

"David, it's in Spanish! Can you read Spanish?"

"Not very well, Luke. How about you?"

"I can give it a try. When I was in the Army, I went through an intensive course in Spanish." Rollins paused. "They can teach a dog anything. In my day, I wasn't too bad, but it's been decades. Let's see how far I can get.

"First, it's a no-brainer. The letter is dated December 16, 1976. That's three weeks after the crash." Rollins' eyes scanned the first page, then he proceeded to translate the letter, line by line:

"Dear Jonah,

"I am writing in very unusual, difficult circumstances. By now you will probably have read or heard that I was killed in an air crash in Mexico. This is obviously not so, a case of mistaken identity and maybe attempted murder, but you must not tell anyone that I have contacted you, or your life—and theirs—will be in serious danger."

"I'm doing better than I thought," he said, looking to Winkler for approval. "No extra charge for translation services."

"Just keep on going, Luke. You're doing great. Thank you, Uncle Sam!"

"You did not know this, but I have been investing ransom monies for the Montonero guerillas in Argentina. This has gone on for many years, and until now I was doing very well for them, growing their capital substantially.

"Recently, however, I incurred serious losses. Some very speculative investments. I told them I would make good, but they have lost patience, and I received information they made a contract on my life. I had to disappear for a while, to get the funds to repay them. I decided I would take 'loans' from a number of the banks in my group. But I needed to be free from their eyes for a few weeks to arrange everything because the amounts were too large to take all at once.

"While I was the financier of the guerillas, I was also a consultant for the U.S. government, providing them with

information on the movements of the guerillas and their internal operations. My information was not that helpful to them, but they paid well. When I told them what had happened, they agreed to help me get the time I needed. The CIA arranged to have me switch places with a man who I was told looked exactly like me, at one of the stops on the flight from New York to Acapulco. I was told to leave my passport and driver's license in the seat pocket in the plane. They were going to give me another set of identification papers to use on a temporary basis.

"I got off in Memphis, went to the men's room, and waited there. I was told he would board in my place, and after my flight left I should quietly slip out the back of the flight lounge, which I did. I never saw the fellow, but I assume he boarded in my place for the continuation of the flight. They left a car for me in the parking lot."

Rollins turned to the next page and continued.

"But the next day I was picked up on the street, arrested, and thrown in prison. It seems that the man who was my double was a convicted criminal who had recently escaped from prison. The CIA must have known this. We had our differences, but I do not know why they would have double-crossed me.

"When I read that the flight crashed, and the story of the missing head and hands—that my —" Rollins paused, searching for the right word. *"—my charred remains consisted only of a torso—I was even more convinced that they were trying to murder me and made the flight go down. I assumed it was the Montoneros.*

"So I am now in his place, in prison, thinking about how to get out of here without revealing my true identity. I must look so much like him that no one even questions who I really am, and they did not even bother to fingerprint me when they brought me here."

Rollins turned to the third and final page.

"For now, I have told no one except you, and you must not tell anyone that you have heard from me. If the guerillas find out, they will certainly be enraged and torture anyone who has information until they find out where I am. No one in my family knows—not my wife, my brother, my parents. They all must believe that I have died, or they will face worse consequences than they are now facing with my death and what will soon be the failure of my banking empire.

"If I cannot sort this out, however, I want you to know that the funds I withdrew from my banks, which would cover only part of my losses, are safe in a Swiss bank, in a numbered account. I am writing a basic Power of Attorney on a separate page I will include with this letter, in blank, which can be used to withdraw them, but without the account number and password—which I will give you by phone when I can—and you can fill in if necessary. It will be effective immediately and remain in effect even if I am disabled or die. If the time comes when you have to use this, contact Klaus Wehrli at the Commerz Bank branch in Arosa, Switzerland. He is the one who handles this account. This information is ultimately only for the use of my family and to be given to them or a representative."

"Can you believe this, Luke?" Winkler interrupted. "Did he ever get himself into a mess! First he screws up big time as banker for the bad guys, then he has to siphon money out of his own banks to keep them at bay but doesn't quite finish the job."

"David, let me finish," replied Rollins, eager to go on with the translation to see if there were any more revelations.

"I have been in prison for three weeks. It is not the worst place, and in this situation probably the safest place I could be. It's good that the guerillas think that I am dead.

"I am giving this letter to the prison psychologist, who seems to feel that I am not like all the others. I trust her. In this way, hopefully it will not be read by the prison authorities—but would they ever believe it anyhow?

"Thank you for your friendship."

"It's signed Ricardo Guttmann."

"Damn, Luke, do you believe it? All these years, and no one could ever prove if he was on the plane or not, and if this letter is authentic—which it probably is—at least we know Guttmann didn't go down with the plane."

"Yes, David, and the Power of Attorney is right here. Short and sweet. He just authorizes the person whose name is to be completed on the form, and I'm filling in your name right now—if that's OK with you—to have full authority over the account, including the power to withdraw funds and close the account."

"Sure, Luke, but we've got to find that account number and password. The rabbi probably hid them apart from the letter, somewhere in the house. Based on the sixties furnishings, it sure doesn't look like he cashed in for himself. Far too modest a place. And unless she's a first-rate actress, Mrs. Weinman wasn't in on it. Let's assume the rabbi played it straight and was just holding on to the letter, as instructed. Or maybe Guttmann never provided the account number and password."

"Sure, that's possible, David. Or maybe there's another envelope stuck inside a book or taped on the underside of a drawer."

"But Mrs. Weinman will be gone tomorrow morning and won't be back for weeks. Luke, I think we're stuck."

"I wasn't thinking of asking her about it, David. She seemed clueless anyhow and clearly wanted to distance herself from the whole affair. I was thinking of going back to the house and doing our own...investigation."

Winkler was aghast. "Are you kidding? You mean breaking and entering? I'm a lawyer, Luke. I couldn't be involved in anything like that."

"Who said anything about breaking and entering?" Rollins reached down into his pants pocket and pulled out a single key on a chain with a label, with the rabbi's street address on it.

"What the hell?! Where did you get that, Luke?"

"While you were saying your goodbyes to Mrs. Weinman, I spotted a rack of keys by the front door. There were actually three with the house address. I figured she wouldn't need them all, now that the rabbi wasn't going to be using one. So, I plucked it off the rack and stuck it in my pocket—just in case. We wouldn't be breaking and entering if we entered with a key. It would be as if we were invited guests," Rollins said.

"Not by a long shot, Luke, not without at least talking to Mrs. Weinman about going through her stuff. I doubt she'd agree. Remember, she's really uncomfortable—"

Suddenly, they both fell unconscious as their heads slumped down onto the table and the music continued to blare in the restaurant around them.

CHAPTER 23

IT WAS NEARLY TEN THE NEXT MORNING when Winkler slowly opened his eyes, head throbbing, to find himself in a hospital bed. He was in a double room, with Rollins sitting at the end of the next bed, pulling up his pants. A man in his late forties, well built with a brush cut, wearing a dark suit, entered the room.

"You guys Winkler and Rollins?" he asked.

"That's us," said Rollins. "And you?"

The man flipped open his wallet and showed them a shiny gold badge and identification card. "Detective Gino Balducci, NYPD. Welcome to the Big Apple. You guys landed in the ER here at Elmhurst Hospital in the middle of the night. The hospital got your ID off your driver's licenses. The intake report says a limo driver dropped you off just after three this morning, both out stone cold. Said you'd been boozin' it up around town. We don't want any 'tourists' dying of excess alcohol. So, they pumped you out and let you sleep it off here."

"That's a crock," Rollins said as he tucked his shirt into his pants. "We were in a Russian restaurant, had one drink and were in the middle of talking over something, then the lights went out. I'd guess it was a little after nine o'clock. I don't know what happened." He threw some water on his face and ran his fingers through his hair to straighten it out.

"You guys missing anything?" asked the detective. "Whatever you had on you when you got admitted is in these plastic bags. Which one's Winkler?"

Winkler raised his hand slightly, still feeling weak, and the detective tossed him a white plastic bag with his name on it in black marker. He pulled his wallet out of the bag and opened it.

"Let's see. I've got my driver's license, American Express card, Blue Cross card, and some cash. Sweet." He counted the cash. "I had at least five hundred after we left Ginsberg," he said, turning to Rollins. "Couple hundred left. Guess he felt he was worth three hundred for the day—"

"Plus whatever he wants to charge to the credit cards," added Rollins.

Winkler dug further into the plastic bag. "Nice guy. He left me my briefcase." He unzipped his black leather envelope-style briefcase and fanned it open, looking in each section. "Left my notepad, some maps and my cell phone. The CD J.B. Winston gave us is gone. Damn! My Platinum VISA and Mastercard, State Bar ID, U.S. passport, and business cards are gone. But I guess he didn't see my Canadian passport, which I kept in this little side pocket just in case. I'm a dual national; never can tell when that could come in handy. How about you, Luke?"

Rollins dumped the contents of the other bag onto the bed: Wallet; cell phone; car keys; house key; drugstore reading glasses; shirt; belt; socks; and shoes. With a final jiggle, loose change rained onto the bed.

"Wallet's got my cash, but there wasn't that much to start. Just some twenties. All my credit cards but my Amex are gone. Passport is gone. Still have my driver's license, car keys, and house key, so if we ever make it home, I can get in! I have my Blue Cross card and some of my business cards, too."

"Where's the manila envelope and the letter?" Winkler asked. "It was right there on the table in the restaurant.

You'd just finished reading the letter, remember?"

"Not in my stuff, David. How about your bag?"

Winkler turned his plastic bag upside down and shook it frantically. "Nada. Nothing else, Luke. It's gone. Poof! We were so close. But what about that other key, Luke? The one we were talking about?"

"Nope, David, not here. Gone, just like the letter. Slipped right through our fingers."

"Detective, I'd like to file a complaint for theft, or whatever it is when someone steals your credit cards and other stuff," Winkler said. "I know the guy's name, the driver who took us to the restaurant—Igor—he must have been behind this."

"Actually, he left his business card," the detective replied. "Not Igor. Gives his name as Nikolai Tabatchnikoff. Big Apple Cars. The company name is bogus—it doesn't exist—and the phone number on the card is the city morgue. Some sense of humor these guys have. We'll run Nikolai through our system and see what we find, but I'll give you odds the name's bogus, too. You fellows pick the restaurant he took you to?"

Winkler paused a moment, still a bit groggy, trying to remember. "Nope. Come to think of it, he suggested the restaurant. Said it was his favorite."

"You remember the name?"

Winkler and Rollins looked at each other.

"I don't think he ever mentioned the name," said Winkler. "Just said it was a good one, his favorite, in Forest Hills. Then he took us there for dinner. The food was great. But I don't remember the name. To tell the truth, I didn't pay much attention. It was late, and raining hard. Russian place. The name was on the front window, but it was in Russian, and if there was any English, I didn't pay attention. I paid cash and didn't take a receipt."

"Did the driver come into the restaurant with you?"

"No," said Winkler. "Looked and acted very professional. He just stayed in his car. Later, he suggested we go back to the same place, for a drink." Winkler was questioning how he could have let himself be taken advantage of this way.

"Gents, this wasn't a random one-off. I've seen other cases, and this one's very similar, could be part of an identity theft operation. How many drinks did you say you had the second time you went to that restaurant?"

"Just one apiece. David had a beer, I had a vodka tonic," said Rollins.

"Yep, I suspect the driver marked you, steered you—literally—to the restaurant, and his comrades spiked your drink with a knockout drug. I've seen it before. You're lucky they didn't just dump you in an alley. They took their sweet time deciding what to do with you before they brought you here."

"Do you think you can go to the restaurant and see if someone there would say something?" asked Winkler. "There was an important document on the table, and it's missing."

"Waste of time, I'd say," the detective answered. "First, you don't know which Russian restaurant, and there are more than I can count. Maybe it was Forest Hills, maybe it wasn't. He could've just said that to put you off track. Then there's the matter of who's gonna say anything. All of a sudden, no one speaks English, if you know what I mean. You know how many times I've heard '*Ya ni panimayu pa Angliski*'? You actually think someone's gonna tell a cop who spiked your drink and ripped you off?

"We can go through the motions and write up a report, but when it's all said and done, we won't know much more than we know right now. Unless you guys have some other suggestions—"

"Detective," said Winkler, "I'm not so worried about the identity theft. I can deal with that. But there was an important letter on the table, and I had a house key, marked with the address. I can't tell you much about it, but it's really important that we get that back. It's a big deal—a really big deal—I assure you."

"Everything's a big deal," replied the detective. "You've been assaulted. Robbed. Identity probably stolen. But you're alive and probably won't have any lingering side effects. And we've got limited resources. What makes you think these guys are interested in any more than your credit?"

Winkler felt he had to get the detective to help them. "The driver, Igor, or Nikolai Tabachnikoff—whatever his name—was constantly yacking on his cell phone in Russian while he was driving. He probably overheard what we were talking about and passed that information to someone else. It probably had to do with the letter. Why would some Russians—and let's assume for a moment they were Russians—leave us with cash and take a letter in Spanish? And why would they take our business cards and passports? Sure, I suppose the passports are worth a few bucks on the black market, but mine could also be useful in connection with the letter."

"How did you get to the driver?" asked the detective. "Just a name in a phonebook? Or an ad on the Internet?"

"I just asked the bellman at the hotel," replied Rollins. "Now that I think of it, he was Russian. He said we shouldn't take a cab; it would be too expensive. He had a friend with a car service that would be much cheaper. He pulled a cell phone out of his pocket and made a call. And within a couple of minutes, a black town car pulled up in the alley next to the hotel. I wondered why it didn't park in the front, where the regular cabs do, but didn't think any more about it."

"Like a gypsy cab," said the detective. "Unlicensed. Unregulated. They charge whatever they want. Sometimes foreign visitors who don't speak English trust them to take the right fare from their wallets, and they pluck hundred dollar bills without giving it a second thought. Scum of the Earth."

"Detective Balducci, it's really important that the house— the house whose key they took—be checked to make sure they didn't rob it." Winkler figured they weren't going to search the place on their own, especially since now they didn't have the key. And it bothered him that Rollins had taken it in the first place. "Do you think you could take us by the place for a minute, just to have a look?"

"I really shouldn't do this. I'm assigned to your case, not to investigate other situations, and your case, as a practical matter, can be closed."

"Detective, please, it'll just take a minute, and it really is related to what happened to us," said Winkler, pleading.

"OK, sure, we can take a run over there. But whose house is that anyway? You guys aren't from here," probed the detective.

"A friend—a widow—gave us the key, just in case we needed to drop by when she wasn't there," said Rollins.

"So why don't you just call your friend and make sure everything's OK and tell her you lost the key and she should get the locks changed?"

"We would do that, but—" said Winkler.

Rollins quickly interjected. "She's out of town, and no one's home."

They both knew if the detective spoke to Mrs. Weinman, they would be exposed, but they also knew they had no choice. They couldn't tell the truth. And they were fairly certain she wouldn't be there to greet them.

Winkler grabbed a sheet of paper and wrote down the address. "84 West 119th Street, Forest Hills. It's etched in my memory."

"OK, get yourself dressed," the detective said to Winkler. "When I came in, the head nurse said you could leave anytime you wanted. I'll bring my car around to the main entrance in a couple of minutes. Black unmarked. Swing by the cashier's office—just before you reach the main door, on your left. No doubt they took your insurance information off your Blue Cross cards, but I was told you should button things up before you leave."

After passing by the cashier's office, Winkler and Rollins rushed to the main entrance, arriving just as Detective Balducci was pulling up to the door. Winkler took the front seat.

"84 West 119th. Not far, maybe twenty minutes if you were driving," the detective said as he pushed a button that triggered his flashing blue lights and siren. He stepped on the gas, and his car raced out of the hospital driveway. "Sorry to be in such a hurry, but I've gotta check this out as quickly as I can, write up my report, and move on to another case with some potential. I know it's not what you want to hear, but yours is about as low a priority as jaywalking."

CHAPTER 24

IN UNDER TEN MINUTES, the car pulled onto the rabbi's street and screeched to a stop. Winkler jumped out of the car, address in hand, and looked at house number 86 on the right, and 82 on the left. Between them was a heap of bricks and plaster, sticks of wood, shingles, and gutters. The wrecking ball had finished its work, and a bulldozer was just starting to remove the rubble. The pile of ruins was what used to be the rabbi's house, number 84.

"Are you sure we're on West 119th Street?" Winkler shouted to the detective, who'd gotten out of his car and was looking at the scene in amazement, looking for number 84.

"No question about it. This is the right street," he replied. "Let me find the crew chief and see what's going on here."

Detective Balducci spotted a tall fellow with a hard hat standing off to one side, who seemed to be directing the action with a Nextel phone. He walked over to him and introduced himself.

"No doubt you have some paperwork that authorizes demolition of this house?" he asked.

"Sure do, back in the truck, and the place was posted as well," the crew chief replied.

He walked back to his truck and pulled out a clipboard with a work order on it and a court order with blue tape on the corners.

"Here's our work order, and this is the court order, which was right on the door. We pulled it off before we started, and also rang the bell to make sure no one was home."

"There was no court order on the door when we left here last night," said Winkler. "Look here, it says EIGHTY-TWO West 119th Street, not EIGHTY-FOUR!"

"Holy shit!" exclaimed the crew chief, pulling the papers from Winkler's hands. "I can't believe it. My guys with the heavy equipment must have pulled up to this house this morning, saw the order on the door, and assumed it was posted on the correct house, and I assumed they knew what they were doing. I guess none of us looked at the house number on the work order. In all my years—" He immediately ordered his crew to stop working.

"I don't think this was an error in posting the notice," said Winkler. "It definitely wasn't posted on number 84 last night, and according to the notice, it had to be posted two weeks prior to demolition to allow time for an appeal."

"Something's rotten here," said Rollins. "Let's take a close look at the door to number 82."

Winkler, Rollins, Detective Balducci, and the crew chief walked over to number 82, and Rollins carefully examined the front of the door without touching it. "You can see here as the light is hitting the door," he said, turning his head at an angle to catch the light just right. "There are three shiny spots—my guess is, they'd have some adhesive on them from tape—just about where the corners of that court order would have been posted. And look here, there's still a corner of white paper with blue tape on it. How many corners does your court order have?" he asked the crew chief.

"Three corners with tape, one corner is ripped off," said the crew chief.

"Gentlemen, I don't know exactly what's going on here, but no one is to touch that door until our crime lab folks are finished with it," Detective Balducci instructed.

"Tell your guys to stop working and leave everything as it is. No clearing of the rubble. You can remove your equipment. I'll need names, addresses, and phone numbers of all your crew in case there are questions—and there's sure to be a lawsuit. And give me that court order. We'll have to check it for prints—and the doors—both number 82 and number 84, which is probably buried in the rubble."

Winkler and Rollins walked with Detective Balducci towards his car.

"This can't be a coincidence," said Rollins. "Last night we visited an occupied residence, and I'd swear there was no court order on the door. We have reason to believe there may be some important information in the house and someone else knows that and has the address—and the key. Sometime late last night—or maybe early this morning—the court order was switched from number 82 to number 84. Whoever did that may have also entered the residence, to look for the information—and maybe the owner, Mrs. Weinman, was still there—or maybe she'd already left."

"Are you suggesting the guys who may have drugged you two are behind all of this—and there may even be someone in the rubble? I thought you said your friend was out of town and that's why she gave you the key?" asked the detective.

"Actually, she was going out of town. She was supposed to leave for Florida on a very early flight this morning," said Winkler.

"Did she live alone?" asked the detective.

"I think so. When we visited her last night, there was no one else there," replied Winkler.

"Do you know where she was going, if she was going to visit someone, so we could check and see if she made it there safely? That would be better than having to sift through all that rubble and bring in the dogs."

"She just said she was going to visit her sister-in-law, in Ft. Lauderdale. I don't know the name," said Winkler. "Can you check the passenger lists of all flights leaving La Guardia for Ft. Lauderdale this morning? The passenger we're looking for is Sarah Weinman."

"Let me see what I can do," replied the detective, who then walked back to his car and called his office.

Rollins pulled Winkler aside, out of earshot of the detective, and spoke in a hushed voice. "David, my guess is that someone—probably the Russians—trashed the place, looking for leads on the Swiss bank account, then played a little game with the demolition crew to cover their tracks. The only questions are whether Mrs. Weinman got in the way and whether they found anything.

"If they found something, they'd be flying high. No reason to do any more than make it look like a robbery, just leave it a mess, take some stuff, maybe eliminate the witness, if she was there. But if they didn't find anything—hell, I think they would have been furious—so close but still missing the key to an incredible fortune. If Mrs. Weinman was there—if I were them—I would take her in the hope that with some 'encouragement' she could remember something. But if she wasn't there, I might be inclined to wreck the place, out of spite, then try to find her. Maybe use the wrecking of her house to prove they're dead serious."

"Luke, we've got to find out if she managed to leave before they arrived. But if she did—and let's say she's on her way to Ft. Lauderdale—how would they have any idea where she is?"

"Don't you think she told at least one of her neighbors she was going to be away, and maybe even where she was going?" said Rollins, looking around at a crowd of over a hundred onlookers attracted by the demolition and flashing blue light on the detective's car. "Hell, they could even be working the crowd right now, asking people if they know where the owner of the house is. And what kindly New Yorker wouldn't share that information at a time like this? Of course they would. We need to find her before they do."

"I've got an idea. The rabbi's death notice would have mentioned family members. His sister's name would probably have been included. I'll get Emma working on it and ask her to see if she can locate the Swiss banker as well," Winkler said, picking up his cell phone.

Two more police cars pulled up, and uniformed officers got out and spoke briefly with Detective Balducci. Two officers started putting crime scene tape around the demolition site; the others moved the crowd back and urged them to disperse.

"Nothing to see here, folks. Just another demolition site in Queens. Go about your business," one of the officers shouted, again and again.

A few minutes later, the detective motioned to Winkler and Rollins to come over to his car. Winkler quickly wrapped up his call with Emma.

"Good news, guys. She made it out on the first flight from LaGuardia to Ft. Lauderdale this morning. Delta Airlines, Flight 966. Left around seven this morning, should be arriving at Ft. Lauderdale right around now. She would have left the house around five. My guess is that our perps came by here sometime after she left. By the time the demolition crews arrived with their equipment, say around seven, the court order would have been on her door, and she wouldn't have had a clue. Now we just have to find out where she is and give her a heads up there may be some people looking to talk to her."

"We've got someone working on that," said Winkler. "If we connect with her, we'll let you know. Can we have your card?"

"Sure," said the detective. "I think we still need an executive decision about whether we sift through the rubble—just in case anyone was in there. My boss will be down here in a few minutes. What did you guys say was all so important, that might have been in the house? I think it had to do with a letter you were reading, which disappeared when you were drugged."

"Yeah, the letter. Well, it's a very long story," Winker said, not sure how much he should reveal. "We're tracking a missing person. A very cold case. The letter was just a piece of the puzzle. We can't be sure if it was a big piece, or nothing, but I think the first thing we need to do is talk to Mrs. Weinman in Florida. Mind if we call you later? Or if you want, you can call us anytime if you need to fill in some blanks," Winkler said, handing his own card to the detective.

Balducci eyed the card. "Detroit, eh? From what I read in the papers, the cops have their hands full."

"Maybe so, like any big city, but I've never been drugged in a restaurant in Detroit, and I've never known anybody to have their house razed by mistake in Detroit," Winkler said, smiling.

CHAPTER 25

WINKLER AND ROLLINS THEN STARTED WALKING DOWN THE STREET, considering their next moves.

"Luke, I've got to get to the Swiss banker before anyone else does, and maybe I should just work that alone. Anyhow, you're grounded from international travel for a while, without a passport. Luckily, I've got my Canadian one. Why don't you just head back to Detroit, and I'll be in touch once I find out if we can locate the banker or someone else at Commerz Bank willing to talk to me."

Rollins agreed, then hailed a cab to take him to LaGuardia. Meanwhile, Winkler stepped into a coffee shop, ordered black coffee, and within minutes his phone rang.

"You're amazing, Emma! Thanks, I've got it," he said, scrawling down the number on the notepad. "And you've already called her to tell her I'll be calling. Great! Keep working on finding that Swiss banker."

She's pure gold, Winkler thought to himself as he punched in the number for Mrs. Weinman's sister-in-law in Ft. Lauderdale.

Mrs. Weinman answered the phone herself and sounded annoyed. "Mr. Winkler, what's all this fuss? I told you I'd let you know if I found anything else, and now—I haven't even unpacked yet—your secretary is calling me down here at my sister-in-law's. She said it was important that you talk to me, but Mr. Winkler—as I already told you—I really don't want to get involved in the story of the letter. There's something very—"

"I'm sorry to cut you off, Mrs. Weinman, but I need you to listen to me very carefully. What's the nicest hotel in Ft. Lauderdale?"

"The Ritz-Carlton, but I don't see what that has to do with anything. I'm staying in a very nice condo with my sister-in-law."

"Mrs. Weinman, I don't want to alarm you, but I need you and your sister-in-law to go to the Ritz immediately. I'm going to have a reservation made for you under the name of Sylvia Greenspan. You should stay there until you hear back from me. There are some very bad people looking for you, and I don't want them to find you. It could be very dangerous for you. Don't have any contact with anyone but your sister-in-law, and don't let anyone know where you're staying."

"Dangerous? What's going on?"

"Mrs. Weinman, somebody drugged us in a restaurant and took the letter, which has very valuable information, but it's only one piece of the puzzle, and I believe whoever did this may think you have more pieces."

"That's ridiculous. I don't know anything. I don't know anything. I'll tell them. They'll believe me," she said, trembling but strong.

"Mrs. Weinman, I'll pick up the tab. Eat whatever you want, but only through room service. You'll have a full suite; consider it a special vacation. These people are ruthless. They won't believe you."

"Mr. Winkler, I appreciate your concern, but really, are you sure there's something so dangerous that we need to check into a hotel?"

"Believe me, Mrs. Weinman, it's serious. They had your house razed—demolished with a wrecking ball—this morning—"

The phone was silent. A few seconds later, Winkler heard a hand go over the mouthpiece as Mrs. Weinman told her sister-in-law what he'd said.

"Mr. Winkler, I want to go back to New York to see my house, what's left of it."

"Please, Mrs. Weinman, give us a few days—maybe a week—to figure out who's behind this. Your house is being watched by the police. There will be an officer there, day and night, so there will be no looting. In the meantime, don't talk to anyone. And if something comes to mind that might help us, please call me on my cell phone, anytime.

"But there's just one more thing, and I really don't want to bother you about this, but it's very important. I know you don't want to be involved with the letter, but there was something in it that suggested there may be one more piece of information, one more letter, or maybe a message from a phone call. We're looking for some numbers Mr. Guttmann would have sent to your husband— a bank account number and a password. If you can think of where he might have put that information, if he received it at all—even someplace outside of the house. Maybe in his office, or with a trusted friend or advisor. If anything at all occurs to you, please jot it down. When things settle down, we may ask you to look into those possibilities. Is that OK?"

"Mr. Winkler, I'll do my best, but this is so upsetting, you can't imagine—"

"Whatever you do, whatever you can think of, Mrs. Weinman, will be most appreciated. No obligation; just keep it in mind. Maybe something will occur to you. We're going to have a team sift through the contents of your house, but in case we don't find what we need there, it's possible he put the information somewhere else—if it even came at all."

What had started out at as a pro bono effort to confirm an accidental death had now turned into a high stakes treasure hunt. Winkler was clearly facing ruthless adversaries who would stop at nothing to claim a huge fortune.

CHAPTER 26

STILL IN THE COFFEE SHOP, which had become Winkler's temporary command headquarters, he dialed his trusted assistant, Emma, for an update.

"Emma, have you been able to track down Klaus Wehrli at the Arosa branch of the Commerz Bank? I know there's a six-hour time difference, but I was just wondering if you were able to find him. After all, he was on the account decades ago."

"You're in luck, David. I just got off the phone and was about to call you back. It's a very common name, but the person I spoke to at the main office in Zurich knew him personally, the Klaus Wehrli who handles special foreign accounts. He's still with the bank, but in a senior position. I spoke to his assistant, who said you'd spoken with her earlier today and set up an appointment for next Monday morning. I'm getting some strange feelings here, David—"

"No way. I didn't talk to anyone at the Commerz Bank. I was waiting for you to do that."

"That's just what I told her. Her boss is on vacation, but she patched him in and told him there's some confusion, and maybe conflicting claims. He's going to call you directly to discuss what's going on—"

At that very moment, another call came in to Winkler's cell phone.

"I think this is it, Emma, I've gotta take this call. I'll call you back." He ended the call with Emma and answered the incoming call.

"Yes, this is David Winkler." It was Klaus Wehrli, confused about hearing from two people, both of whom purported to be him. "Yes, I'd very much like to see you about an account I think has been dormant for several decades. I understand you've been contacted by someone else—I don't know who—but I was given Power of Attorney over the account, and someone stole it from me. My guess is, they're going to try to make a claim to the account."

The banker didn't want to discuss further details over the phone but asked to meet with Winkler before his other meeting scheduled for the following Monday. It was now Thursday. Since the banker was still on vacation, they agreed to meet Saturday at ten in the morning, at the Weisshorngipfel Restaurant on the Weisshorn summit, up the mountain from Arosa, which was a little more than two hours from Zurich. That would give Winkler time to make the overnight flight from New York City to Zurich, and the train from Zurich to Chur, then another from Chur to Arosa, where he'd spend Friday night.

The banker instructed him to have breakfast at the café directly across from the cable car station and keep an eye on his watch. The first cable car to the top would leave at eight thirty, with departures every twenty minutes after that. He was to get on the one leaving at nine thirty, which could be expected to fill up. Just before nine thirty, he should head over to the cable car station and get on just as the doors were closing, to minimize the chance that he'd be followed. It would take twenty-five minutes to get to the top, and the next car wouldn't leave from the village until nine fifty. That would give them some time to talk, uninterrupted.

The banker was either extremely cautious or legitimately concerned someone might attempt to eliminate the competition for the account.

WINKLER COULD HARDLY SLEEP on the flight to Zurich, thinking about the Power of Attorney that had slipped through his hands and was about to be presented by thieves. How would the bank deal with a document that was made out in blank, filled in with his name, but lacking the account number and password? If they date tested the document, they could surely tell the ink was new and the name filled in well after the principal had been presumed dead. Maybe the Russians had altered his passport, or obtained a forged one, so they could represent that one of them was him. Or perhaps they'd say they were acting under the power to delegate authority to a third party and present a forged delegation.

He tried to bury these thoughts in the back of his mind as he continued his journey, from Zurich to Chur, then from Chur to Arosa. Several feet of snow had fallen overnight, and as it continued to fall the snow weighed heavily on the branches of the evergreens to each side of the track. He ventured toward the front of the train, where the snow catcher plowed into mountains of fresh snow, clearing the tracks for the train and its cargo of eager passengers.

When Winkler arrived in Arosa at around one in the afternoon, the sky was clear and bright blue. The views from the valley up to the snow-covered mountains were breathtaking. The gingerbread buildings in Arosa all shared the same old Swiss architectural style, an image of life in simpler times in a place where time had stood still. If he hadn't been on a mission, he would have enjoyed the beautiful mountain scenery, taken lessons at the Swiss Ski School, or even walked the paths that wound up the mountains and meandered through the valleys. Instead, he napped on and off and spent time on his cell phone talking to Rollins, as the two of them thought through the process they'd follow to locate the prison that was Ricardo Guttmann's last known residence.

"SO, LUKE, WHILE I'M OVER HERE for the next day or so, you'll try to find out where Guttmann was when he wrote that letter, which prison breaks occurred within the year prior to the crash, and who was recaptured. Do you think you can get that kind of information?"

"I'll give it a shot. I've got a friend in the FBI who can probably get someone to check the online state and federal prison databases, assuming they go back that far. I'll have to call in some chits—"

"See what you can dig up, Luke. If you get some hits—and I don't expect there are that many prison breaks in a given year—match them up for race and body type, and let's see if any of them fit Guttmann's profile. Hispanics would be high on the list. I can't see any warden mistaking a guy with a heavy Spanish accent for a redneck, even if they are look-alikes. We've got to assume a little bit of good faith and diligence here, even if the system is sloppy at times. I'll touch base with you after I meet Wehrli, but if you need me in the meantime, you know how to get me."

CHAPTER 27

AS THE BANKER HAD INSTRUCTED, Winkler checked out of his hotel on Saturday morning and made his way two blocks down the road to the café directly across from the cable car station. He'd purchased a winter parka, ski pants, and hiking boots in the hotel clothing store, both to keep from freezing and avoid sticking out too badly from the skiers. His suit, shoes, and the trench coat in which he'd traveled were packed in a small duffle. It was a gorgeous sunny day, with bright blue sky, no wind, temperature in the mid-twenties, and the ground was covered with deep, fresh powder snow.

Swiss cable cars, like Swiss trains, run on time. Duffle strapped over his shoulder, Winkler watched attentively from a window seat at the café as the skiers, lined up for the nine thirty departure, loaded into the waiting cable cars. When the last car was about full, he made a dash to be the last one in for the twenty-five minute ride up to the top, in two sections.

All the skiers who filled the cars appeared to be families, young couples, or kids anxious to get to the ski school at the summit. None of them met what he imagined to be the profile of a Russian thief, none except the two fellows who appeared out of nowhere as he looked down to the station after the cable cars jerked and took off on the ride to the top. Burly men in their forties, dressed in navy wool pea coats with black ski caps, without skis, they had angry looks on their faces. He might have been imagining it, but if the banker was right, these two would have been bad company on the way up, and he wondered how he'd avoid them once they got on the next departure and made it to the top. He also wondered how they would have known he was going to meet the Swiss banker.

THE VIEW FROM THE TOP of the mountain was spectacular. A vast panorama of snow-covered peaks all around, the rays of the sun glistening on the snow. But Winkler knew he had only a short time to find the banker and make his case. He quickly entered the restaurant inside the lodge, which was full of breakfast diners, and asked the greeter if she knew where he could find the table of Mr. Klaus Wehrli. She asked Winkler his name, then escorted him to a second dining room off to the side, with a window to the valley.

After brief introductions, the banker had a server bring Winkler a pot of hot coffee, and they immediately started their discussion. He mentioned he thought he was being followed, and the banker shared his sense of urgency. The entire meeting lasted less than twenty minutes. Winkler showed the banker a copy of his engagement letter with Maria Theresa Romero on his smart phone, explaining that it effectively made him a representative of the alleged depositor's family.

He also offered to put the banker in touch with Mrs. Weinman. Although she never saw what was in the envelope, she could verify that she did, indeed, give an envelope to Winkler that indicated that it was to be given only to Ricardo Guttmann, a member of his family or a representative of the family. He explained that the Power of Attorney was stolen from him.

He also pointed the banker to the website he'd set up to publicize and solicit information in connection with the search for Guttmann.

Finally, he presented his Canadian passport, which confirmed he was who he said he was.

"Mr. Winkler, I appreciate what you're saying, and what you've provided to verify your authority here. But this is all very problematic. First of all, I want you to understand our discussion today is altogether hypothetical. Due to our strict bank secrecy laws, I'm not acknowledging we even have any account over which you may or may not have authority. Is that clear? We're only talking about what we might require if someone has a Power of Attorney over an account at our bank. Understood?"

"Absolutely."

"Next, you don't even have the Power of Attorney, which you say was stolen from you. Further, even if you did have it, you indicated it doesn't have the account number and password on it—and you don't have that information. So right now, you have no authority at all over any account in our bank. Even if we had the Power of Attorney, with your name on it, we'd still need the account number and password. The Power of Attorney is specific to one account, not general as to all bank accounts, is that correct?"

"Yes, so let's assume the fellows you're scheduled to meet tomorrow bring the Power of Attorney and have some identification saying one of them is me. You could question that ID, couldn't you?"

"Yes, and I probably would. But let's assume they come up with a sub-delegation—another letter that says David Winkler authorized one of them to act on the account. Even if we agreed to take that authority—and under the circumstances, I'm not entirely certain we would—we would still need the account number and password."

"Let's deal with that possibility right now. If you don't mind, I'd like to formally revoke any sub-delegation I may have given, including any false ones they may say I gave to them. That'll give us one less problem to deal with."

Winkler pulled out a slip of note paper and scrawled out a statement, reading it aloud as he wrote:

"I hereby revoke any sub-delegation I have ever given, from the beginning of time to the date hereof, to anyone, with regard to any account over which I have any authority at the Commerz Bank of Zurich, Switzerland."

He signed and dated it at the bottom, then asked, "Will this work for you?"

"I don't see why not. May I see your passport again so I can verify your signature?"

Winkler readily complied. After comparing the signatures, the banker noted his Canadian passport number at the bottom of the page and took a picture of it with his cell phone.

"But if they somehow got the account number and password, is there any way you'd release the funds to them in these circumstances?" Winkler asked.

"Not likely. But here's what I can assure you. If they show up for the meeting, I'll get the original Power of Attorney and tell them we need it to process their request, which is absolutely true. I don't want to reject it entirely, because it's a critical document for the disposition of this account —I mean the hypothetical account, of course!

"If we can't find a way to sort out who's really authorized to deal with this account—I mean any account over which there's a dispute as to authority—we may have to file a petition with a Swiss court. It would be something like the 'interpleader' action you're familiar with in the States, to determine the rightful owner of the account."

"So what's the next step, Mr. Wehrli?" Winkler asked.

"I would say it would be best, if you want to assert authority over the account, that you come up with the account number and password. At least then we could just deal with the competing claims—yours and those of the 'other' Mr. Winkler.

"I don't want to anticipate how the meeting on Monday will go. You just get your case together, as soon as you can, and I'll take it from there. If the other gentleman presents a Power of Attorney with your name on it, rest assured that we'll consider the situation very carefully. My meeting will certainly be monitored by armed security guards. I would say it's a very good thing that you've come all the way to Switzerland to deal with this situation—and I sincerely apologize for putting you through all this trouble."

"The apology is mine. I've interrupted your ski holiday with a business meeting and a very sticky situation —"

"That's what we're here for, Mr. Winkler. But I really think it's best you leave now. I've arranged for what you might call a 'special' way down. Put your coat on and follow me, please."

Winkler quickly took the last sip of coffee from his cup, slipped on his parka, and followed the banker to the rear door of the dining room. They exited to a vast area outside the lodge, where dozens of skis and poles were lined up in rows, waiting for their owners to start their day of skiing.

"You're not expecting me to ski down the mountain, are you?" Winkler gulped. "It's been years since I've done any downhill skiing—"

"Of course not, Mr. Winkler. That would be too cruel. Take off your eyeglasses, put them inside your parka for a minute, and step back, please."

At that moment, a red and white Swiss Ski Patrol helicopter appeared out of nowhere, rising from the valley just over the rim of the plateau on which the ski lodge was built, its whirring blades blowing snow everywhere. It touched down gently about fifty feet in front of Winkler and the banker, who had to turn their heads to keep the flying snow from hitting them directly in the face.

"Mr. Winkler," the banker said, shouting to be heard over the roar of the helicopter. "Your ride is here, and you don't even need a broken leg! You'll be off just about the time the next cable car reaches this station. Within just a few minutes, you'll be back in the village, at the helipad next to the train station, and you can catch the next train to Chur, which leaves at 10:48 a.m., if I remember the schedule correctly. From there, you take another train for Zurich. That should put some distance between you and your new friends."

The banker shook Winkler's hand, then motioned for the helicopter crew to open the door so Winkler could board. As quickly as it had arrived, the helicopter lifted off, stirring up another snowstorm, then headed down the mountain, with Winkler as its cargo.

As the crowd exited the cable car, those two burly men in their forties, dressed in navy wool pea coats with black ski caps, watched the helicopter as it made its way down the valley. By the time they saw it, the helicopter was already too far away to identify the passenger, but they seemed to know their prey had escaped them. One immediately pulled out his cell phone and made a call.

CHAPTER 28

THOUGH WINKLER HAD THE FEELING he was under surveillance, no one approached him during his train ride back to Zurich, and the two pea-coated men were nowhere to be seen. He spent a peaceful night at the Radisson Blu Hotel at the Zurich Airport, just a short walk from the airport train station. He took the first flight out the next morning for Detroit, with one stop in Amsterdam, arriving back home by early Monday evening.

Tuesday morning, he was back in the office, and the whole place was buzzing. Joshua Green had taken a turn for the worse over the weekend, and hospice had been called. The experimental treatments for his multiple myeloma had just made the disease progress faster. There was nothing more they could do for him except keep him comfortable and hopefully moderate the morphine so he'd be conscious enough to say his last goodbyes to a few close clients and friends. With no wife to care for him, and no children or grandchildren to gather around, he was an icon about to make a lonely departure for another place.

No one from the firm was allowed to visit; instead, everyone was encouraged to submit short anecdotes about their firm-related experiences with him, which would be edited down for a memorial booklet the firm would publish after the funeral.

Emma was in tears when Winkler walked in.

"Did you hear, David, about Mr. Green—"

"Yvonne told me when I walked into the lobby. I kind of knew this was going to happen. He told me about his condition after that big blow-up at the Management Committee meeting. He was so private, and not optimistic about the treatment."

"He was a giant, David, larger than life. Do you remember I worked for him when I first joined the firm?"

"I sure do. He wasn't too happy when we decided he didn't need a full-time secretary and you were assigned to me. You were his crown jewel!"

"I wouldn't go that far, David, but he always treated me with such respect, even after that, and went out of his way with his generosity. Did you know he got us a car when my husband lost his job? And he pulled strings to get my mother admitted to the Executive Suite at St. Anthony's Hospital after we were turned away because there were no beds. The man had real compassion, and power, and didn't hesitate to use it if he sensed you were in need."

"That's the side most people don't know, Emma, unless you were the recipient of that generosity. He never talked about those good deeds. I'll bet there are a hundred stories like that we'll hear in the coming days.

"For most people, Emma, he was a legal genius, a force to be reckoned with. If he was on your side, that was great. You had a real fighter in your corner. But if you were on the other side, you'd better watch out. He never lost a case. Settled, maybe, but never lost."

"David, he sent you a note. Here—"

Emma handed him an envelope with Winkler's name written in big black ink across the front.

"How did this get here? Who saw him?" Winkler asked.

"Mr. Kelly went to see him just before things got real bad. He said Mr. Green had it ready and didn't say anything about it; just wanted you to get it."

Winkler swallowed hard, took the letter in his hand, and thought for a moment before reaching into his drawer for a letter opener. In a sense, although Joshua Green was still alive, it was like getting a message from the grave. He took a deep breath, then opened it. He quickly read it, then passed it back to Emma, who shed a tear as she read it to herself. The note was brief but carried great weight, coming from a man who was revered by clients and colleagues, and respected even by his most ardent opponents:

"David—

Been thinking about your new case. Don't let it go. Whatever pressure you get, keep on digging. There is much, much more here than meets the eye. Get some help if you need it, and consider protection as well. You are walking on the edge of a deep crater, and the stakes are huge. You could be up against governments, maybe even ex-Argentine military, and who knows how many others who lost fortunes when the banker's banks failed. While you may be leading them to the pot of gold, at one point they will consider you dispensable. Be careful, and God Bless."

"Emma, I don't know what to make of that. He doesn't know even half of what's gone on since we took the case."

"Has he ever been wrong?" Emma asked rhetorically. "In all the years I've known him, he's always had an uncanny ability to know what's really happening, even without the full facts. Who's lying and who's getting paid off. He could always tell when it was best to settle a case rather than risk putting the client's future in the hands of a judge or jury."

"Any other messages?"

"Do you want the bad news or the good news first?" Emma knew which news Winkler would always want to start with.

"Let's start with the bad news," he replied.

"Mrs. Davis called, wondering when you'd have her new trust ready. She said she wasn't pushing, knows you're a busy attorney, but she also mentioned you'd met about a month ago, and she thought you had everything you needed. She's so cute. She said to remind you that although she's a young eighty-seven and still playing golf, she isn't getting any younger. The drafts are on your desk for review."

"Have one of the senior associates review them. My file notes should be sufficient to understand the plan, and please call Mrs. Davis back. Let her know we'll be in touch in a few days to schedule a meeting next week to sign the documents. We can review everything together then. She's had a falling out with one of her sons who married a gold digger, and she decided to tie up his share of the estate for his lifetime so the wife won't get her hands on it.

"Anything else, Emma?"

"Mr. Kelly stopped by, wondering how you're doing with the Romero case. He thought he would find you in. I told him you were doing some hands-on and it was taking you out of town for a few days. I didn't volunteer any details, and he didn't ask. He's been hearing grumbling from some of the partners. He said he wasn't concerned himself, just wanted to give you a heads-up that he was getting some pushback."

"I can live with that. What about the good news? This whole situation really has me wound up. What can you tell me to brighten my day?" Winkler asked.

"Luke was able to get information you asked for on prison breaks within a year prior to the crash. Turns out there were five that matched in terms of approximate age and body type."

"What did he find out about those five?"

"One couldn't be your guy. He was never caught. You can also cross off the second. He was caught after the escape but killed in a shoot-out with federal marshals. The third was black, so not your man. Two were Hispanic."

"Are they both still in prison?"

"Yes, one in Illinois, one in Georgia."

"Try to set up meetings with those fellows, tomorrow mid-morning in Illinois, the following day in Georgia, if you can. Call J.B. Winston and ask if he was serious about putting one of his executive jets at our disposal. It'll make him feel like he's helping, and things are moving too fast to lose time sitting around in airports. And arrange for rental cars at each airport where we'll be landing."

"Would you like Luke to go with you?"

"Absolutely, and have him bring his files on these convicts. I'd like to know whatever we can on them, including what got them behind bars. See if the wardens would be available to meet with us, if it comes to that. Maybe we'll find nothing, but maybe we'll have something to talk to one of them about."

CHAPTER 29

THE CESSNA CITATION X TOUCHED DOWN at Joliet Regional Airport in Joliet, Illinois at nine fifteen the next morning. Winkler and Rollins picked up their rental car and arrived at the front gate of the Stateville Correctional Center in Crest Hill, Illinois, about half an hour later. After inspecting their driver's licenses and business cards, the guard at the entry gate directed them to the visitor parking area, where another guard directed them to the visiting center.

"Do you have your completed Doc 148—the Prospective Visitor's Information Form?" asked the guard in the center.

"This is a legal visit," said Rollins, who knew from past experience in prisons the requirement to fill out a long information form would be waived for a lawyer.

"OK, but make sure you leave all your personal items in a locker, including cell phones and wallets, unless you want to go back and lock them in your car," said the guard.

Winkler and Rollins were then directed to a visitor's booth behind two inches of solid plexiglass, where they waited for Prisoner 796823, Juan Gutierrez. Five minutes later, a buzzer sounded and a steel entry door on the other side of the plexiglass wall swung open. The guard stepped back to the rear corner of the room. Gutierrez picked up the phone on his side of the plexiglass wall, and Winkler did the same on his side.

"Mr. Gutierrez, my name is David Winkler. I'm a lawyer and just wanted to ask you a couple of questions." The prisoner listened attentively.

"I appreciate your taking the time to talk to me and my friend, Luke Rollins, who's associated with our firm."

"No problem, señor, I have lots of time, nothing but time. I am here for forty more years, including extra time for attempted escape. Are you going to take my case?"

"What case? I came to ask you some questions. I don't know anything about your case. Anyhow, you've been here for decades, and it would be too late to appeal your conviction."

"No, not that case. I killed a couple of guys—drug dealers—they deserved it. I know I'm guilty, convicted 'fair and square,' as they say. But I've been complaining about safety conditions in this place. Over the past five years, six guys have fallen off the top bunk, including me. I messed up my back pretty bad. One guy actually cracked his head open.

"Do you think they would put a rail on the top bunk? Hell no! Maybe they need a Congressional committee to study the problem. A baby gets choked between the rails of a crib, and whammo! You get a recall of millions of cribs. Prisoners wreck their backs or skulls falling off upper bunks without rails, and what do we get? Zip! Nada! Nobody gives a damn!

"So I filed my complaint with the prison. That got me nowhere, but I've done whatever I can do under their internal administrative procedures. Next, I filed suit against the prison officials under federal law—a Petition for Deprivation of Rights, to get damages. I got lots of time to read up on this stuff.

"My back is screwed up enough as it is. I don't need to be tortured by falling off a top bunk. Wanna see?"

In an instant, the prisoner unbuttoned the top half of his orange jumpsuit and turned around so Winkler and Rollins could see his back. He was a hunchback, with a contorted back and shoulder so incredibly twisted, it was hard for them to look. The guard shouted to the prisoner to get himself buttoned up and announced that the meeting would be over in three minutes.

"You been like this your whole life?" Winkler asked.

"What you can see from the outside, yes, I was born like that. I guess it's ugly, but it never hurt before I fell off that bunk bed. Now I've got broken bones and dislocation, constant pain—"

"I'm going to leave one of my cards for you," said Winkler, holding the card up so the guard could see it. The guard nodded with approval. "If you can get us a copy of your file, we'll review it and see if we can take your case. Or maybe we can find you someone who will."

"What about those questions you wanted to ask me?" asked the prisoner as the guard approached to take him back to his cell.

"I think we found out what we needed from you today. Maybe another time. Thanks again."

"WHAT KIND OF DETECTIVE WORK WAS THAT?" Winkler asked as they walked out of the prisoner visiting room.

"I cross-checked the file for height and weight. The guy was a match. Hispanic to boot. How was I to know his body was twisted up like a pretzel? When the records say five-foot-nine, they don't say if the guy stands straight or is all stooped over."

"He may have a case, though, on the bunk design—maybe against both the manufacturer of the bed and the prison system or officials. I can imagine creative plaintiff's counsel would probably join in the architects or interior design consultants who put together the specs for the bunks—and see how much money the defendants or their insurers would be willing to put on the table to make this go away. I sure wouldn't want to have this guy strip to his waist in front of a jury!"

"Funny how you can sympathize with a two-time killer who's being treated unfairly by the system."

"Luke, beyond the orange jumpsuit and handcuffs, he's a guy, just like you and me. But let's hope the fellow you came up with in prison in Georgia is the guy we're looking for. Otherwise, I'll have to send you back to the drawing board."

CHAPTER 30

AT EIGHT O'CLOCK THAT EVENING, the executive jet touched down at the Griffin-Spalding County Airport, in Griffin, Georgia, about half an hour by car from the William Ewen Correctional Facility. Winkler and Rollins picked up a rental car and checked in to separate rooms at the Holiday Inn Express in Griffin for the night.

Still jet-lagged from his weekend trip to Zurich, and anxious about his next prison visit, Winkler tossed and turned all night long. Just as he was about to fall asleep, his cell phone rang. It was six in the morning and Klaus Wehrli was calling.

"Sorry to disturb you so early, Mr. Winkler, but it's noon here, and I have meetings all afternoon. I met your 'friends' Monday morning but couldn't report back to you until our senior management had an opportunity to discuss this situation internally. They, in turn, felt it was necessary to refer the matter to our general counsel. I just heard back, at least with interim advice."

"Can you tell me what happened at the meeting?" said Winkler.

"They presented a Sub-Delegation with what purported to be your signature on it. Since they said they were acting on your behalf, I'm allowed to talk to you about it. To support the authenticity of your signature, they provided a photocopy of your U.S. passport. I must say, it certainly looked like your signature on the Sub-Delegation. They said you hired them as your business agents to deal with our bank."

"Did they present the original Power of Attorney?"

"They certainly did. And as I told you I would, I kept it. They weren't very happy about that, but I told them I needed the original to process their request. I gave them a photocopy."

"And what exactly is their request, if I may ask?"

"Obviously they wanted to close the account," replied the banker.

"I would expect no less. I assume they wanted a wire transfer."

"They certainly did. To an account in the Cayman Islands, with your name on it no less."

"I suppose from that account, they would transfer it to another. Did you tell them the account balance?" asked Winkler.

"We couldn't even acknowledge that they had authority over the account. I didn't mention that you had contacted us, or that you had withdrawn all Sub-Delegations, but I did point out that the Power of Attorney didn't include the account number and password. I was perfectly candid with them about that."

"How did they react?"

"They said the fact that no account number was included meant it covered all accounts of the depositor at our bank, which is simply not correct. If someone wanted to grant authority over all accounts—or any accounts—the document would simply say so. That wasn't done here."

"And anyhow, you would still need the password, right?"

"Absolutely," said the banker, "and I pointed that out as well."

"How did they react?"

"They seemed surprised, then said they thought you were going to send that information directly to me at the bank. They said you gave them my name."

"Very creative! They got your name from a letter written by Ricardo Guttmann. So, how did you leave things?" Winkler needed to know how far the banker would go to prevent the impostors from draining the account. Once the money was gone, it would be impossible to get it back.

"I took copies of their passports, and wire transfer instructions based on the Sub-Delegation. Since they presented a copy of your U.S. passport, which you said was stolen, I contacted the Zurich Police, who contacted the U.S. Department of State. As it turns out, both their passports were stolen, so we don't know who they really are. They think we're holding the Power of Attorney, Sub-Delegation, and wire transfer instructions until they get back to us with the account number and password. At least that's how I left things with them. I really don't know what they're thinking."

"Did they say when they expect to get back to you?"

"Yes, they said it could take up to a week, no more."

AS WINKLER ENDED HIS CONVERSATION with the banker, Rollins knocked on his door.

"Mr. Wehrli, thank you so much for calling. I appreciate your cooperation, and I'll be back in touch as soon as I know more." He hung up with the banker, then turned his attention to Rollins. "Luke, why are you up so early?"

"I've been up for a while. Maybe I had a feeling you'd get an early morning call from our new best friend, Mr. Wehrli. Anything worth reporting?"

Winkler filled Rollins in on the entire conversation.

"Within a week? They're going to get him the account number and password within a week? Do you think that's just talk, or do they know something we don't?"

"Hard to tell," Winkler said. "But from now on, we'd better be doubly careful. If they think we have that information, they could show up at any time. And I'd better tell Emma things are getting very tense and to have our people crank up our office security a couple of notches.

"We've got some time before she'll be at the office. Let's grab a bite, then head out to our meeting with Prime Suspect No. 2. I sure hope this isn't another wild goose chase, Luke."

CHAPTER 31

IT WAS AROUND SEVEN FORTY-FIVE Wednesday morning when Winkler and Rollins pulled up to the main gate of the William Ewen Correctional Facility, about five miles from the Georgia Diagnostic and Classification State Prison. The new facility, named after Georgia's first governor, was necessary because of overcrowding due to the continuing increase in the prison population.

Winkler handed his business card and driver's license to the guard and advised that they were there to see Juan Martinez and were a little early for an eight o'clock conference.

"Martinez? Sorry, but there's a note here that says you're to meet with Warden Potts. He usually comes in at nine, but I guess he'll be here by eight. Wouldn't want to keep you big city boys waiting. Why don't you just park over there in the staff lot? He should be around any time now."

"Much obliged," said Winkler.

No sooner had he pulled into the space next to the one marked "Reserved for Warden Potts," than a shiny black Hummer squealed around the corner, passed the guard gate, and pulled into that space. Decked out with a ten-gallon hat and fancy cowboy boots, the warden stepped out of his vehicle and greeted his visitors with a hearty handshake. At about six-foot-two, in his mid-sixties with a beer belly, he was an impressive specimen. Winkler's hand felt like it was in a nutcracker.

Georgia born and raised, the warden spoke with a heavy Southern accent.

"Billy Joe Potts is my name. Real pleasure to meet you fellows. Don't often get visitors from Dee-troit. Let's talk in my office."

He led Winkler and Rollins up the stairway, through a reception area, and punched the security code into the door lock.

"Make yourselves comfortable," he said, motioning to them to be seated on the sofa. "I'll put some coffee on." He reached up for a jar of Folger's instant. "We're not much for that fancy drip stuff down here. This'll wake you up just the same as real brew."

He took down three mugs from a shelf, blew the dust out of them, put a plastic spoonful of coffee in each, added hot water from an instant hot tap, then gave each man a mug of coffee with a wooden stirring stick.

"Hope you like it leaded and black, 'cause we're out of milk. But I've got some sugar if that's your preference."

Both men nodded that black was fine. They were there to meet a prisoner, not enjoy coffee.

"Well, I guess I've got some explaining to do. The prisoner you came to see, Juan Martinez, isn't available. Here's here, but he's basically incommunicado. Since his final appeal was denied, he's just counting the days."

"Counting the days until what?" asked Winkler.

"His execution," replied the warden. "It's been a long haul, maybe one of the longest death sentence incarcerations in this state's history. All a waste of time and taxpayer's money, as far as I'm concerned. By next Tuesday evening—in six days, if my math is right—he'll be no more.

"When your office called on Monday—day before yesterday—to set up the meeting for today, we didn't have the final denial on the Application for Clemency. If we had it, we wouldn't have booked your meeting for today. I really apologize. I just realized it last night when I was looking at the prisoner visits scheduled for today. I sure didn't mean to waste your time, coming all the way down here for nothing."

Winkler couldn't believe it. For all they'd been through, and to be so close to perhaps finding the missing banker, only to have the door slammed in their face. He had to probe. Maybe Martinez wasn't Guttmann after all.

"Do you know Martinez?" Winkler asked.

"Sure do. In fact, I knew him back at the Georgia Diagnostic and Classification State Prison, where we used to house the death row inmates. We call 'em 'UDS,' short for 'under death sentence.' We housed 'em there 'til we were bursting at the seams and opened up this place a few years ago. I moved over when he did.

"I was Assistant Warden at Georgia Diagnostic when we took him in, back in 1974. Lived through the break-out in '76, when he and four others escaped in a damn laundry truck! We got 'em all back, one way or the other, 'cept one. Never could get that guy. But we caught two in the next county, brought 'em back peacefully, and one put up a fight with a county SWAT team and got his head blown off. You don't want to mess with those boys."

"And what about Martinez? How did you get him back?" Winkler asked.

"At a routine traffic stop in Memphis, a cop just happened to recognize him. Had no ID and wouldn't say who he was, but the cop recognized him from an APB photo. They had a tip he might be in the area. Just dumb luck. He didn't even try to run."

"Do you have a file on him we could look at? Something that would have his photo and fingerprints?"

"Actually, we don't keep paper files anymore. It's all on computer. Come on over here, and I'll show you what we've got. Our database covers the entire state criminal justice system. It'll just take a minute for Ol' Betsy to boot up."

A couple of minutes later, they were looking at the record of Juan Velasco Martinez, prisoner number 74-762158.

"What are we looking at here?" asked Winkler.

"The photo's more or less current," said the warden. "We update them every so often. We figure it wouldn't do no good if you had a picture from thirty years ago and a prisoner escaped today. This isn't supposed to be a family photo album."

"The photo shows him clean shaven. Do you have a policy on no beards?" asked Rollins.

"Sure do. Don't want prisoners hiding blades or whatever inside a beard. We get First Amendment suits on that from time to time, but this guy's been clean shaven as far back as I can remember."

The only photo Winkler had of Guttmann was bearded, and it was decades old. It was impossible to see any similarity between the old photo of Guttmann and the more or less current photo of Martinez.

"And the prints? When were they taken? I see his date of incarceration was in 1974. Are those the prints that were taken back then?" Rollins was trying to find something to either make or break the argument that Martinez and Guttmann were one and the same.

"Nope. When we went digital a few years ago, we made a point of getting new prints on everyone. That way, we could be sure we had good quality, not just a scan, or a scan of a photocopy in some cases."

"Do you have the original prints from 1974 to compare?" asked Rollins.

"No need to. A person's prints don't change over time, not unless they're altered. Anyhow, the old paper records were destroyed. But what you see there are the prints of Juan Martinez, prisoner 74-762158. I guarantee it."

"Warden, let me get to the point. Is it conceivable that the person who was put back in prison in 1976 as Juan Martinez isn't the person who was convicted as Juan Martinez in 1974? In other words, is it even remotely possible that this is somehow a case of mistaken identity?" Winkler couldn't find a way to ask the question diplomatically.

"Mr. Winkler, I don't know what you big-city boys smoke on your off-hours, but let me make myself perfectly clear. There was no mistake. The guy they picked up and brought back after Juan Velasco Martinez escaped was Juan Velasco Martinez, the same guy who escaped, no one else. The Memphis cops got a tip he might be in the area, and he ran a red light and was picked up. His prison photo was sufficient to identify him. When he was arrested and brought back here, he didn't say we got the wrong guy. If you were picked up as someone else—even if you had the same name—wouldn't you be kickin' and screamin' all the way to prison? How about flashing your own ID to prove who you were? I sure would! Trust me, we got the right guy."

"So, never in all these years," asked Rollins, "did Juan Velasco Martinez take the position that he was being held wrongfully?"

"Oh, sure he did, but not immediately. But don't forget, most of them eventually get educated by a jailhouse lawyer, or get some kid in law school to take their case.

"They take every imaginable position to try to weasel their way out. Error in the trial. Mistaken identity. This one said he got amnesia, said he didn't have a clue why he was here and wasn't who we know he is. And so we give them all their rights—too many rights, if you ask me—until one day they exhaust all their remedies, and that's where he is now.

"Gents, I'm really sorry I couldn't be more helpful..." The warden's tone was sincere, but defensive at the same time. He was clearly fed up with all the effort that had been expended to dispense justice to someone he firmly believed had abused the legal system.

Winkler couldn't leave without probing further. "Warden, if you could just give us another minute of your time. Maybe there's some background that'll help confirm that we're on the wrong track. What was he in for?"

"It's a convoluted story. He was divorced, and he abducted his eight-year-old daughter from his ex-wife, who had legal custody. The police tracked him down, he took off in his truck with the girl, lost control, crashed into a tree, and the kid died. Under Georgia law, you can get life or the death penalty for kidnapping when there's bodily injury. A unanimous jury gave him the death penalty. Open and shut case.

"He's been up and down the court system for decades, in the middle of the whole death penalty debate. But that's how it goes. No more appeals. Yesterday at noon, we got word that the Georgia Board of Pardons and Paroles had denied his request for clemency."

"So now what?" asked Winkler.

"Unless someone pulls a rabbit out of a hat, the play is over. That's the last act. The final curtain comes down at six o'clock next Tuesday evening. That's when they'll inject him and he'll take his last breath."

"So there's really no way we can see Martinez, not even for a few minutes?"

"I suppose if he wanted to talk to you, he could, but you'd have to work that through his attorneys. As things stand right now, he's pretty upset, don't want no visitors. That's typical for a death row inmate when all his appeals are exhausted and the execution date is set. In this case, it's not much of a change for him. In all these years, he's never had any visitors from outside, except attorneys and the prison shrink. No family, not even a letter or phone call from family. It's like the fellow doesn't exist, except for folks who are using his case to fight the death penalty."

"What about his attorneys? Could you give us a name?"

"Sure can—Jeremiah Bean is the main lawyer right now. He's with the Georgia Capital Defenders office over in Peachtree City. He's been on the case for a few months. But it won't do you no good."

"Why's that? Because he's exhausted all his appeals?"

"Yep, and also because Bean's not up to visitors. His car blew up last Friday afternoon on West Highway 16 where it crosses I-75—and from what I hear, he's in really bad shape. The car was probably wired by the family of one of his criminal defendant clients who wasn't happy with his services. The doctors aren't sure if he's going to make it. Bad news travels fast around here. You can find him at Bi-County General Hospital in Jenkinsburg—but you'll probably be wasting your time."

"Warden, would it be too much trouble for you to give me a print of the screen we just looked at, for my file?'

"Sorry, Mr. Winkler, but I'm afraid our printer hasn't worked for a while. Got an order in to have it fixed, but it's not high priority. Don't normally have a need to print."

"Oh, then would you mind if I just take a photo of the screen with the camera in my phone?"

"Help yourself, Mr. Winkler. We've got no secrets. Everything's by the book."

CHAPTER 32

WINKLER AND ROLLINS THANKED THE WARDEN FOR HIS TIME and made their way down to their rental car. As Winkler reached for the door handle, he spotted a piece of paper tightly folded up and jammed into the window molding. He pulled it out and slipped it into his shirt pocket. The warden's Hummer blocked the view from his second floor office.

Once they'd passed through the gate, he handed the note over to Rollins. "What's this about?" he asked.

Rollins unrolled the note and read the message aloud:

"We must talk. Sugar Daddy's Getaway. Main Street. I'll be there in thirty minutes."

"Seems somebody knows we're here," said Rollins. "They must suspect someone is watching them and don't want to leave the prison at the same time as us. Didn't we pass that bar on the way here, right at the center of town?"

"Could there be anything more bizarre? Someone knows we're here and is watching us as we leave," said Winkler. "And the fact that the attorney's car blows up at a time like this, it can't be a coincidence."

When they pulled into the parking lot at Sugar Daddy's, they were surprised to see over a dozen cars so early in the morning. But the day was already hot, the place was air conditioned, and they also served breakfast.

They sat down in a booth in the back and ordered coffee. After their second cups were poured, a grey-haired woman wearing a navy blue skirt and blazer, toting a heavy purse, entered through the back door, just about half an hour after they'd left the prison. She walked over to their table and introduced herself.

"Gentlemen, I'm Alice Hanover, psychologist over at the prison you just visited. I've got something to share with you, and I don't know what you're going to do with it, but you didn't hear it from me. Understood?"

Her voice was soft, and the din of the busy restaurant provided some assurance that their conversation would be relatively private.

"Sure, no problem. I'm attorney David Winkler, and this is Luke Rollins, who's working with me on this case. We were here to meet with Juan Martinez, but I guess you know that. Unfortunately, he's apparently not taking visitors."

"I know all about it," said the psychologist, "and I may be the only one around here who believes his story. Always have. He seemed very credible to me. But he had a string of pro bono lawyers over the years, some good, some not so good, some who just plain dropped the ball. His trial counsel had never handled a capital case. He did no investigation, filed no pre-trial motions, gave no opening statement, didn't raise any mitigating circumstances, and failed to file an appeal."

"Mitigating circumstances?" retorted Winkler. "The warden made it seem like an open-and-shut case. He kidnapped his child, and she died in the process. Seems like the jury could have given him the death penalty on that basis."

The psychologist clearly knew the whole story and wanted to share it. "I'm not surprised he forgot to mention some important facts: The child was dying of leukemia; the mother refused to let her have treatment; the police fired on the truck and caused Martinez to crash; and the mother was the daughter of the local chief of police, who was opposed to his lily white daughter marrying a Mexican.

"Seems to me like a jury might have found mitigating circumstances and given him life instead of the death penalty if they'd been aware of even some of those factors. But the attorney said nothing about them during the trial, not even in his closing statement. Even if the attorney was overburdened by his case load, or just out of his league, he could have argued that Martinez' sentence should be overturned because of inadequate or incompetent counsel. But he didn't even file an appeal!"

"Interesting argument," said Winkler. "But I understand that at this point Martinez is officially at the end of the line."

"It would seem so, unless you're some kind of magician. This case has dragged on for years because of various challenges to the death penalty. His most recent attorney— Jeremiah Bean—was talking about a last-minute plea for a stay. He told me that the fact that the prison destroyed the original paper files with fingerprints on first entry into the system was exceptional and could constitute prosecutorial misconduct. But with what happened to Bean last Friday afternoon—I assume you know someone tried to kill him by blowing up his car—as far as I know, there's nothing in the works. Martinez is just counting the days."

"The warden mentioned the explosion," said Winkler, "but he didn't link it to Martinez. He suspected another of Bean's clients was unhappy about his representation and didn't want to take the trouble to file a malpractice suit—just thought he'd get even by having his attorney vaporized. Do you think there could be some connection to Martinez?"

"If you're asking if Martinez was behind the car bombing, I'd say there isn't a chance in hell. Martinez' only hope at this point was to have Bean make a last-minute appeal to some authority that would see the holes in his incarceration. Bean was talking publicly about how he was getting ready to file a ream of paperwork in the hope of getting a stay."

"Funny, the warden didn't mention anything about that," said Rollins.

"Doesn't surprise me at all. He's not about to point you in any direction that would lead to a stay for Martinez." The psychologist almost seemed to be an advocate for Martinez and had her own ideas about what was going on. "I've got a theory, that he now wants Martinez executed as soon as possible, just to avoid any further digging into his incarceration. If, as I believe, his incarceration—after the escape—was a case of mistaken identity, then it was Warden Potts who was responsible for it. He was the assistant warden at the time and made a big deal of his success in getting four of the five escapees back, though one was in pieces in a box. No one focused on the absolutely ridiculous escape in the laundry truck, or the failure of Potts and his team to take new fingerprints when Martinez was brought back in. So, when the then warden died of a heart attack, Billy Joe Potts was promoted to that position.

"It's a cushy job, but do you know his pay grade? I can't tell you for sure, but he makes somewhere around $100,000 a year. Yet he lives like a king, his wife doesn't work, and neither of them got an inheritance or won the lottery. Did you see that big Hummer he drives? He gets a new one every year and has a tiled barn with a half-dozen exotic cars. We don't see many Lamborghinis and Ferraris around here, Mr. Winkler, but he has them and more.

"Did you notice the new security fencing around the facility? That's only the visible part. There's a complex electronic security system behind it, including a telecommunication system to monitor the phone services. If a prisoner makes an outgoing call which is re-routed to a third party, the call is cut off. All good stuff, but do you know who gets these contracts? A series of companies owned by the warden's brother-in-law. My guess is that either the warden owns a percentage of these companies—and that information isn't public—or he gets some sort of 'consulting fee.' Even the annual facility painting contracts are handled by this group of companies, and they have only a couple of employees. Everything is subcontracted.

"I've got a far-fetched idea the warden has somehow been 'encouraged' over the years to keep Martinez here. It's just a gut feeling, but he's been absolutely unwilling to even admit the slightest possibility of mistaken identity. And it was on his orders that the prior paper records were destroyed. Not scanned and archived, mind you, but destroyed. I've asked around about this. Sometimes they don't destroy them, particularly in a case where questions have been raised."

"What about the records from his original arrest and conviction? Couldn't his lawyers get any of that?" Rollins was reluctant to buy into a conspiracy theory right away.

"Similar story. The stuff was stored in a warehouse in an old building in Jenkinsburg. There was a roof leak that went undiscovered for many months. Hundreds of bankers boxes of court records literally rotted and were converted to pulp. There was no budget to resurrect them by freeze drying, and no perceived need to do so. The criminal defendants had no say in the matter. They were just told the records had been destroyed. I can't say there's no record of a pre-1976 fingerprint of Juan Velasco Martinez, but his string of pro bono lawyers couldn't find it. And it looks like we're about out of time."

"So why do you believe Martinez, Ms. Hanover?" asked Rollins. "Like the warden told us, most convicts eventually come up with an argument as to why they shouldn't be there. Why do you believe this one? Even if the warden is getting rich off the contracts you mention, why would that necessarily mean someone has been encouraging him—I believe you used that word—to keep Martinez behind bars?"

"Look, Mr. Rollins, I met Martinez just after his recapture in 1976. I started my job as prison psychologist a few weeks before he re-entered the system. That was over at Georgia Diagnostic and Classification State Prison. He was quiet, very quiet. He acted like he'd never been there before. He didn't know the day-to-day routine. He was very intelligent, and worldly. Manicured. Dressed in high-end clothing, Italian designer, as I recall. If anything, he would have been a white collar criminal, but not who they said he was. He just didn't fit what they said he'd done. He assured me there was a mistake, but he didn't want to talk about it and certainly didn't want to file a formal protest.

"Then he asked me for newspapers. *The New York Times. The Wall Street Journal.* They don't sell many of those in this town. Martinez was a rough carpenter. How many Mexican rough carpenters do you know who read those newspapers? He asked for an Argentine newspaper, *La Opinion*, but I couldn't get it. Juan Martinez was supposedly Mexican. Why would he want an Argentine newspaper?

"So I got him *The New York Times* and *The Wall Street Journal,* and he read something in them that upset him very much. He asked me for some paper and a pen, and if I would mail a letter for him and make sure no one knew about it. I agreed. He trusted me, and for some reason I was willing to break the rules for him. So, I did it. He addressed the envelope and asked for a second envelope so it would be double wrapped. I mailed it for him. I saw only the outer envelope."

"Do you remember when all that happened, and who the letter was addressed to?" asked Winkler.

"He wrote that letter about three weeks after he re-entered the system—or entered it, whichever you believe. Shortly after that, he was in a terrible fight. An attempted gang rape. He was very good looking and probably considered easy prey. He got beaten very badly and took some heavy blows to the head with a chair. After that beating, he seemed to have lost his memory. He just kept saying he didn't know who he was, or why he was here. Couldn't give me the names of any of his family members—not even his parents or his ex-wife.

"Remember, Martinez was divorced, yet he was wearing a wedding band when he was brought back. Made no sense. I happened to mention this to the prison authorities, who brushed it off as just a ruse; maybe, maybe not. And he never had any visits, letters, or phone calls from family—only from attorneys. His ex-wife probably could have identified him or testified to the misidentification, but she never got involved.

"I think it's a case of true amnesia. It's the only one I've ever seen. Frankly, I think a suit should have been brought for allowing that attack to happen. The guards were too slow to react, and it wouldn't surprise me if somehow the attack was part of a coordinated plan to deal with Martinez cooked up by Billy Joe Potts—or maybe his handler.

"But Martinez' lawyers seemed more interested in getting him out based on problems with the conviction than in getting damages. And his court-appointed Guardian Ad Litem definitely took a back seat. That didn't surprise me. He was appointed by the local Probate Court Judge, who just happens to be the warden's cousin. Need I say more? The Georgia court system is incestuous. Maybe it's the same everywhere—"

"You're not worried about talking so openly about all this?" asked Rollins, looking at the full tables all around them.

"Don't worry about those guys. They're knee-deep yakking about yesterday's sports scores. I guess I'm a little concerned, but I don't think anyone around here considers me a threat.

"Anyhow, I'm retiring at the end of the month. My husband owns this place, or should I say used to own it. It's sold, and the buyers take over this weekend. He sold it to his staff, and we're pulling up roots and retiring to Costa Rica. We can live well—very, very well—with my pension and his sale proceeds. The kids and grandkids have all moved away, so we got a place big enough for all of them to come visit. It's a really beautiful, lush country. And we hope to do volunteer work, helping school kids with their English."

"I guess we were very fortunate to come down here when we did. A week later, and you'd be gone," said Winkler.

"But if you hadn't met me, your life would be much simpler. I really don't know what you can do with all this information, especially with just a few days to go."

"We need some time to digest it, that's for sure. Two more questions: Where does the warden think you are right now? And do you recall who Martinez' letter was addressed to? I don't know how you would remember details that far back, but if you knew, it might help put the pieces of the puzzle together."

"As for the warden, I'm checked out to review cases with an independent clinical psychologist, Dr. Rees Hibblewhite, whose office is located right next door. My car is parked in front of his door. His receptionist, Molly, saw me enter and go into a meeting with Dr. Hibblewhite, with a stack of files under my arm. We gave instructions that we weren't to be disturbed.

"I then quietly left the office through the back door and entered this place through the back door as well, and I'll return the same way. Rees Hibblewhite is an old college friend and will support me 100%. He's the only clinical psychologist for hundreds of miles and doesn't see his flow of second-opinion work from the prison slowing down any time soon, no matter what the warden does. Confidentially, he's been treating the warden's wife for years, and if this got nasty, he could probably make the warden's life unbearable. You'll have to rely on your imagination there. God—this place really is incestuous!"

"No kidding!" exclaimed Winkler. "I hope it never comes to that. Any recollection of the address on that envelope? I know it's a long shot, but I just had to ask—"

"Mr. Winkler, do you know why some ladies' handbags are so heavy? We tend to keep things that just maybe, someday could be important. For example, I believe somewhere down here at the bottom of my bag—"

She stuck her arm down into a large handbag she'd left on the chair next to her and started pulling out things. A wallet. Keys. Cell phone. Hand cream. Perfume. Pens. A transparent accordion folder with store discount coupons. A legal pad in a black leather folio. Even a laptop computer.

With all of that piled on the table, she could finally see the bottom of the bag, where she spotted what she was looking for: A small notepad, about two by four inches, with stitched binding and a black and white speckled cardboard cover.

"Here it is," she said, victoriously, flipping the pages to the end of the notepad. "I must have known someone would ask about this one day."

She read the entry. "*J. Weinman, 84 West 119th Street, Forest Hills, New York.* Does this mean anything to you gentlemen?"

"Sure does," Winkler said. "Would you mind signing an affidavit confirming what you told us today?"

"Look, Mr. Winkler, I have my own ideas about Warden Potts and his motives. I may be right, but I also may be wrong. I want to help you, but I have no interest in hanging Warden Potts."

"What if I limited it to your comments on Martinez' behavior before and after the beating, the request for the Argentine newspaper, and mailing of the letter? I believe we've actually seen that letter, and that could create a reasonable doubt about who he really is."

"You write it up and e-mail it to me. If I can sign it, I will. And if I have a problem with something in it, I'll let you know."

She pulled out a business card from her wallet, scratched out her office e-mail address and wrote in her personal e-mail address, and passed the card to Winkler. "Don't send anything through the prison's e-mail system—I'm sure you'll understand."

"Sure. We'll need to act quickly. If we get it to you by the end of the day, can you get it back to us by tomorrow?" Winkler looked down at his watch. "Would you have a few minutes to stop by the hospital with us to see Jeremiah Bean? I don't know if he can talk, but I'd like to give it a shot."

"Pull your car around back. I'll drive with you. But let's make it quick. I've got to make it back to the prison."

CHAPTER 33

BI-COUNTY GENERAL HOSPITAL was only a short drive from Sugar Daddy's Getaway.

The white-haired volunteer in a red blazer at the information desk told them Jeremiah Bean was in Room 403, in the Burn Unit. Visitors were allowed any time, nine to five, but they should stay no more than fifteen minutes.

A uniformed officer from the County Sheriff's office sat at a desk outside Room 403, playing solitaire to pass the time. In his sixties, balding, around five-foot-seven, what he lacked in height, he made up for in girth, weighing in at over 250 pounds.

Fortunately, Alice Hanover knew him.

"Well, if it isn't Deputy Charlie Parker! How the heck have you been? I haven't see you for...how long has it been, Charlie? Since our kids were in high school together?"

"Time marches on, Alice," replied the deputy. "Chet's married, got four kids, moved West. Ginny was married, had three kids, then her son-of-a-bitch husband up and left her and the kids, so they're all back home with us. What brings you over here, Alice? You mixed up in legal stuff havin' to do with this lawyer? You know I always said it don't pay to take the side of killers and rapists. Ain't no good can come of it.

"This poor guy—he's in really bad shape, Alice. Must have lost a case for somebody who's none too happy about it. His nurse just told me he's talkin' a bit now, just a coupla words, but he's not out of the woods. They took him off the ventilator earlier today and still got him on a huge amount of pain killer."

The psychologist explained that her two friends were visiting from out of town and just wanted a few minutes to talk to the lawyer—if he was up to it—because they were interested in a case he was working on.

"Guess there's no harm in that, as long as they're not from the press. The sheriff doesn't want this to turn into a media circus. They're bringin' in the State Police and the ATF to try to figure out what kinda explosive device was used to blow up his car, and maybe who did it. We're not supposed to talk about the case. You guys got business cards and driver's licenses? I gotta keep a log of who comes and goes."

"Sure, thanks," said Winkler. "We'll be brief."

"Maybe you want to take a look at this story in the newspaper before you go in, so you'll have an idea of what this fellow has been through." The deputy handed Winkler a local newspaper with a front-page story and photo of the charred remains of the lawyer's SUV. It was just a burned out chassis.

"Mind if I keep this?" asked Winkler.

"No problem," replied the deputy. "I can't imagine how the guy got out of that fireball alive!"

"With what he probably has ahead of him, I wonder if he wishes he hadn't," said Rollins as he, Winkler and the psychologist entered the room.

Although Room 403 was in the Burn Unit, it looked like any other ICU. Electronic gadgets covered the wall above the bed, reporting all the patient's vital signs. A bag of IV fluid hung along one side of the bed, and a urinary catheter tube ran to a bag hanging off the other side. The newspaper story reported that Jeremiah Bean had third-degree burns on 80% of his body, and Winkler wondered what part of him hadn't been burned. He was wrapped up like a mummy, the head of the bed propped up at a slight angle. His eyes were closed, and he seemed to be sleeping quietly. The three of them stood there a moment in silence, then the psychologist pulled up a chair to the side of the bed and spoke softly.

"Jeremiah. Jeremiah Bean. Can you hear me? This is Alice Hanover." She hoped he remembered her.

His eyes opened slightly. She got up from the chair and moved closer so he could see her.

"Alice? What are you doing here? What happened? There was a huge blast, then fire—"

"Jeremiah, we're not going to stay long. I brought two fellows with me. They're interested in the Martinez case and have some new information. They're wondering where things stand, if you'd planned to make any more appeals. Your Application for Clemency was denied, and Martinez is scheduled to be executed next Tuesday."

"No, no! You can't let that happen! I was working on more appeals. The files…in my car…my laptop..."

"It's all gone, Jeremiah. Your car is nothing but a burned-out chassis, and everything in it was reduced to ashes. Does anyone else have drafts?"

"No…working alone. Everybody else…given up. This last appeal…my Hail Mary pass." He closed his eyes.

Then, with his eyes still closed, he continued to speak. "If…new information…there may be—" His voice trailed off to a whisper. "—other possible appeals."

Winkler came closer and strained to hear what Jeremiah Bean was suggesting. Words came out slowly, sometimes barely audible. Three minutes later, exhausted, he stopped talking. But Jeremiah Bean had given Winkler his best ideas for a last-ditch effort to spare Martinez' life, or at least get a stay of his execution.

CHAPTER 34

ALICE HANOVER AGREED TO REVIEW HER AFFIDAVIT and get it back to Winkler immediately. She headed back to the prison, leaving him and Rollins to map out their strategy.

Realizing he had no time to lose, Winkler called Emma as he and Rollins walked through the crowded hospital lobby to the parking lot.

"Emma, I need some urgent litigation support," he said, calmly. Winkler was the kind of attorney who could deal with any complex situation by identifying the issues and dealing with them systematically. He knew no one in his blue stocking firm had ever done anything like this before, but that wouldn't stop him. There were probably only a handful of attorneys in the country who'd ever seen a situation even close to this, and there was no time to go looking for one of them.

"Get Dillingham on this. He came from the prosecutor's office and should be able to put something together that'll at least pass the requirements for filing."

Dan Dillingham was a seventh-year associate who'd worked in the Wayne County Prosecutor's office for three years before joining the firm. One of the reasons he left was that he felt criminal defendants often had inadequate counsel. Despite the fact that his job was to put them behind bars, he sympathized with many of them. He'd often told Winkler he wished he were working for the Federal Defenders' Office. Winkler also suspected Dillingham would be willing to give some extra effort to this petition, because he'd soon be up for partnership, and burning the midnight oil would show he was a team player.

"I'm going to need a Petition for Emergency Stay of Execution of Juan Velasco Martinez, Georgia State Prisoner Number 74-762158. He's scheduled to be executed next Tuesday at six in the evening. The Georgia Board of Pardons and Paroles has denied his request for clemency. Unlike most other states, the Governor of Georgia has no direct authority to grant clemency, but we should think about whether he can exercise some political pressure on the board or others." Winkler just wanted a bare bones pleading he could massage.

"We have some new information, and we're going to try several long shots. Ask Dillingham to draft the petition—just the guts of it based on new information—and I'll provide the rest. He can refer to new information discussed in Exhibit 'A' and allude to prosecutorial misconduct. I'll fill in the facts. Further support will be in Exhibit 'B," which will be an Affidavit of Georgia State Prison psychologist Dr. Alice Hanover. I should have both exhibits by tomorrow morning."

"Sure, David. I saw Dan earlier today, so I know he's around. But Afzam has some very important information for you, the veritable 'smoking gun.' He's located old records of the New York State Banking Commission. They date back to when Guttmann applied for a banking license in connection with the purchase of a New York bank. Guttmann's fingerprints are in the file!" Emma was delighted to be the bearer of good news.

"Unbelievable!" said Winkler. "Have Afzam get a certified hard copy via FedEx overnight. Send me a copy of the prints via e-mail. I'm going to e-mail you Martinez' prints from the Georgia prison records. Have them compared with Guttmann's. Dillingham can get someone to do that for us. My guess is, you'll have a match."

"David, there's something else you should know. The office is swarming with police. We had a break-in last night."

"How did they get by the sensors?" asked Winkler. "We invested a fortune a couple of years ago when the partners had a concern about security."

"David, you won't believe it. The intruders passed themselves off as carpet cleaners—with uniforms and cleaning equipment—and literally walked in the front door after hours. They weren't scheduled to clean, but they gave a forged letter from our office manager to the security guard who actually came up to our floor and opened the door for them around ten o'clock last night. The guard became suspicious when they left after only twenty minutes. Apparently, he hadn't been watching the security cameras when they were on our floor.

"David, the only areas that were touched were your office and my desk. They cleared all the papers off your desk and took your laptop from the closet."

"What could they have been after?" Winkler asked.

"My steno pad is gone as well. It had my notes from a couple of days ago, when you asked me to reserve the suite for Mrs. Weinman under the name of Sylvia Greenspan. It's all there in black and white, David, including the name of the hotel and her room number."

"I've got to contact Mrs. Weinman. I'll be back in touch." Winkler was suddenly in panic mode.

"But wait, David, there's one more thing. Mr. Banks from Tricontinental Research has been calling. He said he's looking for an update."

"Damn, I was supposed to touch base with him weekly. Things have been moving so fast, I totally forgot. Does he want me to call?"

Winkler really didn't have the time to talk to Banks and frankly didn't know what he'd tell him. Even if Martinez really was Guttmann, the clock was ticking on his execution, and the last-ditch appeal for a stay was far from a sure thing. Recovering the fortune from the Swiss bank wasn't even on his mind, except that Mrs. Weinman had unwittingly gotten herself into a crossfire.

"No need to call, David, but he does want to meet with you. He'll be in Detroit next Monday and asked me to set aside half an hour for him. Your schedule is clear. Although I wasn't sure you'd be back, I set up an appointment for ten in the morning. I told him I'd get back to him to confirm."

"Fine, Emma, let's just keep putting out fires. As far as I know right now, I should be able to meet him next Monday morning. But have Afzam try to find out as much as he can about Trevor Banks. Something just doesn't sit well with me, and I can't put my finger on it. Get a photo of him off our security cameras, and have Afzam see if he can come up with any matches."

"WE'RE SURE SPREAD THIN, LUKE. We've got a man headed for execution, who presumably doesn't want to meet with us. His attorney has been blown off the case, and we may have what it takes to get his situation reconsidered—if we can put it together, get it filed quickly, and get someone to listen. At the same time, I think the Russians may have enough information to pay a nasty visit to Mrs. Weinman. They'll stop at nothing to get to that account.

"We have to move her out of the Ritz immediately. I expect she'll resist, but I have to try to persuade her."

Winkler punched in the number of the Ritz Hotel and asked for the room of Sylvia Greenspan. The phone range once, twice, three times.

"Yes. Who's calling?" the voice answered.

"This is David Winkler. Who's speaking?"

"Molly Abraham. Mrs. Weinman's sister-in-law. You're the lawyer. It's so nice of you to put us up here. I'd heard about this place, but I've never been here—"

"May I speak with Mrs. Weinman? It's very urgent!"

"She's not here, Mr. Winkler. We were just sitting here, having a nice, late breakfast from room service, like you said, when all of a sudden she went to the ring of keys in her purse and saw one and said, 'That's it!' Then she said something about Joshua having a safe deposit box down here at the First Intercoastal Bank and she had to go check something and would be back in a few minutes."

"How far away is First Intercoastal Bank?"

"Just a short walk down the boardwalk—maybe ten minutes, no more."

"When did she leave?"

"Gosh, it must be over an hour by now. Should I be worried? Has something else happened?"

"Mrs. Abraham, please go downstairs and take a cab to the nearest police station. Then call my office and let them have a phone number for you. We're going to ask you to move to another location. But for now, we need you to leave the hotel immediately."

"And what about Sarah? What if she comes back here? Should I leave her a note?"

"Absolutely not! But when you get to the police station, tell them she went to the First Intercoastal Bank over an hour ago to make a large cash withdrawal and is long overdue. They'll send out a car to find her. Don't you worry!"

Winkler felt sick. In his gut, he knew there could be only one reason why she would have left the hotel. But was she merely delayed talking to folks on the boardwalk, or had the Russians already scoped out the hotel and followed her to the bank?

AS THE EXECUTIVE JET READIED for take-off at the county airport in Griffin, Georgia, Rollins was chatting with the pilots, and Winkler's cell phone rang.

"David, I've got Mrs. Weinman on the phone for you." It was Emma, poised and business-like, as usual. "Should I patch her in?"

"Absolutely," said Winkler, anxious to hear where she was, and feeling great relief that she was able to contact him.

"Mr. Winkler, I'm calling you from the police station in Ft. Lauderdale. I think I have the information you're looking for. When I got down here, it occurred to me that my husband had a safe deposit box in Florida, and when I looked at the ring of keys, I saw that funny safe deposit box key. I just had to go to the bank and see whether he might have put that information in the box. And sure enough—"

"But Mrs. Weinman, you can't go back to the hotel. I have to keep you away from some men who are eager to get their hands on that information."

"Not to worry, Mr. Winkler. I think they'll be busy with the police for a while. When I left the hotel, I had a feeling I was being followed. You know there are certain kinds of people you see around here, mostly in their eighties or older, and two men in their forties, not even very good looking, stick out like a sore thumb! So when I got to the bank, I alerted the manager, and since they were hanging around outside the bank when I finished my business at the box, the manager called the police.

"So, now the police are holding them for questioning. From what I overheard a police officer say, they've asked for a Russian interpreter and a lawyer. Funny how they knew enough English to ask for a lawyer! I had to give the police a statement, and they may want to ask me more questions. I told them I really don't know very much, just that you were looking for some information about a foreign account. I gave them your name and phone number, and they'll probably contact you as well."

"That's fine, Mrs. Weinman, but just to be safe, I'd like you and your sister-in-law to move to another hotel. We don't know if these men have accomplices who may be watching your room at the Ritz. Please stay on the line, and Emma will give you the address for another hotel. Go there, and we'll contact your sister-in-law and make sure she joins you. This time, you'll check in under the name Sophie Adler. Do you have some cash for cab fare?"

"Absolutely, Mr. Winkler. A lady never ventures out—not even to the drugstore—without identification, her health insurance card, and enough cash for cab fare to get home from wherever she may find herself. That much, my mother taught me."

"And as soon as you get to the hotel, Mrs. Weinman, please fax the information you found in the safe deposit box to my office. Emma will give you the fax number. I'm very sorry about all this, Mrs. Weinman, and really appreciate your help."

CHAPTER 35

"DAVID, DAN DILLINGHAM JUST SLIPPED ME A NOTE. He needs to talk to you about the petition. I think you may want to delay your flight until tomorrow. Can you call him back right away?" Emma had already brought Dillingham into the loop.

"Sure, Emma. You finish up with Mrs. Weinman, and I'll call Dan immediately."

Winkler was totally out of his element and really needed a litigator with a can-do attitude. Dillingham had pulled off major litigation coups for Winkler in the past, and he hoped this time he could do so as well. The other cases all involved complex commercial disputes, with millions of dollars at stake; this time, a man's life was on the line.

Winkler dialed Dillingham's direct number and explained the situation.

"David, I get the picture—a Hail Mary appeal for a death row inmate based on mistaken identity—and we'll have new information to prove the mistake. What's this about proving he's not who they say he is by reference to fingerprints in New York Banking Commission records?"

"That's right, Dan. Afzam located a set in the New York Banking Commission files. Those prints were submitted as the prints of an Argentine banker, Ricardo Guttmann, and they were taken by the NYPD based on positive identification. You can get them from Afzam. I'm going to e-mail you a photo of a screenshot of Martinez' prison record with his fingerprints on it. The quality isn't the best, but have those compared to the prints from the Banking

Commission. If they match, I'd say there's every reason to at least stay the execution of Martinez—or Guttmann—and then have a full hearing to have him released. I should also have an affidavit from the prison psychologist for you tomorrow morning."

"OK, David, but there are a couple of problems.

"The first is a big one, and may be a deal-breaker. It's not enough that Martinez—or Guttmann—is innocent, even if we can prove it. We may need to raise a separate constitutional issue. In some cases, it would be that the prosecutor buried crucial evidence, witnesses lied, police hid evidence or coerced false confessions, or defense attorneys performed so poorly that they basically failed to advocate at all. Basically, once the trial has taken place, you need to raise a constitutional issue. Mere innocence isn't enough to support a habeas corpus petition."

"What?! The fact that our guy didn't commit the crime, that they have the wrong person, isn't enough to get him out? I can't believe it! Is this based on some obscure lower court decision?"

"No, David, it's a judicial perversion that's been on the books since the 1993 *Herrera* case in the U.S. Supreme Court. The majority opinion held that Texas courts' refusal even to consider the prisoner's newly discovered evidence didn't violate due process and suggested he file a Clemency Petition with the Texas Board of Pardon and Paroles. In our case, I don't know how far we'll get with the Georgia Board of Pardons and Paroles, since they just rejected a Clemency Petition a few days ago."

Winkler gasped. "But Guttmann was never given a trial! They tried Martinez. If executing Guttmann, an innocent man, isn't a violation of due process and his 8th Amendment right to be free from cruel and unusual punishment, then I don't know what is. Even non-citizens have constitutional rights. What about the destruction of the physical records when they went digital?"

The conversation was interrupted when Winkler's cell phone indicated another call was coming through. From the caller ID, he could see it was Alice Hanover.

"Dan, I'm gonna put you on hold. It'll just be a minute."

He wasn't expecting the psychologist to call and hoped she wasn't going to withdraw her support for fear of retribution from the warden. He listened intently, then thanked her for the call and switched back to Dillingham.

"Dan, you won't believe it. Alice Hanover, the prison psychologist, tracked down a former prison employee, Darcy McManus, who was at Georgia Diagnostic when Martinez was brought back in after his escape. It was her job to take fingerprints of all new arrivals. She distinctly remembers insisting that Martinez be fingerprinted. Potts, then assistant warden, was present, gloating about how he got the escapee back. He refused to allow her to take prints, saying it wasn't necessary, that they knew who they were dealing with. Failure to take his fingerprints violated established procedure, and she pointed that out. She was ticked that he just blew her off, but was afraid to press him on the issue because he was the boss. She'll sign an affidavit."

"My God," said Dillingham. "Combine that with the destruction of the paper records when they went digital, and it looks like we have our constitutional violation. Something like prosecutorial misconduct. So, we go with the prints from the photo of the screenshot from the prison computer system—"

"We don't have a choice, Dan. If we ask Warden Potts to take new fingerprints or e-mail the prison record for a cleaner image, we'll get stonewalled. I guarantee that

100%. Let's go with what we have. I'll attach an affidavit with the two sets of prints and the fingerprint expert's opinion that the two match, assuming that's what he tells us. That should work for now. We can get new prints during the period of the stay. The standard for a stay of execution pending disposition of a habeas corpus petition is that there are 'significant grounds' upon which relief may be granted. The new information should constitute evidence that Guttmann is not the man convicted as Martinez." Winkler was getting a little ahead of himself but felt confident the fingerprints would support his argument of mistaken identity. "You mentioned a second problem, Dan. What other obstacles have you uncovered?"

Dillingham had clearly given a lot of thought to the situation. "We can't just file all our appeals. We need an adverse decision from which to appeal. Up to now, all the appeals and Clemency Petitions have been filed on behalf of Martinez. Now we have a totally different party, Ricardo Guttmann. I think we should start with the Georgia state court that convicted Martinez, and if the judge doesn't buy the mistaken identity argument, then we let loose with the appeals.

"But even before we do that, I think a visit to the county prosecutor, Johnny Morrow, would be the smart way to go. I've already contacted Jeremiah Bean's office, the Georgia Capital Defenders, to send an attorney to meet with you. I don't think you should meet with the prosecutor without local counsel. The soonest Morrow can meet is four tomorrow afternoon, which is fine. It'll give us some time to finish the petition and get the affidavits.

"The prosecutor is up for re-election in a few months, and if he refuses to listen to us, it could look real bad that he let the state execute the wrong man. If he doesn't agree that the wrong guy is about to be executed, then we take it to the judge for an immediate decision, and if that doesn't work, then we launch the appeals."

"Do we have time for all this, Dan?"

"I don't see any choice, David. It's a question of whether we go straight to the judge or play our hand with the prosecutor first. We won't have our petition and affidavits ready until sometime tomorrow, and in any event, we couldn't meet with the judge without the petition and affidavits. I know there's a lot on the line here, and it's a rush, but we have no choice.

"One more thing: What about our representation of the inmate? How is it that we're now his counsel? Have you met with him?" Dillingham didn't want to overlook any technicality.

"No, not yet, and I can't see how that'll happen before we meet with the prosecutor tomorrow." Winkler couldn't escape the facts.

"I have an idea," said Dillingham. "Jeremiah Bean is with the Georgia Capital Defenders. Technically, it's the organization that represents Martinez, not the attorney, so when one of their lawyers tags along, we'll have continuity of counsel, and you just appear as co-counsel. Didn't Jeremiah Bean make you co-counsel when you met with him at the hospital?"

"Hmm...he was real weak, heavily medicated to manage his pain, hard to understand, but he did communicate."

"David, that's when he asked you to be co-counsel! Who's to say that's not true?"

Winkler smiled and nodded. Dillingham continued.

"I've also touched base with the Innocence Project, given their experience with exonerating wrongfully convicted individuals through DNA testing. I've asked them to mobilize their social media network once we get the petitions filed. Within a few hours after we file, I expect we'll have thousands of people and anti-death penalty organizations contacting their Congressmen, the Governor of Georgia, and even the President to set this thing straight.

"Once we compare the fingerprints, I'll contact the Embassy of Argentina. I'm certain they'll lodge an official protest with the State Department that one of their nationals is being wrongly detained and about to be executed. They couldn't have been notified at any point in the process since his true nationality wasn't even known."

Winkler was amazed at how quickly Dillingham brought himself up to speed in areas in which he'd never worked.

"Dan, there's no question this is a clear violation of the Vienna Convention on Consular Relations, but I'm not sure how that's going to help us. That treaty has been in the press with regard to Mexican prisoners on death row in Texas. The police are supposed to tell them of their right to contact the consulate for assistance. Consular officers are supposed to monitor and support defense counsel's efforts, confer regularly with the defendant and his family, and attend court proceedings. But the cases have ended badly. I seem to recall the Mexicans were executed notwithstanding the treaty violations.

"I guess we could invoke the Convention," Winkler continued, "but I certainly wouldn't count on it, and I'm also a little leery about contacting the Argentine Embassy right now. They could want Guttmann for other reasons. Let's take this a step at a time. Get the stay, then get him out and ask for protective custody. We'll deal with the Argentines later.

"Dan, I've got to go. I'm gonna tell the pilot we're not flying tonight. I'll draft what I need to on my end and watch my e-mail for your draft of the petition. Thanks for your help."

"Remember me at the next annual review meeting," Dillingham replied. "Anyhow, it's a nice change from corporate litigation. Let's see if we can make the justice system work."

CHAPTER 36

"MR. VINKLER, YOUR INSTINCTS WERE RIGHT. Trevor Banks is not who he says he is."

It was Thursday morning. Winkler was busy in his motel room, reviewing Dillingham's petition and polishing his affidavit, when Afzam called him with some shocking news.

"It wasn't easy, but I used facial recognition software on the image of Banks we got off our security surveillance system, after enhancing it to sharpen it up. Then I went out on the Web and looked for matches but came up with nothing. But then I had the system age whatever was on the Web, based on the number of years between the Web photo and the current date, and we got a couple of matches, and they are very, very interesting. I just e-mailed some photos to you."

"I have your e-mail with several attachments," said Winkler.

"The first is the current photo," said Afzam. "This is the fellow you know as Trevor Banks, taken within the past few days. The other photos are the matches. If you just look at the original photos, you won't see much of a resemblance. Too many years have passed, and they haven't been very kind to him. But once you age enhance them, the similarity is amazing.

"These photos are from news articles, archived from the late 1970s, and in each case he is pictured with a group of Argentine military leaders. In photo #2 he's in the back row, right behind the big shot. Same as in the next one.

Each time pictured with the same fellow, Colonel Raoul Vincenti."

"So who is Trevor Banks?" asked Winkler.

"Based on the captions and the accompanying news stories, he is Alejandro Ramos and was a high level aide to the colonel," said Afzam.

"Were you able to find out any more about him?" asked Winkler.

"His name was only mentioned in one more item," replied Afzam. "This is what I think you would refer to as a 'home run.' I found a confidential, top-secret, classified internal State Department memorandum, now declassified and made available after a Freedom of Information Act request. The memo is a transcript of a meeting which took place in 1976 between representatives of the Argentine Government and Henry Kissinger, then Secretary of State.

"The Argentines were fed up with the left-wing Montonero guerillas and asked Kissinger for political support in their decision to use the full force of the military to stamp them out.

"He urged them to finish the job and eradicate the rebels before Congress would get back in session. He was concerned about a new human rights law which would require the White House to certify that a government was not violating human rights before providing U.S. aid. He was hoping the Argentine generals would wrap up their murderous eradication of the left before the law took effect."

"And what was Ramos—or Banks—doing at that meeting?"

"He was the representative of the Argentine military. He made the point, loud and clear, that human rights had to step aside for the greater good of the country—to save the nation."

"What about Colonel Vincenti? Could you find anything on him?"

"He was convicted of torture in Argentina in the early eighties, as part of the Dirty War prosecutions. He was at the very top of a group which engaged in electroshock, water-boarding, and what were euphemistically called 'transfers' of prisoners. The prisoners were actually drugged, stripped, then thrown out of airplanes into the ocean, never to be seen again. Then he was pardoned, so he never did time. However, I did a search for his image on the Web, aging the ones I found where he was pictured with Banks, and look what I found. It's photo #3."

The third photo was from a front page article in a recent edition of *The New York Times*. The title of the article read: "New Secretary of Homeland Security Set for Approval."

"But this is Eduardo Cruz, a Congressman from Florida who's in the process of being appointed Secretary of Homeland Security. He's just awaiting Senate approval. What does this have to do with Colonel Raoul Vincenti? Are Cruz and Vincenti the same guy?" Winkler was stymied.

"It certainly looks like it to me," said Afzam. "Have a look at photo #4, another current photo of Cruz. He is accompanied by an aide, none other than the man we know as Trevor Banks. Seems to me that a couple of people have tried to bury their past, and one is about to ascend to a very important position of power in the United States, quite possibly without the Senate having the benefit of full information on him."

Winkler's heart stopped. What had he gotten himself into? Was he about to blow the cover of a man who aspired to lead one of America's top security organizations? Or did the President really know who he was and want someone like him to help quash our own internal dissent?

Even if that's so, he thought, *there must still be a few reasonable voices in the Senate who'll want to know the person whose appointment they're being asked to approve is a cold-blooded killer and torturer.*

"Afzam, see if Dan Dillingham can get Senator Harden's office to pull their file on this nomination, and at least let us know if there were any name changes mentioned. We may not be able to see the entire file, but maybe we can open the door to closer scrutiny if there was no disclosure of name changes and we bring up this apparent inconsistency. If they can get their hands on Congressman Cruz' immigration records, I'd be very interested to see if he disclosed his checkered past, or buried it."

"Certainly, Mr. Vinkler, but there is one more thing. Your private investigator, Luke Rollins. What do you know about him?"

"Not very much, Afzam, except that he's had a career in law enforcement and came highly recommended."

"Were you aware that he served in the U.S. military?"

"Yes, he mentioned that, but we didn't discuss details."

"Mr. Vinkler, did you know that he spoke Spanish?"

"Yes, and in fact he did a great job translating Ricardo Guttmann's letter. But he didn't profess any great language expertise."

"Well, Mr. Vinkler, I don't think he has been totally candid with you. The memorandum of the meeting with Secretary Kissinger indicates that Mr. Rollins was present, that he was in fact the Military Attaché at the Embassy in Buenos Aires and acted as interpreter at that meeting.

"I don't want to speculate, but it would not surprise me if he knew Trevor Banks—or Alejandro Ramos— from his days with the military in Buenos Aires. The U.S. and Argentine military had a very close relationship. In fact, it wouldn't surprise me if Mr. Rollins brought Mr. Banks to you. My concern is that he may be feeding information to Banks, and possibly those other people who are trying to find Ricardo Guttmann or the missing fortune."

"Oh my God! Afzam, thank you so much! I have to figure out how to cut ties with Rollins immediately. We certainly don't need a mole in this operation."

Winkler ended the call with Afzam and stood for a moment, gazing out the window. He was shocked by the revelation that Rollins had been in Argentina and supported the Argentine military during the Dirty War. How could Rollins not have mentioned this to him? Should he confront Rollins directly on this? Did it matter? Did he need Rollins anymore, or had his role as an investigator come to an end? Would a blow-up with Rollins be worse for him as he continued to deal with Trevor Banks, or Ramos?

There was a knock on the door. It was Rollins.

"Morning, David. How's the paperwork going?"

"Fine, Luke. Should be wrapping it up shortly. You know, Luke, I think from this point onward it's all legal work. What I mean is, I don't think we really need your talents as an investigator anymore, now that we've figured it all out and found our man, so to speak."

"I agree, and I'm just as happy to stop the clock and get back to the office. I just had a call, and there's a juicy assignment waiting for me as soon as I get back. Something about a judge who's been leading a double life and has a second family in another state. Wife number one has a divorce attorney who'd like me to help him work up the case."

"Just tally up your hours," said Winkler, relieved that Rollins was so willing to step aside, "and Emma will get you a check. Thanks for all your help. I really mean it."

At this point, Winkler didn't need the drama of a confrontation with Rollins about who he was really working for. Whatever information had been passed along was yesterday's news, and Winkler needed to focus his energy and efforts on getting the stay of execution.

CHAPTER 37

IT WAS ALL FALLING NICELY INTO PLACE. Winkler didn't know if the petition would win the day, but it said all the right things.

New information supported the position that the prisoner wasn't who the prison records said he was, that there was a clear case of mistaken identity. The fingerprints spoke for themselves. The set from the New York Banking Commission, taken by the NYPD, represented the prints of Ricardo Guttmann. The prints from the screenshot off the prison's own computer were a perfect match, according to a report and affidavit of a credentialed fingerprint expert. Winkler's own affidavit accompanied the screenshot of the prints, and if there was any doubt as to their authenticity, the court could either order the prison to print another copy or order that new prints of the prisoner be taken.

The affidavit of Darcy McManus, the former prison employee, supported the position that there was official misconduct when Martinez—or Guttmann—was admitted after the escape, without taking his fingerprints, in clear violation of prison rules. The destruction of the paper records in this case wasn't consistent with any written policy. Winkler was optimistic his meeting with the prosecutor would be fruitful, but at the same time he realized things rarely go as expected.

Winkler arrived at the County Building just before four o'clock. He was to meet Mary Ellen Palmer, an attorney with Georgia Capital Defenders, outside the prosecutor's office on the third floor.

The County Building was a classic nineteenth century government building that housed the county courtrooms, as well as the prosecutor's office and other county offices. The roof was domed, and the front bore classic pillars. The ceilings were twenty feet high, the floors were marble, and the doors to each office were solid oak, with heavy trim and brass hardware.

Winkler paced nervously, wondering if Mary Ellen Palmer was going to be on time. She appeared a minute after four.

"Sorry I'm a little late," she said. "I'd hoped to be here earlier so we could talk about your petition, but I've read what you e-mailed me, and anyhow, you're the one who's going to make the presentation. I'm just window dressing, right?"

"Kind of," said Winkler. "I'm not admitted in Georgia, and there's no time for a *pro hac vice* admission. Officially, your office is counsel to Martinez, and when I met with Jeremiah Bean in the hospital, he asked me to come on as co-counsel. One of my colleagues, who drafted the petition, thought we should start with the prosecutor rather than just file the petition with the court. So, let's go in and see what we can do."

As they entered the prosecutor's office, the secretary said the prosecutor was waiting for them and ushered them in. Mary Ellen Palmer made the introductions, then turned the meeting over to Winkler.

"Mr. Morrow, sir, I appreciate your taking the time to meet with us. I know the hour is late, and in fact, the clock is ticking on the execution of Mr. Martinez, which is scheduled to take place next Tuesday evening at six o'clock."

"I'm very much aware of that, Mr. Winkler. Our office has been involved in this matter for years, and I argued our case to the Georgia State Board of Pardons and Paroles.

You know his request for clemency was recently denied, don't you?"

"Yes, sir, I certainly do. I'm here for a completely different reason. We have evidence that the prisoner who's scheduled to be executed is not Juan Martinez, but is in fact Ricardo Guttmann, an Argentine banker. There's a clear case of mistaken identity. Mr. Guttmann was never tried for any crime and shouldn't be executed. We're asking you to take the initiative and order a stay of execution so the new evidence we have can be thoroughly reviewed and he can be released."

The prosecutor, surprised by the information, abruptly sat up in his chair and leaned forward. "And what might that evidence be, Mr. Winkler?"

"I have it right here, Mr. Morrow, fingerprints showing the person who's incarcerated as Juan Martinez is, in fact, Ricardo Guttmann. I have an opinion of a credentialed fingerprint expert comparing the prints of Ricardo Guttmann, taken by the New York City Police Department. The expert examined both the fingerprints of Ricardo Guttmann and the fingerprints of the prisoner known as Juan Martinez, which appear in the prison records. They're a perfect match.

"The prisoner is, in fact, Ricardo Guttmann. Let me give you a copy of the expert's report and the two sets of fingerprints. I also have my own affidavit with regard to Martinez' prints from the prison record, and our Petitions for Habeas Corpus and Stay of Execution, which I hope we won't have to file. We've made them on behalf of Martinez and Guttmann."

The prosecutor laid the papers on his desk as his eyes moved from one set of fingerprints to the other, then to the expert's report, then the petitions.

"Mr. Winkler, where did you get these fingerprints? This case has been bouncing around for decades, and this is the first time anyone has raised an issue about the identity of the prisoner."

"The prints from the prison record are from a photo I took of the record on the warden's computer, with his consent. I asked him to print the record, but he said he couldn't because his printer wasn't working. He allowed me to take the photo. The quality isn't the best, but it was good enough for the expert to conclude there was a 100% match. The second set of prints is from the files of the New York State Banking Commission. The prints were taken by the NYPD based on positive identification of Guttmann, who at the time was applying for a banking license. I'm in the process of getting a certified copy. The expert's report was just faxed to me."

"Hmm…" The prosecutor was silent as he took off his glasses and laid them down on the desk, picked up the two sets of prints and expert's report, and stroked his chin, squinting as he reviewed the last-minute material, thinking about how to respond.

"Mr. Winkler, I don't get it. How the hell did Guttmann get into prison in the place of Martinez?"

"As the affidavit of the former prison employee indicates, sir, there was an irregularity in the intake procedure at the prison. Martinez escaped. Someone who looked just like him—Guttmann—was brought back in. Fingerprints weren't taken, even though prison procedure required them. The person in charge of that process tried to take the prints but was told by a superior it wasn't necessary. That's covered in the affidavit of the former prison employee, Darcy McManus. Her superior who directed her not to take the prints was the current warden, who was the assistant warden at that facility at the time."

"So you're asking me to call off an execution based on this expert report. Is that right, Mr. Winkler?"

"Yes, sir, based on the expert's report, and this affidavit of a former prison employee, which supports the fact that no fingerprints were taken when the prisoner known as Juan Martinez was admitted after the escape of Juan Martinez. According to what the warden told me, fingerprints of Martinez taken at the time of his original admission were destroyed somewhere along the way when the prison went digital, without retaining digital copies. So, the prints in the prison's computer system were taken months, or maybe years after the escape, when the prison went digital. They are, indeed, the prints of the prisoner known as Juan Martinez, who's really Ricardo Guttmann. Based on this new evidence, we're just asking you to grant a stay to allow for a thorough review. Thirty days should do it."

"And how do I know any of this is authentic? I'm sure you can appreciate how it looks from this side of the desk. After several decades of no one raising this issue, you come waltzing in here at the eleventh hour—I'm guessing you're from out of state, acting as co-counsel—with what purports to be evidence of a major screw-up on the state's end. To the best of my recollection, there's never been any suggestion that we had the wrong guy. Why wouldn't he have said something?"

"It's a long story, Mr. Morrow, but actually he's repeatedly said he isn't Martinez, but he's been unable to say who he is because of amnesia due to injuries suffered in prison. His assertions were simply rejected, just like the allegations of innocence made by so many prisoners. The point is, we've just determined who he is—and he is *not* Juan Martinez."

"So, Mr. Winkler, on the strength of your affidavit, an opinion of an out-of-state fingerprint expert, and an affidavit of a former prison employee alleging a breach of protocol decades ago, you want me to grant a stay of execution. Is that what you're asking?"

"Yes, sir, that's the idea."

The prosecutor took a deep breath and was silent for what seemed to Winkler to be an eternity.

"Mr. Winkler, I'm sorry, but I just can't make a major decision like this based on the very late and flimsy evidence you're presenting to me. For all I know, the fingerprints aren't authentic, or if they are, they're not a match. I don't mean to insult you or suggest any impropriety—and I'm well aware that a man's life is on the line—but it could all be phony. I would need to see originals or certified copies of anything you're going to rely on, including the expert's opinion, and original fingerprints would have to be reviewed by our own expert.

"I'd suggest we see how the judge feels about this. The Chief Judge, Terry Barnes, may still be around. I know the other judges were going to be out of town this week at a judicial conference. Let me call his chambers."

The prosecutor picked up the phone and dialed Judge Barnes' chambers. His assistant picked up.

"Good afternoon, Nelly. Is Judge Barnes available for a brief visit? I have an important matter I'd like to run by him."

The assistant explained that the judge had left earlier in the afternoon, to take a long weekend hunting. He was going alone and wasn't going to be back in town until Monday evening. He'd specifically told his assistant he didn't want to be bothered and was going to turn off his cell phone. He was in the middle of a lengthy trial and was burned out. She had no idea where he was headed.

"Mr. Winkler," said the prosecutor, "I'm really sorry, but I don't see how Judge Barnes is going to be of any help.

I suppose you could wait until Monday, when the other judges will be back—"

Winkler looked at Mary Ellen Palmer, and they both shook their heads in amazement. Was the judge's absence legitimate? Or had he made a last-minute decision to go hunting when he learned of Winkler's visit, to avoid having to weigh in on the Martinez case? The bottom line, however, was that they hadn't obtained even a denial from which they could appeal. There was no way they could risk waiting until Monday.

As they left the prosecutor's office, Winkler pulled out his cell phone and called Dan Dillingham.

CHAPTER 38

DILLINGHAM AGREED THAT THEY NOW HAD NO CHOICE but to start filing their petitions.

He'd received the affidavit of the prison psychologist, Alice Hanover, but decided to hold it back because it merely made the story more confusing and could have put her in jeopardy.

At this point, there was no need to get into any further details about Guttmann, or any motivation of Warden Potts to get Guttmann into prison as Martinez, or to have Guttmann executed. All that mattered was to get the stay and have Guttmann removed from the prison and placed into protective custody. They'd just focus their petition on mistaken identity and misconduct on behalf of the prison system in not taking Guttmann's fingerprints when he was admitted after Martinez escaped.

Winkler's experience with the prosecutor proved that if anything can go wrong, it will. What should have been an easy decision for the prosecutor left them hoping this wasn't an indication of things to come.

He asked Dillingham what he could expect of the various appeals. "Dan, I don't want to be a naysayer, but do we have a shot, even with all our proof?"

"David, it's worth doing, but it certainly won't be a slam dunk. Half of all court cases are probably wrongly decided."

"I know, Dan. Do you remember the case of the Mexican national I mentioned? He'd been convicted in clear violation of the Vienna Convention. Despite tremendous pressure from the public and anti-death penalty organizations, the court denied a petition for a stay, and he was executed. There was something about how a treaty isn't law, and the law hadn't been enacted which would have given it effect. Wouldn't they need to give reasons to deny our appeals?" asked Winkler.

"Sometimes they do, sometimes they don't. In this case, the State can denigrate the petition by arguing that the issue should have been raised earlier, the case has taken enough of the government's resources, and whatever information is being presented now isn't 'new,' but has existed for decades and it's simply too late. There's nothing you can do about it if they take that position. If you get a hearing, you can argue that an innocent man shouldn't be executed because of the failure of prior counsel to find fingerprints buried in the files of the New York Banking Commission, which are totally unrelated to this case.

"The State could also argue that the petition was improper because it wasn't filed by counsel of record, who lays dying in the hospital after his car was bombed. I think you'll be OK on that score," said Dillingham, "since the petitions will show Georgia Capital Defenders as co-counsel."

Winkler and Dillingham agreed they would simultaneously file Habeas Corpus Petitions also styled as Petition for Stay of Execution, with the Superior Court in Georgia, Georgia State Board of Pardons and Paroles, the Georgia Supreme Court, the Federal District Court, the 11th Federal Circuit Court of Appeals, and the U.S. Supreme Court.

Dillingham continued. "I don't expect much from the Governor of Georgia, but we'll serve the petition on the governor's office as well. He's proud of the number of death row inmates they've executed and has already turned down a petition in another case, based on violation of the Vienna Convention. Even though we're only asking for a thirty-day stay until a court can rule on the mistaken identity issue, I think it'll be hard to get his attention.

"David, I wonder if our firm has any relationships in Georgia that might be able to bring pressure on the governor and appeal to his self-interest." Dillingham was definitely thinking outside the box.

"I've got it," said Winkler. "Our firm represents Armando Velasquez, a Mexican-American former baseball all-star and multi-millionaire, who's the new owner of the Atlanta Braves. He's been very vocal on the anti-death penalty front.

"They've been negotiating a new stadium lease for months, and there have been rumors that if the negotiations don't go in Velasquez' favor—to the tune of millions in subsidies for stadium improvements—he may well move the team to Los Angeles, his hometown. I know Velasquez—I set up a private foundation for him not too long ago—and based on our conversations, I'm fairly sure he's going to stay put.

"But recently there was a story in *The Sports News* suggesting he's considering all of his options. It's got the local and state officials on edge. My guess is, the governor would prefer to see the lease negotiations successfully concluded and finish his term with the team firmly planted in Atlanta for at least another decade."

"You're not suggesting a deal linking the two, are you? Stadium lease for a thirty-day stay of execution?" said Dillingham.

"Not at all," replied Winkler. "But let's just keep this in our back pocket. If we have to, we might enlist Velasquez' support. He could be subtle, thanking the governor for his support in the past, and the governor would, of course, say how much he appreciates the contributions the team makes to the economy and national standing of the Great State of Georgia. Velasquez could then offer how executing a foreign national based on mistaken identity would be a travesty, something even a pro-death penalty advocate such as the governor would certainly want to avoid!

"Right now, there are a couple of calls we need to make," said Winkler, "and I think Emma can handle them. First, to Alice Hanover. If she's still in town, I'd like her to come with us to the prison tomorrow to meet with Guttmann. Other than his attorney, she's the only one who has his confidence. If he insists on no visitors, maybe she can break through that barrier. Emma can explain this to her.

"Next, I'd like Emma to talk to Maria Theresa Romero and get her on the next plane to Atlanta. Hopefully, she'll be able to arrive tomorrow morning, and we can connect with her at the airport and fly down to the prison on the Executive Air jet."

"David, you're thinking that even if Guttmann is willing to shut everyone out—resigned to die and not interested in fighting anymore—he might make an exception if it's his daughter who makes the plea to allow you to take one last shot?"

"Right. And even if he rejects the offer, at least he will have had the opportunity to meet her, and she will have met her real father."

CHAPTER 39

THEY WERE IN LUCK. Alice Hanover was still in town and agreed to meet Winkler at the prison. The meeting was tentatively set for the following day at eleven.

Emma was able to contact Maria Theresa Romero and coordinate her overnight flight from Montevideo to Miami, and onward to Atlanta, to arrive at nine. Winkler would meet Maria Theresa at the Atlanta airport and continue on the executive jet flight to Griffin, Georgia, and from there it was just a short drive to the prison.

Alice Hanover had agreed to contact Warden Potts and set up a meeting with Guttmann, Winkler, and a member of Guttmann's family, supposedly to say final farewells. She was not to mention anything about the petitions. The psychologist assured Emma that Potts would schedule that meeting, even if Guttmann maintained a 'no visits' position. She was prepared to bring up Warden Potts' wife's therapy with Dr. Hibblewhite if the warden didn't provide his full cooperation.

Dan Dillingham had decided to have local counsel file the petitions in Atlanta, and they were standing by, awaiting word that Guttmann was on board. Dan would file the petition with the U.S. Supreme Court and—for dramatic effect, if nothing else—with the chief of staff of the President of the United States, all about the same time, after receiving Winkler's call.

Simultaneously, press releases would be e-mailed to all the major news organizations worldwide, to hundreds of human rights organizations, and to all the anti-death penalty organizations in the U.S. and abroad.

Afzam had set up a Facebook page for the "Save Ricardo Guttmann Movement," a place where supporters could sign to show their moral support for the petitions, and a Twitter feed for moment-by-moment developments, starting with the first petition being filed.

The case was described as a classic one of mistaken identity, which proves the danger to the justice system when a person's life can be taken, with an air of legitimacy, even though he isn't guilty of any crime. A website would contain copies of all the petitions, fingerprints, and expert's report as to the fact that they were the prints of Ricardo Guttmann.

Billings Ryan, the firm's public relations consultants, had scheduled a major press conference, to take place on the steps of the county courthouse, just down the road from the prison, at five o'clock.

Winkler was hopeful Guttmann would go along with the petitions, but he really had no idea how he'd be received. If life were a Disney movie, he'd be greeted with open arms and a smile, Guttmann would sign on the dotted line, the stay would be granted, Guttmann would be vindicated, and Maria Theresa would be reunited with her father. But Winkler knew life wasn't a Disney movie and the psyche of a death row inmate could be marked by profound distrust and resignation.

CHAPTER 40

WINKLER COULD SEE FROM THE ARRIVAL BOARD at Atlanta's Hartfield International Airport that Maria Theresa's flight from Miami had landed at 9:05 a.m., right on schedule. He figured it would take her just a few minutes to make it to the Arrivals Hall, as she'd cleared Customs & Immigration in Miami and was traveling with only a carry-on bag.

Even though he'd met her only once before, over lunch in Aruba, he easily picked her out of the crowd. They exchanged greetings, including a polite kiss on the cheek, as is the custom in Latin America. He took her bag and they waited only briefly for a taxi to the private jet terminal where their executive jet was waiting.

Although Maria Theresa had hardly slept during the eleven-hour flight from Uruguay, and she was exhausted, adrenalin was pumping through her body. Not knowing where to start, she remained silent until they were seated in the aircraft and Winkler opened the conversation.

"How do you feel about this?" he asked. "You're finally going to meet your real father!"

"Very nervous, David. I have been thinking about it ever since we met. I can't stop thinking about my life to this point. It has only been lies, my so-called parents raising me as their own, without ever telling me of my history. Nothing but lies, and there is no one I can scream at about it because they are both dead. Yes, they probably saved me from death, but at the same time, I have to believe that my 'father' was involved in the death of my real mother. It's terrible, David, something which is tormenting me.

"And now, if I can look forward, I am about to meet my real father. My biological father. A man I have never known. Over and over during the long flight from Uruguay, I asked why I am doing this to myself, and to him. What does it matter? It's just a biological accident that I am his daughter."

Winkler could only imagine the inner turmoil that was ripping her apart. "Yes, I understand, but still, it must mean something. When you found out your 'parents' weren't your real parents, you must have felt a void—a big, empty space, a hole in your heart—something you wanted to fill by finding your real father, if you could. And now it looks like that may be possible."

"I suppose so, and that's why I hired you, and why I have come all this way. But then there is the matter of his fate. To meet your father a few days before his execution may be worse than never meeting him at all—"

"But Maria Theresa, we think we have a good chance to prove he isn't the prisoner they think he is. We're filing court papers to show they have the wrong person, asking that they put off his execution for thirty days to allow for a thorough review of our documentation."

Emma had only told her she had to come to the United States urgently, that they'd located her father, who was in prison and scheduled to be executed in a few days. Emma had decided it would be too complicated to get into the details of the petition, matching of the fingerprints, and all the steps being taken to get a stay of execution. Now that Winkler had Maria Theresa in front of him, he could get into some of these details, which he did, as she listened intently.

"This is incredible, David, all of these things falling into place. Do you think you will be successful? I have heard that in America—which is supposedly the champion of human rights—the justice system works in strange ways. Sometimes the innocents are found guilty, just like in Latin America."

"In this case, that's already happened. Your father has suffered decades— a major part of his life—in prison, because of a series of events that are mostly not of his doing. I can't guarantee the system will correct itself and free him, but we're certainly doing everything we can, and I'm very optimistic. Let's just take one step at a time."

"Whatever you say, David. I suppose he will be just as shocked to know that I exist as I was to find out that he was my father."

As the Executive Air jet began its descent into Griffin-Spalding County Airport, Winkler briefed her on the people she was about to meet, Warden Billy Joe Potts and the prison psychologist, Alice Hanover.

CHAPTER 41

IT WAS JUST BEFORE ELEVEN when Winkler pulled into the parking lot at the William Ewen Correctional Facility. Alice Hanover was already there, waiting nervously. After brief introductions, they marched up to the warden's office. He was on the phone but waved them in and motioned them to sit down as he ended his call and closed his office door.

Winkler started the conversation.

"Warden," he said, clearing his throat, "I want to thank you for scheduling this meeting. I'd like to introduce you to Maria Theresa Romero, the daughter of the prisoner you're holding as Juan Martinez."

"Yessir, Mr. Winkler, nice to see you again," he said, politely but mildly annoyed. "Ma'am," he said, turning his head to Maria Theresa, "nice to meet you as well, and good to see you, too, Alice. But as I told Alice over the phone, I'm not sure Mr. Martinez is willing to see you. As his last day is coming up real soon, we've been asking if he wants to see anyone, and he still maintains his 'no visits' policy. Don't want no priests or pastors either.

"I asked our attorney, Tyree Johnson, in the state's Attorney General's office, the fellow who answers all our questions about prisoner rights and the like. Matter of fact, that's who I was talkin' to when you came in. He told me there's no two ways about it: We have to respect the prisoner's wishes. If he says, 'no visits,' then 'no visits' it is. Unless you get a court order."

Winkler wasn't sure how much he should tell the warden but decided to lay at least some of his cards on the table.

"Warden Potts, the thing is, Mr. Martinez doesn't know his daughter is here. Actually, he doesn't even know he has a daughter. So, if we could just talk to him briefly and explain the situation, we think there may be a good chance he'll want to meet her, if only for a few minutes."

"Mr. Winkler, this is all rather strange. First, you come in here and tell me you think our prisoner isn't who we think he is. Now you tell me this young lady is his daughter, and he doesn't even know he has a daughter. He's been here for decades, and never once—not one single time—has he had a visit, a phone call, or even a letter from any member of his family. And now, just a couple of days before his execution, you show up here with someone you say is his daughter—and a newly discovered daughter at that! Mr. Winkler, this is not a circus, and I don't intend to let you make it into one!"

"Warden, I understand how strange this must seem to you, and believe me, we don't want to upset anyone—not you, and not Mr. Martinez. But if you just give us a few minutes with Mr. Martinez, if he doesn't want to continue the discussion, we'll politely go on our way."

Winkler was reluctant to say anything about the petitions. If Warden Potts even suspected something was happening that could result in a stay, he could keep Winkler away from Martinez and conceivably do something to jeopardize his chances of success.

Winkler glanced over to Alice Hanover, in desperation.

"Mr. Winkler," she said, "would you and Ms. Romero just give the warden and me two minutes to chat, just between ourselves? You can wait in the hallway."

Clearly, the psychologist felt it was time to call in some chits.

Winkler and Maria Theresa stepped outside into the hall. Though they couldn't hear exactly what was going on behind Warden Potts' closed door, what started out as a quiet conversation had some really loud exchanges. The private meeting with the warden lasted more than five minutes.

When the door opened, Alice Hanover had a smile on her face; Warden Potts, on the other hand, was red-faced and had clearly conceded the point.

"Mr. Winkler," said the warden, swallowing hard and taking some time to find just the right words. "I've decided it would do no harm to let you and Alice meet with Mr. Martinez for a few minutes, and if he wants to meet Ms. Romero after that, then that's up to him. If he refuses to see you, or if he wants to end the meeting, then you've got to honor that request. I think we can say if we follow that procedure, we're honoring the prisoner's wishes. We'll leave it up to him. Since Alice has worked with him over the years, and she's prison staff—at least for a few more days—she can go with you.

"Alice, why don't you just go on down to Block Four? I'll call ahead and let them know you're on your way."

CHAPTER 42

"DO I DARE ASK WHAT YOU TOLD HIM, Alice, to make him change his mind?"

"I don't think you really want to know, David, and anyhow, I told the warden I wouldn't share that information. I'm sure you'll understand."

"Gotcha. No problem. You sure made your point, and it didn't take very long."

"I took a risk," she said, "but let's say no more about it. As far as anyone's concerned, he rationalized in his own mind that it was the right way to handle it, to let us go down there and let the prisoner decide. But I mentioned nothing about the petitions, and when that information gets back to the warden...well, let's just say I'm glad I'm about to retire.

"Let's take my car. It'll save us some time since they know me and I have a facility pass on the windshield." The psychologist took the wheel. Winkler rode shotgun, and Maria Theresa took the back seat.

What Winkler had seen of the prison facility on his first visit was no more than the front gate and administrative offices, located right off the main highway at the north end of the property. The prisoner detention facility itself was located several miles into the property, on a new blacktop road. The land was flat and cleared on either side of the road, probably to make it easier to track escapees.

While they saw no one in the fields, the place conjured up images of prison guards on horseback overseeing prisoners doing field work for a few dollars a day. The only wildlife in sight were giant, black vultures, too fattened by roadkill to take flight as the car approached, so they simply hopped away.

"How close are we to the Air Force base, Alice? I remember seeing a turn-off just before the last turn to the prison," said Winkler.

"As the crow flies," she replied, "maybe five miles due east of here, but it's been shut down for decades. When it was operating, it created a fair amount of economic activity in this region. But that was years ago, way back when we had lots of B-52s based around the country, even in the south— including Florida and Louisiana, as well as Georgia— which would have been sent out to annihilate Russia if war had broken out.

"After the Cold War ended, there was no support in Congress for keeping it open, so it was shut down, and the town just next to it, Amityville, lost most of its residents.

"The base and the old prison were built about the same time. Seems rather clever to warehouse your high-risk prisoners near an Air Force base. You certainly wouldn't want them wandering around the post-nuclear wasteland, and the base—and incidentally, the prison—would be almost sure to get nuked early and often in any war.

"I wouldn't be surprised if some smart politician figured that after the bombs fall, it would be hard enough for any survivors to make ends meet without having to deal with rampaging escaped convicts, and it would be better for post-apocalyptic society to have hardened convicts instantly vaporized."

Winkler grinned as Alice provided some comic relief for an otherwise grim situation.

"All that's left of Amityville, in terms of businesses, is a seedy motel that provides a cheap place to stay for inmates' visitors from downstate, and an old gas station, so old it's not even self-serve. The rest of the businesses around here are in the town where we met at Sugar Daddy's Getaway."

A few minutes later, they approached another gatehouse, with armed guards. Their arrival had been announced, and they needed to do no more than show their IDs. The visitors' lot was to the right, with several empty cars in it, and people sat on the grass next to the lot in the shade of large trees.

"What's all that about?" asked Maria Theresa. "Are we before normal visiting hours?"

"Not really, but those folks are probably here to visit family and can't get in because the guards haven't finished their count. Before anyone can get in, they have to physically count the prisoners. The problem is, the guards can't count. So, they don't get the right number and have to do the count over again, and sometimes a few times.

"These poor souls get here on time but have to wait until they're told the count is done. They prefer to wait patiently under a tree, rather than in their cars, which are baking in the sun. And they sure don't have enough money to pay for gas to keep the cars and air conditioning going while they wait, which could be several hours. They hardly have enough money to pay for the gas to get here in the first place."

At that moment, a message came over the loudspeakers that visiting hours had begun, and the family members starting picking up their things and making their way to the various cell blocks, which had large numbers painted on them in bright yellow paint.

Block Four was at the far end, an ugly two-story brick building with narrow slit medieval castle style windows spaced every ten feet or so. The entire perimeter was enclosed by two rings of parallel fences spaced about six feet apart. An outer twenty-foot high chain link fence was topped with razor wire, and an inner twenty-foot high fence consisted of five stacked four-foot high coils of razor wire.

They also saw four guard towers, one at each corner of the area that housed the four cell blocks.

As Winkler and the others got out of the car, they could see an exercise yard off to the left, closer to Blocks One through Three. Prisoners were wearing orange shorts and grey shirts and were marching around a small oval track. Even though the temperature was already in the mid-nineties and it was very humid, a few prisoners were shooting hoops on a cement basketball court.

The entrance to Block Four had a grey steel door, with a security camera to identify the visitors. A buzzer indicated when the door was unlocked and visitors could pass through.

Once inside, they saw a small reception area with a short, middle-aged guard wearing a prison corrections officer uniform; however, he didn't look like he'd be much good at quelling a riot. He was yakking with another guard about catfish fishing.

Alice gave them a minute to finish their conversation, then politely cleared her throat to get their attention.

"Well, if it isn't Alice Hanover, prison shrink! There's a rumor 'round here that you're gonna hang it up and retire! Is that true, Alice?"

Ray Simkins knew it was true but just liked to make retirement small talk. He was five years from retiring, had a pin-up calendar on the inside of his locker where he crossed off the days, and everyone in the place knew about it. It was only a question of whether he'd live that long. He was grossly overweight, had always been a heavy smoker, and coughed like his lungs were ready to give up on him.

The other guards made bets each year as to whether Ray would make it to Christmas, with the bets being evenly split.

"Ray, this is Mr. Winkler, a lawyer, and Ms. Romero, who is Martinez' daughter. Ms. Romero hasn't been in touch with her father because she didn't know where he was, so we're here to talk to Martinez for a couple of minutes to see if he'll reverse his 'no visits' instruction. If he agrees, then we'll come back out and bring the daughter down to see him. OK?"

"Yep, that's what the warden said would be the procedure. You can leave the daughter out here with me. I don't bite." He directed Maria Theresa to sit down on a bench along the wall. "Just give me the IDs for the lawyer and daughter so I can take a picture of them, for the record."

Ray then asked if they wanted a no-contact visit. Winkler looked at Alice; he didn't know the difference and said they'd do whatever was easiest for the guards. The guard replied that a no-contact visit would be easier, so Winkler agreed. A no-contact visit involved talking to the inmate over the phone while separated by two inches of bulletproof glass. The facility had two such booths.

At that point, it dawned on Ray that the phone had been ripped out of one of the no-contact booths and the other one was tied up. "Sorry, Mr. Winkler, but we've got only one no-contact booth working. Looks like you'll have a contact visit after all, unless you want to wait a while."

"No problem," said Winkler, thinking for a moment that if he were visiting any death row prisoner other than Guttmann, he'd really prefer a no-contact visit.

Ray then phoned someone in the back and announced that Martinez had some visitors. They were soon joined by another corrections officer, much more imposing, about six-foot-six and extremely muscular. He had a giant blue tattoo of a Celtic cross on his forearm, and, unlike the first guard, looked like he'd be useful in quelling a riot; he might even enjoy the chance.

The corrections officers' uniforms—black cargo pants, a grey shirt with a small logo of the prison system, and a black baseball cap—were vaguely fascist.

At that point, the first guard issued Winkler and Alice each a bar-coded sheet of paper. Celtic Cross led them around the corner of the reception area, where they stopped at an automatic folding door made of two-inch thick plexiglass, secured by an imposing steel lock.

To the right was the no-contact visiting area, where one old guy on the inside was yelling at another old guy on the visitor's side of the glass.

Celtic Cross hit a buzzer, and the folding door opened. They were now in a twenty-by-twenty-foot airlock between the outside world and the prison proper. In addition to the plexiglass folding door behind them that led to the outside world, a steel door with a plexiglass window to their right led to the prisoner cells.

About a third of the airlock was occupied by a control booth filled with monitors and phones, off to the right and against the far wall. The control booth monitored movement in both the airlock and the cell block and was manned by two more corrections officers.

Having already locked their wallets, keys, and cell phones in lockers in the reception area, they passed through a metal detector without incident. Celtic Cross then asked Winkler to turn around and raise his arms, after which he gently, but thoroughly, patted him down.

The two men in the control booth asked Winkler if he wanted to be accompanied by an officer during the visit.

He quickly declined; he didn't want anyone to get wind of the petitions. They then said they'd monitor the visit on a video camera.

Celtic Cross scanned the bar-coded papers the first guard gave them, saying he wouldn't want to lose anyone in there. He then buzzed them through the inner door of the airlock and escorted them to a rather large but private visiting room, maybe ten by twenty, with a long table in the center of the room, one chair on one side, two on the other, another chair alongside the wall. Three sides of the room were windowless. The third wall had a large window, which Winkler suspected was one-way glass, with a viewing area on the other side. He arranged the chairs so the two chairs had their backs to the window, then they waited for what seemed to be an eternity until the prisoner known as Juan Martinez was brought down to the visiting room.

CHAPTER 43

CELTIC CROSS AND ANOTHER GUARD finally brought the prisoner into the visiting room and indicated they'd be waiting outside.

"Press the button on the table if you need us, or when you're ready to leave. Visits are thirty minutes unless you need more time. But if Martinez wants to cut it short, that's his call."

Alice had seen the man she now knew was Guttmann many times over the years, but not in recent months. She was visibly shocked at what she saw. He was a small man, especially in contrast to Celtic Cross. Extremely gaunt and pale, with thin arms, he was wearing a new 'execution' uniform, which was clearly too large for him. It was badly wrinkled, as if he'd slept in it, but he looked as if he hadn't slept in days. His eyes were red, his head shaven.

The uniform had no belt, and he was wearing prison-issue slippers. His belt and shoes with laces had been taken away for his own safety, so he couldn't hang himself. He was on suicide watch. Only the State could determine how and when he would die.

Guttmann sat down without uttering a word, first staring into space, then turning his eyes, first to Alice, then to Winkler.

"What is this all about? I specifically asked for no visitors. Dr. Hanover, did you bring a clergyman? I'm not a man of faith and don't want any clergy—"

"Juan, this is David Winkler, a lawyer, not a clergyman."

Standing up, Guttmann became extremely agitated. "No more lawyers! Lawyers cannot be trusted! They'll tell you anything, promise you the moon, just to keep you alive so they can file more appeals and continue their fight against the death penalty. That's all well and good. I know the system is flawed and should be fixed, but not at my expense.

"Enough is enough! Even if they get a stay, what will probably happen is my sentence will be commuted to life in prison. What's the point? Do I really want to spend the rest of my life in prison? This is no life. They've taken most of my freedom, but I still have the freedom to choose to die rather than continue the appeals. We've been at this all too long. I've had decades to read about the American justice system. It's all words. There is no justice. I've given up waiting for miracles—"

Finally he sat down, seemingly exhausted, physically and emotionally.

Winkler decided he had to make his case quickly before Guttmann ended the meeting and felt it best to address the new evidence of mistaken identity first.

"Mr. Martinez, I can't even pretend to know what you've gone through, and what you're feeling right now. But what I'm here to tell you is that we have new evidence that'll persuade the powers that be that your execution should not go forward as scheduled, that a stay should be granted. We're prepared to immediately file Petitions for Habeas Corpus to get you out of here, and for a stay of execution pending a full hearing. We can prove there's been a gross miscarriage of justice, that you are not Juan Martinez."

"I've been saying that for years, Mr. Winkler. They look at me like a mad man. No one cares. Juan Martinez kidnapped his daughter, and she died. Juan Martinez was convicted and sentenced to death. Juan Martinez is going to die. Justice will be done, and the victim's family will at last find peace."

"But justice is not being done if they execute the wrong man. You are not Juan Martinez, and we can prove who you are."

"Who am I then, Mr. Winkler?"

"Ricardo Guttmann. An Argentine banker. You are not Mexican, but Argentine."

"What? How can you prove this?"

"Believe me, sir. We have credible, compelling evidence, fingerprints of Ricardo Guttmann, an Argentine banker, which are a perfect match to yours. There can be no mistake. Every person's fingerprints are unique."

Guttmann was stunned and sat in silence for several seconds. Finally, he said, "Where did you get these fingerprints of Ricardo Guttmann, and why are you bringing me this information? Where is Joshua Bean, the lawyer I've been working with?"

"I can review all of this with you, but I assure you, we've done extensive research, which led us to your fingerprints. Dr. Hanover can vouch for my integrity."

Alice nodded in agreement. "What he's telling you is correct. You've told me since the first day I met you that they have the wrong person, and now you finally have someone who can prove it."

"Why isn't my lawyer, Joshua Bean, here to tell me this?"

Alice replied, "We saw him yesterday. He's in the hospital. His car was bombed. He can't help you anymore. He asked Mr. Winkler to come here to meet you and file the papers necessary to stay your execution and get you released."

"So you, Mr. Winkler, will be my attorney, with Joshua Bean?"

"Yes, if that's OK with you," said Winkler. "Please just sign this short engagement letter, making me your co-counsel."

Guttmann looked over to Alice, who nodded her approval, then scrawled a signature at the bottom of the engagement letter and pushed it back over to Winkler.

"You don't have much time, Mr. Winkler, even if you have the proof. We can't control the system. I know they have the wrong man. You may know it as well. But that doesn't mean your appeal will be successful. The system has rules, technicalities, prejudices.

"I'm not going to celebrate, or even get my hopes up, until you tell me I've been vindicated. I don't feel sorry for myself. I've made many friends in this terrible place over the years. I believe many of those people weren't guilty, or at least shouldn't have received the death sentence.

"The real pain doesn't come from your own death, Mr. Winkler. It comes when you see another human being, a friend, someone you've known for years, being escorted off death row to be executed. It tears you apart because there's absolutely nothing you can do about it. This is legalized murder. We're no different here than in Russia, or some countries in the Middle East.

"Those who complain about it, even if there are grounds for appeal, are brushed aside. Each of the wrongly convicted is just a pawn in the system. We're executed just to assure the masses that the rule of law will protect them from evil."

"With your permission, sir, we'll go ahead and file the papers as co-counsel," Winkler said. "But I have something else to tell you. We've brought someone else I want you to meet—"

"No, no one else. I've had enough for today. I may not be free to walk out of here, but I am free to go back to my cell and be alone. Come back another day when you have some news of the appeal."

And with that, Guttmann pushed the button on the table, and the guard immediately took him out of the room.

CHAPTER 44

"HE WON'T EVEN MEET ME? How is this possible? I came all this way, and he won't even have a brief meeting?!" Maria Theresa was beside herself.

"I didn't even have a chance to tell him about you," Winkler replied. "We started talking about filing for a stay of execution. Initially, he was resigned to dying and didn't want any more appeals. Then I told him we had proof of mistaken identity—proof that he wasn't Martinez—and he agreed we could go forward. It was all we could do to get him to that point. Then he abruptly called for the guard, and the meeting was over."

"But David, maybe if I just ask to go back and talk to him alone—"

"I wouldn't even try," said Winkler. "He won't talk again until we know whether our efforts to get a stay have been successful. He made that very clear.

"Maria Theresa, things are moving very quickly. I need to call my office and check on the filing of the petitions. I suggest I take you to the motel in Amityville and you wait until you hear from us. If we get the stay, I'm confident he'll be willing to hear about you, and even meet you."

Winkler knew the clock was ticking. He thanked Alice Hanover and asked if she could stay around town for another couple of days, just in case they needed her for another meeting with Guttmann. She agreed.

He then sped over with Maria Theresa to the B-52 Inn in Amityville, which was every bit the dump Alice Hanover had described. A one-story metal roof building, with a dozen motel units side by side. A rusty metal armchair sat outside each unit. A couple of units had window air conditioners. The air was hot and humid and there wasn't a hint of a breeze. The poor souls who rented the units without air conditioning would be better off sleeping in their cars with the windows open.

The manager was surprised to see a guest arrive early in the day, as most came late at night after a long drive, the day before a prison visit. However, he assured them Maria Theresa would have a clean, quiet room in the back, off the highway. When asked if it had air conditioning, he said it did, but it would be best to just take the armchair over to the big oak tree and get a soft drink from the machine in front of his office. After nightfall, he said, things would cool down a bit, and the air conditioner wouldn't have to work as hard.

As for food, he suggested Maria Theresa try the gas station across the street, as they had snacks and frozen pizza that could be heated up in their microwave oven.

Reluctantly, Winkler left Maria Theresa for what he hoped would be a short stay.

On his way back to the airport, he called his office to authorize filing of the petitions; however, Dillingham had decided to file all the petitions, showing Winkler as co-counsel for Martinez, on the assumption that Martinez— or Guttmann—would agree.

All but one of the petitions had been filed. The attempt to file with the Dougherty County Superior Court had been rejected because it was presented a few minutes after four, and the clerk said it was too late. He suggested trying again Monday morning. When asked if it was possible to file electronically, which was common in most courts, the clerk said it would normally be allowed but the facility was down for maintenance.

CHAPTER 45

WINKLER RETURNED TO THE OFFICE on Monday morning to find a stack of messages from Trevor Banks. Under duress, Emma had set up a meeting with him for Monday at ten in the large conference room. Banks arrived right on time.

"Mr. Winkler, I'm sorry to come on such short notice, but I'm really confused, and I don't mind telling you I'm very upset. I've had no reports at all on your search for Guttmann. I've been extremely patient, figuring you were busy with the investigation. Now it's all over the news that not only have you located him, alive, but he's on death row and about to be executed!

"My people are very upset to get this news on cable TV, not from you. Don't you think a $500,000 client deserves this kind of information first, before the media?"

"I apologize, Mr. Banks, but this situation is evolving very quickly, and I admit, we've done a poor job of keeping you informed. But the press coverage is part of our effort to get a stay of execution, and you were next on our list to be contacted."

"How do you rate your chance of success?"

"It's hard to tell at this point. We've filed petitions at every level we could think of, all the way to the President. We have proof of mistaken identity, if anyone wants to listen."

"So you've met with Guttmann?"

"Yes, but it was a very brief meeting, only long enough to get his OK to file the petitions on his behalf."

"Did he give you any leads on the missing money?"

"We didn't get that far. He cut us off, won't talk further until we get the stay. And if we don't get it, my guess is, he'll take his secrets with him to his grave."

"You can't let that happen, Mr. Winkler. It's too important. You have to find out how to get to that money."

"We'll certainly try, Mr. Banks, but Guttmann is bitter, very bitter, and I can't predict what'll happen if the stay is denied. Mr. Banks, since you're with the government, maybe you can use your connections to help us get a stay, perhaps through the Office of the President."

"Mr. Winkler, I can't work magic—"

"But if it's so important to the United States government that you find Guttmann, one would think a couple of phone calls to your superiors would pave the way for a positive response to our petitions—or maybe you're not really who you say you are."

"What do you mean by that?" Banks said, in an accusatory tone.

"You know full well what I mean! You're not just a government bureaucrat on a mission to find a missing fortune and bail out Argentina. You have your own agenda, Señor Ramos."

"*Ramos*—why do you call me *Ramos*?"

"Because that's who you are—or were—before you changed your name. We know all about your past. You and your cronies took over the government of Argentina in the 1970s. You were a senior advisor to the right-wing military junta and played a key role in the disappearance, torture, and murders of 30,000 people in Argentina."

"You're crazy, Mr. Winkler! I have no idea what you're talking about."

"We have evidence, archival photos we found on the Internet." Winkler laid one of the photos on the table, which showed Ramos as a young man, along with a computer-aged photo laid side-by-side with a current photo. "There's no denying it. This is one and the same person, Señor Ramos."

He was furious. "What do you know about the political reality of Argentina? There was no choice. We had to take over the government to save the country from the rebels. Do you believe the figures about how many disappeared? Those numbers were invented by leftist sympathizers and were pure propaganda. People left Argentina and went to other countries, like Switzerland, came back when things settled down, but never took their names off the lists."

"So how many did you kill, Señor Ramos?"

"Maybe 8,000, or 8,500. This wasn't random. They were all leftist guerillas or sympathizers. We had to eliminate them. They were a threat to the nation. Look, Mr. Winkler, all of this is ancient history, totally irrelevant to our business with each other. My prior life has nothing to do with our engagement of your law firm to find Guttmann."

"I beg to differ. If your motive is other than as represented to me, then I may not have to deliver Guttmann to you."

"Mr. Winkler, don't get on your high horse. You don't know what you're dealing with here!"

"I don't? You think I'm unaware of your relationship with Congressman Eduardo Cruz, formerly known as Colonel Raoul Vincenti, whom the President has nominated for Secretary of Homeland Security? He's pictured in the photos as well. A few minutes with Google shows you were tied at the hip in Argentina, and you're his senior advisor today as well."

"I can see you've done your homework, Mr. Winkler, but where are you going with all this?"

"May I ask you what kinds of policies you and Representative Cruz intend to bring to Homeland Security? Would I be incorrect in assuming you still feel anything is justified to save a country under siege?"

"Don't be naïve, Mr. Winkler. The ends do justify the means. The United States is in a war with Islam, brought on by Islam. Muslims number 1.6 billion worldwide out of a total population of maybe 7.4 billion, or around 23%, and they're growing fast. Europe has already lost the fight as far as I and many others are concerned. Very soon—in a matter of just a few years—either Western Europe will be Muslim, or there will be civil war. If the U.S. continues with its current policies and doesn't take drastic action to eliminate this threat, it will surely meet the same fate. But with some policy changes—which you may think are radical—we may be able to stem the tide."

"What types of changes?"

"For starters, no more Muslims will be allowed entry into the U.S. We must stop the inbound flow. We won't discriminate between Sunnis, Shiites, or whatever. We can't tell our friends from our enemies anyhow, so we just keep them all out. We'll do this as a temporary measure but continue it indefinitely."

"So you stabilize the Muslim population in the United States, ignoring the normal growth of that population. How does that solve the problem?"

"That's just the beginning. Then we deport any Muslims who either don't have U.S. citizenship or have dual nationality. If they have dual nationality, we take away their U.S. citizenship, then deport them. We have no good reason to allow foreigners with allegiance to a religion that's targeted the non-Muslim world to remain on U.S. soil."

"But what about Muslims who have only U.S. citizenship?"

"That's the next step. We identify the rest of them by whatever means necessary. Those who frequent mosques. We get lists or use video surveillance, even drone surveillance. Academics in universities. Muslim community leaders. Subscribers to Al Jazeera. Those who make phone calls or e-mail to Muslim countries. Those who live in Muslim enclaves, such as Dearborn, Michigan. We'll monitor Internet traffic, including e-mail, Facebook, FaceTime, and Skype. We'll then cross-match all these and zero in on Muslims."

"And then what? Do you put them in internment camps, like the Japanese in World War II?" Winkler couldn't believe his ears.

"That would be too costly, and it would only stir up protests from left-wing groups. Our plan will be much more elegant. They'll just disappear, like in Argentina. No administrative or court proceedings. No army of lawyers. No need to pay for their support, as you would if they were in internment camps. After a short time, the others will get the message and leave the country. Self-deportation. They'll take the initiative because they will know what will happen to them and their families if they stay."

"You'll do this based strictly on ethnic or religious grounds, without any evidence that they're in any way engaged in terrorist activities?"

"There's no time for niceties, Mr. Winkler. No need for accusations and trials. The only hope for this country is to uproot them and return the balance in favor of non-Muslims."

"But you'll be ignoring their right to due process under the Constitution. Many, if not most of those you propose to 'disappear' would be U.S. citizens. Their constitutional rights don't matter?"

"Mr. Winkler, there's a time and place for constitutional rights, and this is neither the time nor the place. This is war. You may not realize it, because the nightly news intentionally focuses on petty crimes, murders, car accidents, and natural disasters. The real role of most of the media, as well as law enforcement in this country, is to give the population the impression that everything is under control, aside from these minor incidents. But in reality, everything is not OK. There's a cancer in our society, and it must be removed."

"And Representative Cruz is going to tell the Senate this is his plan?"

"Of course not. The policies will be implemented after he's in place, over a short period of time, with no press. Quietly, behind closed doors. If questions are raised, we won't respond. If formal inquiries are made, we'll claim national security. That's how you wage a dirty war, Mr. Winkler. Plausible deniability."

"So why are you telling me all this? Personally, I'd be 100% against this type of plan. It's disgusting. It's the Dirty War all over again. Aren't you concerned I may take it to the press? Or the government?"

"Mr. Winkler, you're far too smart for that. You have little to gain, and much to lose. If one word of what I've said here today finds its way outside of this room, your beautiful wife will suffer dearly. I know you wouldn't want anything to happen to her, would you? And of course we'll deny anything you say. Who's going to believe a lawyer on a death penalty case over a Presidential nominee trying to save the nation as Secretary of Homeland Security?"

"Mr. Banks—or Ramos—your organization, Tri-Continental Research, isn't really a U.S. government entity, is it?"

"Of course not. I just said that to encourage you to take the case. Guttmann had millions of Montonero money. He stole it, and we want it. You'd better be successful in getting the stay of execution, because we expect to find out from him where the money is, and how to get it. You've taken our $500,000, and unless you want some really bad things to happen to you and your wife, you'd better get us that money."

"Have you heard enough?" said Winkler, looking at his cell phone on the table.

"What?" said Banks, perplexed by the question.

The conference room door opened, and three men entered. The first wore a navy blue suit; the other two were uniformed ICE officers.

"I've heard it all, and recorded it as well," said the first man, flashing his ID with a badge. "Mr. Banks, I'm FBI Special Agent Tom Gilmore, and I have a few questions for you. These gentlemen from Immigration and Customs Enforcement would like to talk to you as well. From what we've just heard, you may be charged with crimes involving misrepresenting your identity and relationship to the federal government, extortion, and a host of immigration and naturalization violations.

"We've also reviewed your application for naturalization, and you did not indicate that you had a prior name, that you were involved in overthrowing a government, and in torture. Your application for U.S. citizenship was clearly false and is punishable by imprisonment, fines, or deportation."

"But there was a deal back then to overlook—"

"Tell it to the magistrate," said the FBI agent.

Winkler followed them out of the conference room to the lobby, then asked the receptionist to see if Dan Dillingham could give him an update on the status of the petitions. It was Monday at ten thirty, and there was only a little over a day to go until Martinez' execution.

CHAPTER 46

"DAVID, I DON'T HAVE A LOT OF GOOD NEWS AT THIS POINT."

Winkler sat at his desk as Dan Dillingham started to run through his notes on an iPad.

"Nothing concrete from the U.S. Supreme Court. I spoke to the clerk this morning, and they reviewed the petition over the weekend but need some time to consider it. It's unlikely they'll be able to grant the petition on a timely basis. They're very skeptical about what they perceive as a last-minute discovery of information in support of our case. They don't want to encourage these types of petitions and feel some other court or administrative body should deal with it. But this is just based on off-the-record comments. Nothing official yet."

"What about the White House?"

"Chief of staff says we won't get any traction with the President. He's likely not to respond at all. He doesn't want to get in the middle of the death penalty debate and has too many supporters who would love to see any foreigner executed, even if they got the wrong guy.

"The 11th Circuit Court of Appeals faxed me a denial of the petition a few minutes ago. Just a one-liner. 'Petition denied.' I want to call them to ask for an explanation, but frankly it would probably be a waste of time, and we don't have any of that to waste.

"Nothing yet from the Georgia Supreme Court, but I wouldn't bank on a positive response. Although death sentences have been on a sharp decline in Georgia in the past few years, Georgia has carried out several controversial executions of defendants who would likely not get death sentences today. In some cases, there was even evidence that the defendant might have been innocent. We'll have to wait and see."

"What's left, Dan?" asked Winkler.

"Federal District Court is still considering our petition. No word on when they'll have a decision.

"We're also waiting on the Dougherty County Superior Court Judge. We couldn't file that one on Friday because we were a couple of minutes late. We filed this morning, but none of the judges were back from a judicial conference. Something about weather-related travel delays. The one judge who was supposed to be on duty was off hunting, not expected back in court until Tuesday.

"There's something strange going on there. His clerk said he's out hunting, but I found out from another person at the court—off-the-record— that the judge only decided to take the trip after he got wind of your impending visit with the prosecutor on Friday. Sounds to me like he doesn't want to deal with our petition. I wouldn't write him off, but whether we get to him in time is anyone's guess."

"So that leaves us with the Georgia Board of Pardons and Paroles, and the governor himself," said Winkler. "The governor doesn't have direct authority to grant a stay, but he may be able to exercise influence over the Board of Pardons and Paroles."

"I was just on the phone with the clerk of the board," said Dillingham, "and they're extremely reluctant to consider this again. They just reviewed the matter and denied clemency only a few days ago. Now Martinez has new co-counsel, a new argument, and facts some think could have been known decades ago. Reluctantly, they're calling a meeting of the board for tomorrow afternoon at two, but the fellow I spoke with wasn't optimistic they could get a quorum on such short notice. If you ask me, they're just going through the motions. They may well just let the clock run."

"And the governor? Any luck there?"

"He's on a trade mission to China. But I spoke to his chief of staff, who was inclined to take a pass. Even though Georgia prosecutors are seeking and juries are imposing fewer and fewer death sentences, the governor has still been in favor of the death penalty and takes great pride in every execution. His 'tough on crime' record may be what gets him re-elected."

"Damn! I can't believe it!" Winkler shouted as he ran his hands through his hair, staring out of his office window, shaking his head in disbelief. "We're so close! We've got proof positive the wrong man is about to be executed, and all the powers that be want to punt it over to the next guy. Isn't there anything else we can do? Get the governor's chief of staff on the line—and get me Armando Velasquez' number as well! What time is it right now in China?"

Dillingham checked the world clock on his iPhone. "Beijing is twelve hours ahead of Detroit," he replied.

Winkler was committed to pursuing every option. "It may be the middle of the night when we finally get him, but I'm going to set up a conference call with the governor and Armando Velasquez. It may be the only chance we have to avoid the State snuffing out a life without any good reason.

"I'll do what I can overnight, then I'd like to take the executive jet down to the prison around ten tomorrow morning. I'd like to be there with Martinez—Guttmann—

hopefully to bring good news but if not, then at least when his end comes.

"Have Emma call Maria Theresa and let her know I'll swing by on my way from the airport to pick her up. Tell her we still don't know if we're going to be getting a stay of execution but that we're hopeful."

CHAPTER 47

IT WAS THE LONGEST NIGHT OF WINKLER'S LIFE.

He had several false starts with the governor's chief of staff, who absolutely refused to allow a direct conversation with the governor. He eventually got Armando Velasquez on the line, and the governor's chief of staff had the poor taste to suggest maybe it wasn't really Velasquez at all, but an impostor. With the clock ticking on Martinez' execution, that didn't sit well with Velasquez. He made it clear to the chief of staff that the team was extremely important to the State of Georgia and he needed only a few minutes of the governor's urgent attention.

Unfortunately, the governor was traveling with the trade mission in a remote area of China, with only sporadic cell phone service, visiting industrial facilities whose owners were considering setting up factories in the United States. By the time they were able to get the governor, his chief of staff, Velasquez, and Winkler on a conference call, it was late afternoon Georgia time. Winkler was already at the prison, in the warden's office. Maria Theresa was waiting outside in the hall.

The governor understood the need to placate Velasquez, although there were no direct threats to abort discussions about the stadium lease or move the team to another state. While the governor didn't have authority to grant a stay, he said he'd be willing to review the matter urgently with the Board of Pardons and Paroles. The message was subtle. The governor convinced himself he wasn't giving up an execution, just recommending a thirty-day stay to investigate the new factual allegations. Velasquez seemed satisfied and dropped off the call.

The chairman of the Board of Pardons and Paroles was then conferenced in. In light of the new information, he agreed to grant the thirty-day stay in advance of the full meeting of the board. He felt confident that, in view of the governor's support, the board would ratify this action.

The warden participated in the last part of the conference call but insisted he needed something in writing. A fax signed by the chairman of the Georgia Board of Pardons and Paroles arrived on the warden's fax machine at 5:45 p.m. local time, just fifteen minutes before the scheduled execution.

The fax contained an order granting a stay of execution of up to thirty days to allow more time to examine claims from Martinez' representatives that the inmate identified as Juan Velasco Martinez, prisoner number 74-762158, was not, in fact, Juan Velasco Martinez. The evidence would be reviewed at a full hearing to review the new claims, at the conclusion of which it may lift the stay and grant clemency, commute the sentence, or deny clemency. The governor would avoid any direct responsibility for the outcome.

CHAPTER 48

RESIGNED TO HIS FATE, the prisoner waited in his cell to be taken down to the execution chamber. Six o'clock came and went. He sat silently, somewhat anxious, but mostly numb, having lost confidence in the judicial system years ago. He didn't have even the slightest hope that the stay would be granted. The delay, he thought, was probably due to some technicality in setting things up for the execution.

"Got someone who wants to see you," said the guard as he unlocked the cell and swung open the door. He put handcuffs on the prisoner and guided him down the hallway to the same room Winkler had used for the contact visit a few days before. The guard sat the prisoner down at the table, and Winkler entered the room, Maria Theresa Romero at his side.

"I've got some great news," said Winkler. "The Board of Pardons and Paroles has granted our petition for a thirty-day stay of execution and will do a complete review of our allegations. With the evidence we have that you're really Ricardo Guttmann, it's only a matter of time before you'll be released." Winkler slid a copy of the faxed order over to Guttmann, who eyed it with disbelief.

"You'll see it still refers to the matter of Juan Velasco Martinez, but it's crystal clear now you aren't Martinez, but Ricardo Guttmann. I think the hearing will just be a formality. You should be out of here within a few days."

"It's not true...I don't believe it." Guttmann closed his eyes, and his body began to shake.

"Yes," said Winkler. "Everything I've said is true. It took a lot of work, and good luck, but we've convinced the powers that be that they made a terrible mistake."

"This is overwhelming. I can't thank you enough. It's all a blur, all these years, and yet no memories of what happened before I found myself in this terrible place."

"We'll get help for you, counseling and therapy, and maybe some of those memories will come back. For now, I want you to take a deep breath, because what I'm going to tell you will also come as a great shock: You have a daughter—this beautiful woman—a daughter you never got to know, and who didn't know you existed either. I'm pleased to introduce you to your daughter, Maria Theresa Romero."

"Are you for real?" asked Guttmann, clearly stunned by the revelation.

"It's a long story, but it's the truth," replied Winkler.

Maria Theresa got up from the table, went over to Guttmann, squeezed his hand, and both of them shed a tear.

CHAPTER 49

WINKLER FLEW BACK TO DETROIT late that evening. Working from home the next morning, he contacted Emma for the Swiss account number and password she'd obtained from Mrs. Weinman, the rabbi's widow.

Winkler then spoke with Klaus Wehrli, the Swiss banker. The current value of the account was almost $10 billion, invested in a diversified portfolio of marketable securities. Technically, Guttmann could assert control over the account but, under the circumstances, Winkler agreed it would be best if the Commerz Bank started a court action to determine the rightful owners of the funds.

Winkler would discuss the options with Guttmann; however, he expected Guttmann wouldn't be up for a fight over this money. Frail and suffering from years of imprisonment, he'd probably just be happy to live out his remaining years in freedom. In all likelihood, depositors and creditors of Guttmann's failed banks would have a first claim, with any surplus transferred back to the government of Argentina.

Winkler was satisfied with the results of his efforts, having given a man his life back and reunited a father and his daughter. He asked Emma to convene a celebratory luncheon with Dan Dillingham and Afzam to toast their victory. Emma was to join them as well. Winkler's wife, Eve, was traveling back to Detroit from New York and would arrive at Detroit Metropolitan Airport around six. He would pick her up, and they'd stop for dinner on the way home.

Winkler arrived at the Detroit Club a little before noon. It was the right spot to celebrate a major event such as this. Built in the 1880s, the majestic red brick private social club was one of the oldest in Detroit and had been one of the most prestigious in the country. The high ceilings, fine woodwork, classic paintings, and oriental rugs all spoke to a kind of elegance from a bygone era, missing from today's clean lines and modern design.

The Detroit Club brought back decades of memories of high-level business meetings with bankers and lawyers, high-stakes negotiations, and gatherings of politicians and foreign diplomats. It had also been the site of years of law firm holiday parties with one hundred or more guests, before the firm outgrew the space of the Club's main dining room.

Dan Dillingham and Emma arrived right at noon, but Afzam wasn't with them.

"Won't Afzam be joining us?" asked Winkler. "His efforts were largely responsible for our victory!"

"David, I don't think so," said Emma. "He's tied up with the transition. I didn't get a chance to tell you—"

"What transition? What are you talking about, Emma?"

"Big changes are happening at the firm. Not exactly a merger, but the firm is splitting up. The Litigation Group was being wooed by another law firm, and the Transactional Group by yet another. What I understand is that there couldn't be a merger of our firm into another firm. There wasn't one firm that wanted to take on all our practices, so those two groups have split off into two other firms. It was all hush-hush."

"When is all this effective?" Winkler asked.

"Today, as I understand it. The movers are at our building right now. They're all lined up around the block. It looks like a traffic jam at the Ambassador Bridge!"

"I didn't see any e-mails about this. And I wasn't advised of any Management Committee meetings either."

"Just one meeting, this morning. They came around and pulled everyone into the conference room and explained what was happening. It's a done deal." Emma was visibly shaken. The firm she'd been a part of for decades was imploding before her very eyes.

"Dan, where do you stand with all this? Are you going with the Litigation Group?" Winkler asked, confused. Dillingham was very close to being made a partner, and he was clearly a litigator. *How did he have time for a lunch on moving day?* Winkler thought.

"David, what's left of the old Kelly, Friedman & Green is just the Private Client Group. The two outside firms are taking people and pending cases. They're also covering the rent on space occupied by the Litigation and Transactional Groups until the end of the lease, if they can't negotiate termination fees with the landlord or sublease the space. Accounts receivable will be divided up among the equity partners who were at the firm on the day of the split. That's the biggest piece of the puzzle. Work in process will stay with whatever group generated it.

"The bottom line is that what's left is the Private Client Group. That's you and whoever you can cajole into staying. I figure you're going to need some help, and I don't like the way all this went down. So, if you'll have me, I'd like to stick around and re-tool, so to speak, and get out of the litigation game. I suppose we'll have to change the firm name, but if you'll take me as a partner, I'd be delighted to have my name on the front door with yours!"

Winkler was shocked at what was happening. He realized attorneys clearly had the right to leave the firm, but never in his life had he ever imagined a mass exodus such as this.

"I guess this takes the wind out of my sails. But we can toast to our victory in the Guttmann matter, while we eulogize a law firm we all love and respect," said Winkler, clearly overcome by the news of the firm's demise.

"David, I know when I bring you bad news, you like a little good news stirred into the pot. So, why don't you ask if there's any good news?" Emma asked, with a grin.

"What are you talking about, Emma? It sounds to me like this is just a bad news day. What have you got that'll lift my spirits?"

Dillingham took the floor. "David, I suspect it must bother you that so much money could be involved in the Guttmann matter and the retainer is used to pay expenses, while the firm receives nothing in fees. Am I right on that?"

"Sure, it bothers me, but that's the deal. There's $10 billion in the account, but that money isn't his, nor is it ours. That's a fact of life."

"So, assuming you'd find that result unjust, I spent some time looking into possible claims that could be brought on Guttmann's behalf that would result in fees under the 40% contingent fee arrangement, assuming Mr. Guttmann would agree, and I'm fairly confident he would."

"Go on, Dan. I'm listening."

"There are probably many claims that could be made: False arrest; false imprisonment; and negligent hiring of prison staff are a few that come to mind. It's not exactly wrongful conviction," said Dillingham. "Guttmann isn't the one who was convicted. What arguably happened is that an overzealous prison official was sloppy in the way he handled Guttmann after his arrest. There should have been a new set of fingerprints, and those prints should have been compared against those already in the prison record. They just went too fast, then refused to re-evaluate when Guttmann protested repeatedly over the years.

"If this had happened in many other states, or even with a federal conviction, Guttmann would have been entitled to a fixed amount per year, by statute, and more since he was on death row all that time. But not in Georgia. It's one of eighteen or so states that don't have a statute providing for compensation for those wrongfully convicted.

"The legislature has to take up each case individually and may or may not pass a private bill. I've done a little research, and in a handful of cases, people wrongfully convicted in Georgia have managed to get awards ranging from a few hundred thousand dollars up to over $1 million, depending mostly on how many years they were wrongfully incarcerated."

"So, in other words, Dan, it'll depend on the appetite of the Georgia Legislature whether Guttmann gets anything. Is that what you're telling me?"

"It would be an uphill battle, definitely not a sure thing. But there's something I just came across that could be a winner," said Dillingham. "Based on the letter from Guttmann to Rabbi Weinman, Guttmann was working for the U.S. government. They were trying to keep tabs on the Montonero guerillas, and what better way than to have a direct line to their banker? So, we looked for documents having to do with Guttmann's relationship with the U.S. government.

"Someone filed a FOIA request after Guttmann allegedly died in the crash, in connection with the failure of his banking empire. Have a look at this."

"Oh my God," said Winkler, as he flipped through the pages of the contract. "Guttmann was getting $250,000 a year in consulting fees. This contract started in 1973 and has an indefinite term, not a fixed end date. It continues in effect until terminated by either party on thirty days' written notice. And the only thing it says about the services to be provided is that Guttmann has to make himself available to the CIA from time to time for consulting services, upon request.

"Dan, do you think the U.S. government ever terminated this agreement?"

"I doubt it. The party making the FOIA request posted a copy of the request online. It was broad enough to cover not only contracts, but also correspondence, documents amending or terminating contracts, and records of compensation paid under contracts. From what I could see, payments just stopped when Guttmann was put in prison in Georgia. I'd say he probably has a claim for past compensation under the contract, which provides that unpaid amounts are subject to late payment interest at 8% per year."

"How much are we talking about, Dan? Millions?"

"It's been more than forty-three years. At $250,000 per year, forty-three years, 8% interest—we're talking about a ballpark figure of over $80 million. Forty percent of that would be around $32 million! $32 million!"

WINKLER AND HIS TEAM enjoyed a long lunch as they chatted about converting the Private Client Practice Group into a boutique law firm specializing in tax and estate planning. Winkler eventually suggested they all head back to the office to make sure the movers weren't taking any of their files and furniture. Winkler also decided to send out notices to all the private clients, to make sure the clients weren't confused by the departure of the Litigation and Transactional Groups. For the most part, those clients would still be serviced by the part of the firm that had worked with them over the years.

After what had been a grueling few weeks, Winkler picked up Eve at the airport, and they had dinner at one of their favorite spots, Moro's, an old school Italian restaurant with tuxedo-clad waiters who prepared some of the dishes tableside. Eve brought him up to date on her yoga experience and hiking in the hills of upstate New York. Later, Winkler briefed her on his whirlwind pursuit of the missing banker, and the positive outcome for all.

They were both exhausted and decided to skip dessert and head home so they could turn in early.

"David, I really congratulate you on solving this mystery. When we met Maria Theresa in Aruba, I had no idea this would lead you on such a journey. I never imagined you'd end up going to the snow-covered peaks of the Swiss Alps, being drugged by Russian goons, and saving a man on death row," Eve said as she slipped into her favorite red nightgown, with thin straps. Did you get a photo of the banker when he got the news that he was going to be a free man, and that he had a daughter?"

"I sure did. Here's a selfie, with the three of us."

"Yes, that's the woman I remember, from our trip to Aruba. David, did you notice she's got a cute dimple on her left cheek, just like you? That's curious, isn't it?"

Winkler paused, looking a little sheepish. As he turned over to switch out the light, he said, "Honey, I haven't told you everything."

EPILOGUE

To Save the Nation is a work of fiction, but it was inspired by actual events, including the disappearances of tens of thousands of people perceived to be anti-government in Argentina in the 1970s.

Although the Argentina disappearances took place decades ago, there are parallels in current events. In this epilogue, the author provides background for further study, in the hope that by learning more about these events, we will avoid repeating the errors of the past.

***

"Some men arrive. They force their way into a family's home, rich or poor, house, hovel or hut, in a city or in a village anywhere. They come at any time of the day or night, usually in plain clothes, sometimes in uniform, always carrying weapons. Giving no reason, producing no arrest warrant, frequently without saying who they are or on whose authority they are acting, they drag off one or more members of the family towards a car, using violence in the process if necessary."

So begins a United Nations booklet on enforced disappearances,[1] which are not a thing of the past. They're very much a current phenomenon, and on the rise.

In 1980, the United Nations Commission on Human Rights established a Working Group on Enforced or Involuntary Disappearances, which continues its work today. One of the Working Group's primary tasks is to assist families

---

[1] Office of the United Nations High Commissioner for Human Rights, "Enforced or Involuntary Disappearances," Fact Sheet No. 6/Rev. 3, page. 1. Annex I to that publication contains a form to submit a communication on a victim of an enforced or involuntary disappearance.

in determining the fate of their family members who are reportedly disappeared. It serves as a channel of communication between family members of victims of enforced disappearance, other sources reporting cases of disappearances, and the governments concerned.

In 2010, the International Convention for the Protection of all Persons from Enforced Disappearances entered into force. As of this writing, the Convention has 98 signatories, but not the United States.

The Committee on Enforced Disappearances was established further to the convention. The Committee on Enforced Disappearances and the Working Group on Enforced or Involuntary Disappearances co-exist side by side and seek to coordinate their activities to prevent and eradicate enforced disappearances.

According to the U.N., an enforced disappearance is defined by three elements:

(1) Deprivation of liberty against the will of the person;

(2) Involvement of government officials, at least by acquiescence; and

(3) Refusal to acknowledge the deprivation of liberty or concealment of the fate or whereabouts of the disappeared person.

Since its inception in 1980, the Working Group has transmitted a total of 57,149 cases of enforced disappearance to 108 countries.

As of its 2018 report, there were 45,499 cases under active consideration in 92 countries. Those countries and the number of cases in each included the following: Algeria (3,179), Argentina (3,241), Chile (785), Colombia (973), Republic of Korea (167), Egypt (258), El Salvador (2,282), Ethiopia (113), Guatemala (2,897), Honduras (130), India

(368), Indonesia (163), Islamic Republic of Iran (528), Iraq (16,416), Lebanon (313), Mexico (377), Morocco (140), Nepal (470), Nicaragua (103), Pakistan (723), Peru (2,365), Philippines (625), Russian Federation (808), Sri Lanka (5,859), Syrian Arab Republic (218), and Timor-Leste (428). The other countries each had less than 100 cases outstanding at the beginning of the 2018 period.

For further information on the work of the U.N. with regard to enforced disappearances, links to additional material on forced disappearances, and special reports on disappearances in a number of countries in recent times, see the author's website, www.robertekass.com.

There will you will also find a link to a video report of a child of a "disappeared" couple in Argentina, raised by a military family.

For films about Argentina's Dirty War, see the following:

•   "Our Disappeared" (2008) (a documentary by a Boston-based Argentine filmmaker about his personal search to find friends and loved ones caught in the vise of the military and who "disappeared" in Argentina during the Dirty War);

•   "Imagining Argentina" (2003) (a political thriller centered around a couple living through the dictatorship during the Dirty War; the husband has the power to see the fate of missing people, except his own wife); and

•   "The Official Story" (1985) (the story of an upper middle-class couple who live in Buenos Aires with an illegally adopted child, and the mother finally comes to realize her daughter may be the child of the one of the "disappeared").

---

[2]United Nations General Assembly, "Report of the Working Group on Enforced or Involuntary Disappearances," A/HRC/39/46, July 30, 2018.

AUTHOR'S NOTE

To Save the Nation is a work of fiction, but because it was inspired by actual events, readers will invariably ask: "How much of this is true?"

The Dirty War actually happened during the military dictatorship in Argentina during the 1970s. Thousands of people 'disappeared,' although the actual number has been disputed. Those representing the disappeared estimate 30,000 disappeared. The military says it was more like 8,000.

Among the disappeared were about 500 pregnant women. Their babies were taken from them under C-section, and the babies were adopted by third parties or the military. More than 100 of those children of the disappeared have been reunited with their biological families over the years, due in part to DNA testing.

I had a personal relationship to what was happening in Argentina. As a young American lawyer practicing international law in Brussels, Belgium, I met a woman from Argentina who had left the country to wait out the dictatorship in Brussels. She told me that prior to leaving Buenos Aires, she and her friends would call each other at the end of each day, just to see if they were still there. Those wearing blue jeans, or with beards, or who were labor activists were at risk of disappearing, being tortured, and possibly killed.

I also had a client who was an Argentine banker, whose private jet crashed on a flight from New York to Acapulco, and whose international banking empire collapsed within a few weeks thereafter. There was speculation in the press, including major financial magazines, that he might not have died in the crash, that it may have been a set-up. I learned that his in-house counsel, who was my friend and with whom I worked on business deals, died under torture in Argentina after the banks collapsed.

I left Brussels while the story was still unfolding and years later started my research to see what had finally been determined. While my research was extensive, many important issues were still unresolved.

I decided to create a purely fictional work that would bring together many of the things I'd learned in my research. I hoped the story would provide an entertaining way to encourage serious debate on how far a government should go in quashing dissent, even if those in power feel it's necessary to do so "to save the nation."

The story would be that of a Uruguayan woman whose mother dies. She learns from her mother's papers that her parents weren't her real parents, and the man she always knew as her father was actually Argentine ex-military and involved in the murder of her mother. She also learns her real father was an Argentine banker who allegedly died in a plane crash and whose banking empire crashed shortly thereafter. She would meet an American lawyer who knew something about the story and hire him, to either confirm the official story—that her real father died in the crash—or find him.

I worked on the story off and on but didn't write the chapters sequentially. I found it difficult to imagine how the woman would feel when she learned her parents weren't her real parents, that her entire life she'd been living a lie. Would she hate her adoptive parents for lying to her, and her adoptive father, in particular, for being involved in the murder of her real mother? Or would she love her adoptive parents nonetheless, because they saved her life? I felt the only way I could deal with this appropriately would be to go to Argentina and interview children of the disappeared.

Working through the Grandmothers of the Plaza de Mayo (Las Abuelas de la Plaza de Mayo), an organization that has been pursuing numerous issues related to the disappeared since the 1970s, I interviewed several children of the disappeared. I also had a lengthy meeting with a former colonel from the dictatorship, who explained what they did and why they felt it was justified.

Later I also interviewed a former U.S. military attaché at the U.S. Embassy in Buenos Aires, who explained what the U.S. government knew about what was happening in Argentina during the Dirty War. His wife, who was Argentine, shared thoughts about what it was like to live in Argentina during this period.

ABOUT THE AUTHOR

Robert E. Kass is a Detroit-based lawyer and author of three highly-acclaimed non-fiction books.

To Save the Nation is his long-awaited first novel. It was inspired by actual events which occurred in the 1970s while Kass was a young attorney practicing in an international law firm in Brussels, Belgium.

His initial motivation in writing this book was to raise public awareness of the disappearance of tens of thousands of people which took place in Argentina in the 1970s, so that they would not be forgotten.

However, his research has brought him to the current day, where disappearances continue in nearly 100 countries around the world. What started out as a legal thriller has become a tool to draw attention to these human rights abuses. He hopes to provoke a serious conversation about how far a country should go in violating human rights when its leaders believe the nation is under a threat.

Kass is an honors graduate of the University of Michigan Law School and was the recipient of a Fulbright-Swiss University Fellowship to study East-West trade at the Graduate Institute of International Studies in Geneva, Switzerland.

He landed his first position as an attorney in Brussels, where he practiced for five years, serving a multinational corporate clientele. He returned to the U.S. to earn a Master's Degree in Taxation at New York University.

He then returned to Detroit where he has built a highly regarded practice in estate planning and administration, and planned charitable giving.

A Fellow of the esteemed American College of Trust and Estate Counsel, he serves on the Professional Advisory Committees of numerous charities.

He is a frequent and highly-rated lecturer in continuing legal education programs, as well as to civic and professional organizations. In connection with his previous non-fiction works, he has been quoted in the press, interviewed on radio across the country, and has appeared on local and national television.

ACKNOWLEDGMENTS

With thanks to:

My Argentine friend, Natalio Kogan,
who has kept prodding me to finish this book

To another Argentine friend, Jorge Singman,
who helped me make important connections

To Jo Venet, a former Belgian bank executive,
whose words have kept a mystery alive

To Alejandro Fontana Sandoval, son of
one of the "disappeared," who graciously hosted us
for hours at his home in Buenos Aires to tell his story

To B. Scott Custer, Jr., one of the partners in
my law firm in Brussels in the 70s, who told me
what it takes to be a good lawyer

To Leo Gibson, who knows why

To Donald Barris, Herb Sott, David Denn
and Eugene Driker, who mentored me
and allowed me a career full of legal thrillers

To my daughter, Adena Rose, and my former colleague
in Brussels, Francis Camerlinckx, both of whom
took the time to review drafts of the manuscript

To Judy Meshefski and Anna Hansen, my
assistants, each of whom has made it a
real pleasure to go to the office each day

To my wonderful clients—too many to mention—
who have shown an interest in the message of
this book and encouraged me

And last, but not least, to my wife, Sonja, who
has tolerated my obsession with this story, even
during vacations in Belgium, Switzerland, Aruba,
Argentina and Mexico over the last
two decades

DISCUSSION GUIDE

1. How did you feel about the main characters? Were they believable?
   a. The lawyer
   b. The private investigator
   c. The Argentine banker's daughter
   d. The Argentine banker
   e. The lawyer's assistant
   f. The law firm's computer support person
   g. The man from Tricontinental (Mr. Banks)
      Who did you relate to the most/least?

2. Are there any quotes, passages or scenes that stood out to you?

3. How did the book make you feel?

   a. Were you amused, upset, bored, angry, or intrigued?

   b. Did the pacing of the story keep your attention? Did you have to force yourself to get through it, or were you unable to put it down?

   c. Are you glad you read it?

4. How do you feel about how the story was told?

   a. Was it too predictable or progress in a way that was too systematic?

   b. Did it jump around too much?

   c. Did it hold you in suspense?

   d. Was the ultimate resolution acceptable to you, or too sappy?

   e. What did you find particularly compelling, or upsetting?

   f. Were there parts of the book you thought were unique, thought-provoking or disturbing?

5. What were the main points the author was trying to make?

6. What do you think about the ending?

a. Were you satisfied or disappointed with how the story ended?

b. Is anything left unresolved or ambiguous and, if so, do you feel it was intentional?

c. How do you picture the main characters' lives after the end of the story?

d. What do you think is going to happen to the former Argentine military (Mr. Banks) who was about to ascend to a position of power in U.S. Homeland Security?

7. What is your impression of the author?

a. What do you think about the author's writing style?

b. What do you think about the author's storytelling ability?

c. Why do you think the author picked this story to write about?

8. What changes would you hope for if the book were turned into a movie?

a. Which sections would you cut?

b. What parts would you definitely want to retain?

c. Who would you cast to play the main characters?

9. How does this book compare to other legal thrillers you have read?

a. Did you like it more or less than other legal thrillers?

b. Is the book different in any way from books you usually read?

10. Ultimately the author wanted to provoke a serious discussion about human rights.

a. Did you find the statements made about things some people believe should be done "to save the nation" troubling?

b. Before you read the book, were you aware of events during the Dirty War in Argentina in the 1970s?

c. Before you read this book were you aware of the issue of enforced disappearances, generally?

d. Were you surprised to learn from the Epilogue that enforced disappearances are going on today in nearly 100 countries worldwide?

d. Admitting that these are difficult issues, did this book change your mind in any way about human rights?

11. Did you enjoy the book? Would you recommend it to other readers? To a close friend?